Alex, the dog and the unopenable door

'Who are you?'

'I'm Alex Jennings,' said Alex.

Martha frowned. 'What, the famous explorer?'

'No, his son. I'm running away from the police because they think my dad's some kind of maniac terrorist and I'm helping him, but I'm not. I just like dogs.'

'I see,' said Martha.

About the Author

Ross Montgomery is a first-time author. He started writing stories as a teenager, when he really should have been doing homework, and continued doing so at university. After graduating, he experimented with working as a pig farmer and a postman before deciding to channel these skills into teaching at a primary school. He wrote *Alex, the Dog and the Unopenable Doo*r when he really should have been marking homework. He lives in Brixton, London, with his girlfriend and many, many dead plants.

Alex, the dog and the unopenable door

Ross Montgomery

ff
faber and faber

First published in 2013
by Faber and Faber Limited
Bloomsbury House,
74–77 Great Russell Street,
London, WC1B 3DA

Typeset by Faber and Faber
Printed in England by CPI Group (UK) Ltd, Croydon, CR0 4YY

A CIP record for this book
is available from the British Library

ISBN 978–0–571–29461–9

2 4 6 8 10 9 7 5 3 1

To my family:
There's not much to say in the face of twenty six years of love, support, guidance and understanding (so far).
Thanks.

HOWLER WOODS
TOWN

A MAP OF
The Outskirts
INCLUDING PORTIONS OF
THE CUSP AND THE FORBIDDEN LAND
CUSP
KEEP OUT

Prologue

Cloisters Boarding School for Boys
Annual Essay Writing Competition

Subject: A Great Day in the History of the Cusp
(Maximum 200 words)
NAME: Alex Jennings
AGE: 12 (nearly)

The 1000th Anniversary of the Order of the Sword and Torch was a momentous day indeed for history. Lots of days are important in history for lots of different reasons. Some are important because of great deeds that have been committed on those historic days. But the day of the 1000th Anniversary of the Order of the Sword and Torch was most especially important. This was because it was the day that the world's biggest dog and the world's smallest dog finally met each other, at the Grand Expedition Centre, which is of course located in the Cusp.

The world's biggest dog was a Great Dane called Gibson, who was 107 cm tall, or 42 inches, which is about as big as a 42-inch television screen. Great Danes are seriously massive, I saw one once that no jokes I could have ridden like a horse. The world's smallest dog was a toy Chihuahua called Boo Boo, who unlike Gibson was only 10.16 cm tall. I deduce that he could have fitted inside Gibson's head, even though I don't think that is really possible. Maths is not my strength.

Here is an artistic interpretation of that fateful event:

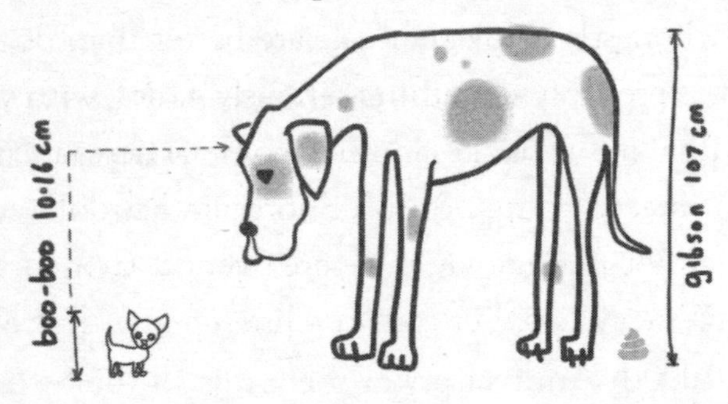

The glorious meeting was part of a series of events to celebrate the day that the Order was first formed, and its members left the Cusp and set out to explore the land that lies beyond the invisible boundary surrounding the Forbidden Land. It was their solemn oath that not one of them would rest until they had finally discovered what mysteries lay at the very centre of the unexplored region, and returned to the Cusp as heroes.

The reason why these two fine specimens were brought together at the Cusp was to symbolise the fact that, unlike people, dogs can somehow cross the boundary and walk over the 'Forbidden Land' without anything trying to push them back out.

No one really knows why this is and we can't ask the dogs (see my earlier point). But this is not why I think it was a great day in history.

The reason why I think that this was a great day in history is as follows. Some people think cats are better than dogs and I have no real opinion on the matter but if you really honestly think that cats are better than dogs then there is probably something seriously wrong with you.

Allow me to make another point. There are 73 different breeds of cats, British Shorthair, Ragdoll, etc. etc. etc., although some say there are over 80. Quite frankly I couldn't care less. Put cats in a line-up and they all look like this:

That's right – exactly the same. The fur changes and some have longer hair and maybe bigger or smaller ears but that's it, they still look like cats. This is because the family name for the domestic cat is *Felis catus*. They all come from the same family and so it makes sense they would all look very much the same. You can't help looking like your family, even if you don't want to. Everyone says I look like my dad.

But dogs are also all in the same family, *Canis lupus familiaris*. Look it up if you don't believe me. The Kennel Club says there are over 150 different breeds but that's a bit of a misunderestimation as it doesn't include mongrels, who some believe can often be even more delightful than their pedigree brethren (myself included). But do dogs all look the same? Do they squat. Gibson and Boo Boo don't look anything like each other. And they're not the only ones – observe this particular line-up:

The Sheepdog, the Dachshund, the Pointer, the Poodle, to name only four, all look completely different. Even though they're in the same family. They could almost be completely different animals. And I don't know about you but I think that is quite something.

And here's where I get to my point. When Gibson the Great Dane finally met Boo Boo the toy Chihuahua in the Cusp on that fateful day, and they saw how different they both were, did they *know* that each other was a dog like them? Or did they think they were both something else? Perhaps an even better question is, when dogs look at us, do they see us as people or some other type of dog?

And in conclusion in a nutshell to sum it all up that is why the 1000th Anniversary of the Order of the Sword and Torch was indeed a momentous day in history.

WORD COUNT: 763 words

GRADE: F

COMMENTS:

Alex, there is no such word as 'misunderestimation'.

And for the last time, you were not asked to provide illustrations.

— Mrs Beaumont

Part One

The Outskirts

1

The morning sunlight shone onto Cloisters Boarding School for Boys. It shone as best it could, but it was no use. No amount of sunlight could disguise the coldness that clung to its black bricks like ancient robes. The sun might as well have shone on a gravestone.

The view from the front gates didn't exactly leave the best impression on newcomers. The first thing they'd see would of course be the gates, wrought iron and rusted. The plaque on the bars was the only part that was ever cleaned nowadays. Its words gleamed to a high sheen in the sunlight:

*** CLOISTERS ***

A BOARDING SCHOOL FOR BOYS

BUILT BY THE ESTEEMED MEMBERS

OF

THE ORDER OF THE SWORD AND TORCH

IN ITS 500TH GLORIOUS YEAR,

. . .

FOR THE PURPOSES OF EDUCATING THE YOUNG

IN THEIR SACRED RESPONSIBILITY:

. . .

TO STEP BEYOND THE CUSP

AND

FINALLY TRIUMPH OVER

THE FORBIDDEN LAND

The plaque was a grim reminder of how many years had passed since the school was first built. Back then, the Outskirts had been filled with towns and villages, but they had long ago been abandoned. Except for the barbed-wire fences lining the horizon, where the secretive world of the Cusp was hidden from view, and where the outermost edges of the Forbidden Land finally began, the school was the only sign of life for miles around.

You could forgive those standing at the wrought-iron gates for imagining that the black and crumbling building ahead had been long abandoned too. With nothing else but barren fields to look at, visitors would have no choice but to stare at the grand entranceway lying at the base of the tallest tower before them. It was a miserable sight.

No matter how many times you stood before the tower, it always looked like it was plummeting down on top of you.

Matthew was no exception. It didn't help matters that he was an hour late for his first day at school, and that he was soaked to the skin in old ditchwater. And it certainly didn't help that he was wearing a blazer two sizes too big for him.

Or that he was supposed to be starting as the new Headmaster.

'Hello?' he called out, banging his briefcase against the railings. 'Er . . . can someone let me in, please?'

Silence. He wiped his mud-smeared glasses with a baggy sleeve.

'Anyone?'

A woman appeared at the grand black entranceway. Her hair was in a neat bob, and she was wearing a bright pink jacket that boasted a truly awe-inspiring pair of shoulder pads. She didn't look very pleased to see him. Even from down at the gates Matthew was certain he could see her nostrils flaring.

'Good morning, Mrs Beaumont,' he called up, giving a meek wave.

'More like "good afternoon", Matthew!' she said furiously. She marched down the steps towards him, pulling a set of keys out her pocket. 'Where on *earth* have you been?'

'Sorry Mrs Beaumont,' he mumbled. 'I got lost in the Outskirts.'

The woman stared at him in disbelief.

'*The Outskirts?*' she gasped. 'You went through the Outskirts on foot? For heaven's sake, Matthew, that's nearly twenty miles! I suggest you get yourself a bike, and in future come along the ditches . . .'

'I did,' said Matthew.

Mrs Beaumont threw open the gate, and thinned her eyes suspiciously.

'*Really*,' she said. 'Then where's your bike?'

'In a ditch,' said Matthew. He held up a plastic bag filled with sodden clothes. 'A farmer lent me the blazer. I had to get changed in a bush.'

Mrs Beaumont gave him a glare of intense disapproval.

'Matthew,' she said calmly. 'This cannot happen again. The new Headmaster of Cloisters cannot be an hour late.'

'I know, Mrs Beaumont,' he said apologetically. 'But it wasn't my fault, honestly! I was cycling as fast as I could to get here, and then this girl just ran out in front of me and I tried to swerve and . . .'

'Stop talking, Matthew,' sighed Mrs Beaumont. 'Look up there for me, please.'

She pointed to the top of the tallest tower. Matthew turned around without protest and squinted his eyes against the harsh morning sun.

On the roof of the belfry stood a stone statue, at least twice his size. It was a knight in full armour. In one hand it held up a great flaming torch. The other thrust forward an enormous sword, its point aimed towards the horizon. From that height, you could almost see beyond the barbed-wire fencing that cut through the countryside and make out the distant boundary that separated the Outskirts from the Forbidden Land. In Matthew's day children used to sneak up onto the belfry roof in break times to see if they could make out of the mythical world that lay across the boundary, fooling themselves into believing that they might even see all the way to the centre – the place where no man had ever set foot, or even laid eyes upon.

Matthew doubted the boys cared about that sort of thing nowadays. If they did sneak up the tower, it was probably to catch a glimpse of what lay immediately past the fences: to the giant ring of the Cusp, whose watch-towers and security perimeters surrounded the Forbidden Land and prevented anyone from going within even a mile of the boundary. No one knew what went on there – probably not even the statue. Matthew looked closely at it. Its head had long since fallen off, and had been replaced by a weathervane.

'That man', said Mrs Beaumont solemnly, 'symbolises what this school was built for. A purpose greater than either of us, one that a huge number have worked and died for. A purpose that was born over a thousand years ago – one your father has dedicated his entire life to, Matthew. To educate young minds in discovering what lies beyond the Cusp, and to finally find a way to the centre of the Forbidden Land – no matter what it takes.'

Matthew had heard the speech a hundred times before. They were the words with which his father began his own speech each year at the annual Cloisters assembly. They had also been used, word for word, at the beginning of their annual man-to-man talk. This one even had its own personalised ending. *Being Headmaster of Cloisters is not simply a job, Matthew*, his father would say, placing a hand on his shoulder, *it is a responsibility. A heavy one to bear. And one day, Matthew, it will be your turn.*

'Do you understand, Matthew?' said Mrs Beaumont.

Matthew nodded. 'Of course, Mrs Beaumont. It won't happen again.'

Mrs Beaumont spun on her heel, and strode back through the enormous doorway. Matthew scampered after her, his shoes squelching loudly on the grey stones. He glanced around nervously. The corridor inside was wide, and cold.

'Wow,' said Matthew, glancing round him. 'It looks . . . exactly the same as when I was here, Mrs Beaumont.'

'Your father has kept things in fine form these last forty

years,' she said proudly, marching ahead. 'How is he? Improving, I hope?'

'Er . . .' said Matthew. 'Yes, I suppose. Far too slowly for him. Can't get out the hospital quickly enough.'

'I'm sure you'll do an admirable job while he's away,' said Mrs Beaumont, although Matthew sensed she didn't really mean it. 'Especially now the First Day Festivities are in full swing.'

'Ah, yes,' said Matthew warmly. 'First Day Festivities. I remember them well.'

'Nothing out of the ordinary this year,' said Mrs Beaumont, weaving through the corridors. 'Somebody tried to set fire to the cricket pavilion, as usual.'

'Ah yes, a classic,' said Matthew.

'And Laurence Davy was caught trying to break into staff cars with a coathanger. Again.'

'Oh,' said Matthew. 'That's a new one . . .'

'And we've had to send Jeremy Butterworth to his dorm for bucketing Alex Jennings.'

'Erm . . .' said Matthew.

'It's when you make someone hold a bucket of water against the ceiling with a long pole,' Mrs Beaumont explained. 'One move, and you drop the bucket. Poor Alex was stuck in the Chapel all night. Ten hours! The organist found him honking for help this morning. They'd glued a French horn to his lips, you see. You'll be pleased to know we've confiscated the horn.'

Matthew gulped. 'Well, maybe things have changed a little since my day . . .'

'Indeed, Matthew,' said Mrs Beaumont. 'The boys nowadays take to criminality like ducks to water. You have to *punish* the badness out of them.'

'Blimey,' said Matthew. 'And to think I brought muffins in for them.' He pulled a small bag of slightly squashed clingfilmed blobs from his pocket. 'Do you want one, by the way? They've got linseeds in them.'

Mrs Beaumont ignored him. She stopped outside a familiar door and turned back to face him.

'The Headmaster's office,' she said. 'Your office now, of course.'

Matthew gulped. 'Of course.'

'Oh, and Matthew,' she said. 'One final word of advice.'

She took a step towards him. Matthew fought the desire to take a step backwards.

'You must make it your own. You have to set an example, right away. Strike hard, and fast. No mercy. One sign of weakness, and the whole system falls apart. Do you understand?'

Matthew nodded silently.

'Good luck,' said Mrs Beaumont.

A bell suddenly rang out, high and shrill and piercing. Matthew's eyes widened.

'First break – already?' he cried. 'Good grief . . . I have to get changed! They can't see me like this . . . !'

Mrs Beaumont had already disappeared. Matthew was alone in the shadow of the doorway. He took a breath, and stepped inside.

The office was exactly as his father had left it. Behind the old wooden desk stood his armchair, turned to the wall, as rigid as a coffin and the colour of a sickly toad. Above it, an enormous portrait of a stern-looking man hung at an angle, looming over the room. From the doorway it almost seemed as if he was glaring down at you, which was of course the exact intention. Matthew looked back up at the familiar cold eyes of his father.

'"One day, Matthew, it will be your turn,"' he sighed. '". . . And I hope you won't let me down like you normally do."'

'Who are you talking to?' said a voice.

'Aaaargh!' said Matthew, leaping several feet in the air.

The sickly-green armchair spun round. Seated inside it was a small boy. Matthew clutched at his chest, his heart thumping. The boy smiled eagerly, and looked Matthew up and down.

'You must be lost,' he said. 'This is the Headmaster's office, and between you and me you don't really look like a Headmaster.'

2

Matthew glared at the boy before him. He was wearing a very large hand-knitted jumper in a colour that Matthew would struggle to describe, and a school tie that he had somehow managed to work into a sailor's knot. In his hands was a wooden clipboard, held in front of him like a tray of biscuits. The expression on his face indicated he had no idea that he wasn't welcome.

'What are you doing here?' Matthew gasped. 'You're not supposed to come into my father's offi . . . I mean, into *my* office without first . . .'

'Who are you?' the boy asked.

'I . . . I . . .' Matthew said, wheezing for breath. 'I'm the Headmaster! You're not supposed to . . .'

'Where's Mr Price?'

'Mr Price is away,' Matthew glowered. 'I'm . . . Mr Price. I'm taking his place until he gets back. Now . . .'

'Technically then that makes you Acting Headmaster,' said the boy. 'As opposed to the actual Headmaster.'

'Yes, technically, it does,' Matthew spluttered, going red in the face. 'Now for heaven's sake, *get out of that chair*!'

The boy quickly slid to the floor and shuffled out from behind the desk. He was very small, even for his age. The jumper almost reached his knees.

'Sorry, sir,' he muttered quietly, looking at the carpet.

Matthew glared at him. 'For the last time, who are you?' he snapped. 'What do you think you're doing, waltzing into my office without first . . .'

'I'm Alex Jennings, sir,' said the boy.

Matthew stopped dead, and stared back at him.

'Alex Jennings,' he repeated.

The boy nodded.

'The boy they bucketed,' said Matthew. 'That was you?'

Alex nodded. 'Yes, sir.'

'Oh,' said Matthew. 'And . . . you're fine now?'

Alex shrugged. 'Yeah, I guess.'

'Ah,' said Matthew. 'That's good to hear.'

The two of them stood in silence for a moment.

'Well?' said Matthew.

Alex looked up. 'Yes, sir?'

Matthew sighed. 'What are you *doing* here, Alex?'

The boy's eyes lit up. 'Oh, yeah.'

Without another moment's pause he leaped forward, wielding the clipboard like a steering wheel.

'Do you like *dogs*, Mr Price?' he began enthusiastically.

'No,' said Matthew.

'Well, lots of people do,' said Alex, not missing a beat. 'Myself included. I love dogs, but my mum says if I ever bring one home again she'll kill me. So I propose that each child in school is given a dog that can live with them in their dorm rooms. Everybody loves dogs, so financially speaking it's a sound investment.'

Matthew let the information settle.

'Er . . .' he began.

'Only twenty-five per cent of dogs in shelters ever find homes,' Alex continued. 'And that's an optimistic estimation. So by rehousing these dogs we would be providing a public service, as well as a profitable scheme for the school.'

Matthew looked back at him.

'Dogs,' he said.

'Yes, sir,' said Alex. 'They are intelligent and noble beasts, and you can teach them to do tricks. We could have them collect mail and dirty laundry during school hours. Better yet, we could train them in the art of stunts and form them into a troupe of show dogs ready for Spring Term.'

He held up a colourful handmade poster of a dog

wearing a top hat being fired out of a cannon. Matthew looked at the poster, and then at Alex.

'Dogs,' he said.

'Five hundred of them, sir,' Alex grinned. 'Somersaulting through hoops, swallowing fire, you name it. A feast for the eyes and ears. *And* I've got over forty signatures of support from fellow students.' Alex thrust the clipboard into Matthew's hands. 'That makes it officially ready for approval by the Headmaster, or Acting Headmaster, which in this case is you.'

Matthew took a moment to collect himself. He looked down at the clipboard for a moment, and then back to Alex, who was nodding encouragingly.

'*Dogs*,' he repeated.

'Some say man's best friend, sir,' said Alex, giving a theatrical wink.

Matthew looked back at the clipboard, and then back at the boy.

'Well, Alex,' he began, 'owning a dog is a great responsibility. One that a person should not simply jump into.'

'Yes, yes,' said Alex, nodding enthusiastically.

'That's not to mention the school's budget,' Matthew continued, 'which is usually spent on things like wages, or new computers. I have to say that the logistics of the school suddenly housing five hundred dogs makes your ambitious performing-dog plan an unlikelihood, before we even begin to consider the moral issues of training them to perform potentially fatal stunts.'

'Mmm, yes, I see,' said Alex, still nodding. 'We can work on that.'

'Besides,' Matthew continued, 'most of the names on this petition are actually made up.' He held up the clip-board. 'I don't think there's a pupil in the school called "Get Bent, Alex". And this one here is just a drawing of you being savaged by a Rottweiler.'

Alex nodded.

'The plan has come up against some resistance,' the boy admitted. 'But I challenge you, Mr Price, to name me one great plan that wasn't ridiculed in its time. Besides, most of the ridicule is from Jeremy Butterworth, who between you and me is an idiot, and whose French horn I have to pick up, by the way.'

Alex pointed over to a black case on Matthew's desk. It was covered in swear words written in Tipp-Ex.

'Oh, he wants his horn back?' Matthew asked. 'And why are you getting it for him, Alex?'

'I'm his roommate, sir,' said Alex.

Matthew snorted. 'He can come and talk to me about it himself if he wants it so badly.'

'I appreciate that, sir,' said Alex. 'But he's just been asked to stand in for a special concert, and the bus is picking him up in less than an hour. I'm obviously loath to bring it to him myself as I've had it glued to my face all night, but if I don't do what he says he'll use me as a pillow for the next week.'

Matthew's face dropped. 'You're not serious, Alex.'

'Oh yeah,' said Alex, with a shrug. 'I get beaten to a paste anyway, whether I do what he says or not. The others have bucketed me so many times now I've gotten pretty good at it.'

'You just . . . put up with it?' said Matthew.

'Pretty much,' said Alex, nodding. 'Besides, things are looking up this year – I've started a dog-walking service in the town, so I won't be onsite during the prime post-prep bucketing hours. Would you like a business card?'

He reached into his pocket and offered Matthew a card. Matthew looked down at it. *Alex Jennings: Bone-a Fido Dog Walker*.

'*The town?*' said Matthew. 'Alex, that's an hour away on the bus.'

Alex nodded. 'Actually it's two buses.'

Matthew looked down at the business card, and back up again.

'Alex, do you have many friends?'

Alex fiddled with his jumper. 'You mean who aren't dogs, I'm guessing?'

Matthew nodded.

'Then no,' said Alex. 'I just like dogs.'

'I see,' said Matthew.

There was an awkward pause. Matthew looked at the boy. He had absolutely no idea what to say.

'Muffin?' he hazarded.

Alex looked back up, blankly. Matthew reached into his pocket and pulled out a slightly squashed clingfilmed blob.

'Muffins,' said Matthew. 'Please. Have one.'

Alex reached out. Matthew suddenly grabbed it back. 'You can eat linseed, can't you?'

Alex looked blank. 'What's linseed?'

'Never mind.'

Alex took the muffin, looked at it and put it in his pocket. There was another awkward silence.

'Would you like to talk about it?' said Matthew eventually.

Alex looked confused. 'The muffin?'

Matthew frowned. 'The bullying, Alex.'

'Oh,' said Alex. 'No thanks, sir. I'd prefer not to.'

'That's fine, Alex,' said Matthew kindly.

Slowly, he reached out and placed a hand on the boy's shoulder. 'You know, Alex,' Matthew said warmly, 'you share your name with a very important person. Someone who liked dogs . . . well, probably even more than you do.' He smiled. 'Have you ever heard of Alex J. Jennings?'

Alex's face paled.

'Years ago,' Matthew began, 'probably before you were even born, there was a man named Alex J. Jennings.'

'Sir . . .' said Alex weakly.

'He was a great and famous explorer,' Matthew continued, ignoring him. 'Probably the greatest in the world. He scaled mountains that no one had ever scaled before, and mapped out jungles that had never been explored. So when the Order of the Sword and Torch decided to launch a new Expedition across the boundary and into the Forbidden Land, they decided he was the ideal man to lead it. They made him the "Official Head of Expeditions". Ever heard of it, Alex?'

Alex was silent. Matthew shrugged.

'No, I guess you wouldn't have,' he said. 'Your generation haven't even had the chance to see an Expedition being launched, have you? Well, I can tell you it's a very important job, Alex. They don't give it to just anyone. I was just a young boy when Alex J. Jennings took the job, and it was very big news. Remember, at that time nobody had tried to set foot past the boundary for years – centuries, even!'

Matthew turned to the enormous map that hung on the wall behind them. It showed the school grounds, the rugby pitches and tracks, stretching far into the desolate Outskirts beyond. The road to town snaked up from the bottom edge of the map, winding past the school and up towards the enormous shape that dominated the top. There – as if some mistake had been made at the printers – the barren fields suddenly and abruptly ended, like a circle of blank paper had been stuck to the map itself.

'The Forbidden Land,' said Matthew. 'The one place that no one had ever managed to explore. By the time Jennings took the job people had tried everything to get past the boundary and discover what lay at its centre. And I mean, everything! Walking on special stilts, flying with enormous wooden wings, being fired out of a cannon . . . they even tried building a giant pier to the centre at one point.

'Of course,' Matthew continued, 'they didn't succeed. It was no use. As you know, once you cross the boundary, everything changes. For as long as anyone can remember, no man, woman or child has ever managed to cross over the boundary into the Forbidden Land without being irresistibly, forcibly pushed out again.'

Matthew reached up to the map and pulled out a newspaper clipping that had been tagged to its side.

'But Alex J. Jennings was the first person to realise that *dogs* weren't affected by the power of the Forbidden Land,' he continued. 'Dogs had been running over the boundary without getting forcibly pushed out for hundreds of years. It's almost like a magnet draws them to the centre. So why not use them?'

Matthew held up the newspaper clipping. It was a faded sketch drawing of a man in an antique metal diving suit, an airpipe trailing from the back of his helmet. He was sitting on top of what looked like an enormous metal throne. The throne was bolted onto a giant sledge, and at the front of the sledge stood a pack of harnessed dogs.

'So that's exactly what Jennings did,' said the Headmaster. 'He built a wheeled sledge, pulled by packs of dogs, and strapped himself to a great metal seat on top. That way he couldn't be pushed out again once the sledge crossed the boundary, and there was no chance of him accidentally setting a foot on the ground either – of course, we all know the consequences of *that* happening . . .'

Matthew held out the newspaper clipping for Alex. The boy did not take it. He stood perfectly still, his eyes fixed to the carpet. Matthew awkwardly took back the clipping.

'Well, I can tell you they were very exciting times, Alex,' he said. 'Everyone was certain Jennings would be the one to finally make it to the heart of the Forbidden Land and find out what was in the centre. When I was a child, Alex J. Jennings was my absolute hero. I remember watching the television with my whole family the day he set off from the Grand Expedition Centre, strapped to the chair in his metal suit. I thought he was the bravest man in the entire world.'

Matthew sighed.

'Unfortunately the story doesn't end very happily,' he said. 'No one heard back from him for weeks, and when they did he'd lost the dogs. And the sledge. Turns out he hadn't reached the centre of the Forbidden Land at all, he'd just gone bonkers. In fact, he thought he was a dog. They had to lock him up, I think. He was in a coma the last I heard of him. Er . . .'

Matthew trailed off, and turned back to the boy. Alex was still staring at the floor, his face flushed.

'But that's not the point,' said the Headmaster emphatically, grabbing Alex by the shoulder again. 'The point is, you shouldn't let *anyone* treat you like you've been treated. Ever.'

Alex nodded, his eyes locked to the carpet.

'And the next time anyone tries to,' said Matthew, 'I want you to think about what Alex J. Jennings would have done. Will you, Alex?'

Alex nodded furiously. 'Yes, Mr Price.'

Matthew looked down at the boy still staring at the carpet, fumbling his knitted jumper into a mass of knots and holes.

'Look, Alex,' he said gently. 'Don't worry about it. I'll let you take the horn this time. I know that standing up for yourself . . . well, it's not always easily done, is it?' He paused for a moment, and turned to look up at the oil painting of his father that loomed above them both. 'No,' he muttered again. 'It's not always easily done.'

The phone on the desk suddenly rang. Matthew sighed, and thrust the clipboard back into Alex's hands.

'Well, off you go, Alex,' he said. 'Take Jeremy his horn. But the next time he tries anything, make sure I know about it.'

'Yes Mr Price,' Alex muttered meekly, grabbing the horn and making a frantic break for the door.

'Excellent,' said Matthew, beaming with triumph and shoving the phone to his ear. 'Have a good day, Alex . . . Er, hello?'

'*Is that Alex Jennings with you?*' came an anxious voice. It was Mrs Beaumont.

'Yes, he's just leaving,' said Matthew, looking up. Alex was at the office door.

'*Don't let him leave*,' said Mrs Beaumont.

Matthew started. 'Er pardon?'

'*The police are here to see him.*'

Matthew looked up.

'The police . . . ?'

'*His father's escaped from hospital*,' said Mrs Beaumont.

Matthew stopped dead.

'His father . . .'

'*Alex J. Jennings!*' came the voice impatiently. '*Alex J. Jennings the explorer*.'

Matthew looked up in horror. Alex was standing at the open doorway, his exit blocked by two great policemen. One had a moustache, and the other was totally bald, but they were the exact same height, their mouths hardened into identical lines. They looked down at the boy in the enormous jumper, his hair as messy and ragged as a tiny dog's.

'Alex Jennings,' said the one with the moustache. 'We're here to talk about your father.'

3

Alex shifted back against the red plastic chair. It gave a little squeak.

Squeak.

He did it again.

Squeak, squeak, squeak.

He looked back up. The two policemen were sitting uneasily on identical red chairs opposite him, twiddling their thumbs and gazing around the prep room. At one point it had been the school's in-house abattoir, and the corners of the room were still decorated with carved wooden stag heads. Nowadays the children came here to do their homework before lights out, and the room was stacked with unused desks and tiny chairs. A weekly timetable hung from a pair of antlers.

'Has anyone told my mum?' Alex asked eventually.

The policeman with the moustache nodded. 'She

knows all about it.'

'Is she on her way here now?' said Alex nervously.

The policemen shared a glance.

'Sure,' said the bald one.

Alex sighed with relief. 'Good.'

There was another pause.

'Do either of you like dogs?' he tried.

There was a knock at the door, and Matthew's head popped cautiously inside. He gave Alex a nod. 'Everything OK, Alex?' he asked gently.

Alex nodded. 'Yes thank you, Mr Price.'

'Ah. Good,' Matthew smiled. He looked over at the policemen, and held up a blue plastic bag. 'They only had tuna.'

The bald one beamed with triumph and punched the air. The one with the moustache rolled his eyes. Matthew stepped over and gingerly deposited the bag on the table.

'You're sure there's nothing else I can do?' he asked the policemen.

'Not right now, son,' said the one with the moustache. 'Just send in the Headmaster when he gets back.'

'I am the Headmaster,' said Matthew miserably.

'Oh,' said the policeman. He looked over at Alex with genuine pity. 'Well, you'd better sit down then.'

Matthew shifted a tiny red chair up to the table and sat down. The prep room descended into silence once more.

They all watched the bald policeman tear the clingfilm off his roll and stuff a good third of it into his mouth, going cross-eyed with pleasure.

'Did anyone actually see him wake up?' Alex asked, breaking the silence.

There was a pause. The policemen shared another glance.

'The notebook, Duncan,' the policeman with the moustache muttered irritably.

Officer Duncan pointed at his full mouth and shook his head.

The first policeman muttered under his breath and pulled a notebook out of his pocket. He scanned the pages.

'Only one person saw it happen,' he said. 'One of the nurses was doing the rounds when Mr Jennings suddenly woke from the coma. Very disoriented, she said. He fought against a dozen orderlies before leaping out of the second-floor window and jumping the fence.'

Alex's eyes widened. 'My father did *that*?'

The policemen nodded.

'Why?' said Alex.

Officer Duncan swallowed, hard.

'We were kind of hoping you might be able to answer that one for us,' he said sheepishly.

There was another knock at the door, and everyone

turned round. Mrs Beaumont's head and shoulder pads emerged into view. She gave Alex a smile of genuine warmth.

'Hello, Alex,' she said.

'Hello, Mrs Beaumont,' said Alex quietly.

Mrs Beaumont turned to the policemen, and her face suddenly took on a weight of seriousness.

'He's here,' she said.

The policemen exchanged a nervous glance. Alex paled, and sank further into his chair. Mrs Beaumont disappeared from the doorway.

'I think I'd better go,' said Matthew, blissfully oblivious. 'Alex, I'm sure Officer Mike and Officer Duncan will both look after you until I . . .'

'Actually Mr Price,' Alex said, cutting him off, 'if it's all right with you and you don't mind I'd prefer you to stay.'

The Headmaster stopped in his tracks. He looked back at Alex.

'What was that?'

Alex fidgeted with the cuffs of his jumper.

'I'd like you to stay with me, please, Mr Price,' Alex repeated. 'If you're not too busy.'

A smile crept across Matthew's face. He nodded.

'Of course not, Alex,' he said gently, sitting back down. 'I've got all the time in the world.'

'*Ahem*.'

The cough cut through the room like a cold draught. Everyone turned round. There was a man at the door.

The policemen immediately straightened up. Officer Duncan hid his roll under the chair. Matthew was certain he felt Alex tense up beside him.

The man took up the entire doorway. He stepped into the light of the prep room, his heels clacking and cricking against the floorboards. Matthew stared in disbelief. The man was wearing a metal helmet with an enormous plume of purple feathers sticking out the top. He came to the table and slowly straightened himself. It was only then that Matthew could see that the man was, in fact, very short. He was dressed immaculately in black velvet tie and tails.

'Sorry about the helmet,' the man said quietly. 'Dress rehearsal.'

No one said anything. The man looked around the room and turned to the policemen.

'Chair,' he spat. 'A normal chair. Get three. You look ridiculous.'

Officer Mike immediately sped out the room without another word. The man turned to Matthew and stared at him. Matthew shifted uncomfortably. It was like being stared at by a snake.

'Who are you?' said the man.

Matthew got to his feet and offered his hand.

'I'm Matthew Price,' he said, 'Acting Headmaster of . . .'

'Do you need to be here?' the man said. He made no effort to take Matthew's hand. Matthew dropped it awkwardly.

'Alex has, er . . .' Matthew stepped aside to indicate the boy beside him, '. . . requested that I be present.'

Alex was hiding his face. The man raised his eyebrows.

'Ah,' he said quietly, staring down on Alex. 'I see.'

The man lifted his arms, and started the careful procedure of removing his helmet. It took some time. Officer Mike returned with three chairs under his arms, and set them down. Matthew optimistically offered his hand once again.

'I'm sorry, I don't think I quite got . . .'

'Let's get started,' the man snapped, ignoring him. 'Mr Price, if you must be here then don't interrupt.'

The man sat down, and placed the helmet on the table in front of him. Matthew glanced down at it. Carved into the gleaming silver of the forehead was the image of a knight, a torch in one hand and a sword in the other. The man turned with a sigh to Alex.

'Well, Alex,' said the man. 'I suppose there's no need to introduce myself, is there? We've met before.'

Alex kept his head bowed. The man smiled. His eyes were locked onto him.

'I suppose you must be wondering why I'm here,' he said.

It was not really a question, and Alex didn't answer. After some time the man sighed, and carefully crossed his fingers in front of him.

'Let me explain the current situation, Alex,' he said. 'Early this morning the security guards at the Cusp reported an intruder trying to break over the security fences. There's no need for me to explain who that man was, is there?'

Again, it was not a question. Alex kept silent.

'This time,' the man continued, 'he almost made it to the boundary. I hope you understand how dangerous an unplanned and unsolicited attempt to enter the Forbidden Land is, Alex.'

Alex stayed with his head bowed. There was silence.

'It is a very serious crime,' the man said slowly. 'One of the most serious there is. You know what the Order does to people who try to break into the Cusp.'

The room was still. The man patiently rubbed the tips of his thumbs together.

'Now, I've been told, Alex', the man continued, 'that when your father woke up last night he seemed . . . frantic. Almost as if he was desperate to get to something. Kept repeating the same word, over and over. Do you find that unusual, Alex?'

Alex didn't reply.

'Well, I certainly do,' said the man. 'It's not often that a man lies for months in a coma before suddenly waking up with so much strength. Leaped across the room like a grasshopper, I'm told. And twelve strong orderlies – twelve! – couldn't drag him back. And all the time, repeating the same word, over and over.'

Alex kept his head bowed.

'I'm sure you know what that word was, Alex,' he said quietly. The silence in the room was crisp. The man leaned forwards.

'"Squiggles",' he said.

He let the word hang in the air. Alex stayed as still as a statue, his face hidden from view. The man's eyes never left him.

'"Squiggles",' the man repeated. 'Does that word mean anything to you, Alex?'

Alex didn't respond. The man held still for another moment, before nodding and slowly sinking back in his chair.

'Nothing,' he said. 'I see. You don't know anything. Indeed, you probably told these gentlemen here you couldn't think *why* your father would escape from hospital in the first place. Am I correct?'

Alex's face suddenly flushed. The man smiled.

'Yes,' he said quietly. 'Yes, I thought as much.'

The man turned to the Headmaster. His eyes had taken on a glint.

'Headmaster, Alex's family and I have become – how shall I say? – *well acquainted* over the years,' the man sighed. 'We've had quite a few meetings like this now, haven't we, Alex? Every time we catch Alex's father trying to break into the Cusp, of course . . . How many times has it been now, Alex – twenty? Thirty? What do you think?'

Alex was no longer looking at the carpet. He was glaring across the table at the man, his face turning slowly red. The man smiled triumphantly, and leaned back in his chair as if telling a favourite anecdote.

'Yes, who'd have thought,' he smiled. 'Alex J. Jennings, my old boss! Ever since that *disaster* of an Expedition he led years ago he's been nothing but a nuisance to us at the Cusp. Desperate to get himself back across the boundary, no matter what it takes! Never mind that he had his chance already and messed it up. His fall from grace was a bit . . . *difficult* for him, I think. The last time we apprehended him he was caught on the fence by the belt of his hospital gown, barking like a dog, running round and around in circles . . .'

In a moment Alex had leaped up and thrown himself clear across the table, fists flailing. He was like an animal. At once the policemen had him by the shoulders and were pressing him back down into his chair as he scrambled furiously against their grip, baring his teeth and growling, his chest heaving.

'Calm down, Alex, calm down!' Matthew cried, placing a hand on the boy's ribcage. Across the table, the man smiled. He hadn't moved so much as a muscle the entire time. Alex glared at him with hate.

'Leave him alone,' the boy gasped, his voice broken to bursting by his chest.

The man raised his arms triumphantly.

'At last, it speaks!' he cried. 'What was that, Alex?'

Alex trembled and clutched the table, calming his breathing.

'I said, *Davidus*,' he hissed through gritted teeth, 'leave – him – alone. He's sick. Leave my family alone.'

Matthew's eyes widened. He dropped his hand from Alex's chest.

'Davidus,' he repeated quietly.

The policemen exchanged a glance. Matthew turned around to face the man.

'Davidus Kyte,' he said. 'You're Davidus Kyte? The Official Head of Expeditions?'

The man gazed idly back at Matthew, rubbing his fingernails against one another, filing them into little points.

'What are you doing here, Mr Kyte?' said Matthew.

The man smiled. 'I'm trying to find out the *truth*, Mr Price. The truth about Alex's father. No one repeatedly tries to break into a top-secret base for no reason . . . I'm just trying to find out what that reason is. And as far as I'm concerned, young Alex here knows something that he's not letting on.'

Alex flung his head back miserably. 'I've told you before – I don't know *anything*! I don't know anything about "squiggles", or why my dad wants to get into the Forbidden Land so badly – I haven't even seen him in years . . . He's sick! *Just leave him alone!*'

Kyte shook his head sadly.

'No, Alex,' he said. 'Not this time. We've let you and your father off far too many times. He's put years of top-secret planning in jeopardy. He could have even *stepped* over the boundary. Do you know what happens when someone does that, Alex? How dangerous it is?'

Alex didn't reply.

'Of course you do,' hissed Kyte. 'Because you know much more than you let on, young Alex Jennings, and don't think I don't know it. Any idea what the punishment is for keeping secrets from the Official Head of Expeditions?'

Alex looked away, his eyes filling with furious tears.

'I'll tell you,' Kyte snapped. 'Prison. And not just any normal prison, Alex. They've made a special one for enemies of the Order, like you and your lunatic father. It's right on the other side of the Outskirts, where no one ever goes. I can see to it you both spend the rest of your lives there.'

Matthew stood up in disgust. 'Now, hang on just one second . . .'

At once the policemen were on their feet.

'Better sit down, sonny,' said Officer Mike, clamping a hand on the Headmaster's shoulder. 'He's not joking.'

Matthew looked at the two policemen, and glanced over at Kyte.

Davidus was smiling, his eyes glinting. 'Sit down, Mr Price,' he said.

'You don't have the power to put a child in prison,' Matthew snorted. 'That's just ridiculous.'

'I have the power to do whatever I want, Mr Price,' said Kyte. He nodded to Officer Duncan. Officer Duncan pulled out a sealed brown envelope from inside his jacket. Kyte's smile widened.

'Signed by the Grand High Pooh-Bah himself,' he said with relish. 'That letter gives me the power to arrest anyone I choose for the good of the Order. That means that if I decide to send a boy to prison for the rest of his life – or even his meddling teacher – then I can. And no one can stop me.'

The policemen each put a hand on Matthew's shoulders, and forced him back down into his chair. Kyte smiled, and turned once again to Alex.

'But of course, it doesn't have to be that way,' he said gently. 'Not for Alex. Not if he co-operates.'

Kyte slowly leaned over the table, and once again fixed his eyes on the boy.

'Tell me everything you know,' he said quietly, 'and you're safe. We'll deal with your father ourselves, and you'll never hear from us again. I'll give you one final chance to be honest with me, Alex. You know what I'm talking about.'

Alex stayed still on his chair, lowering his eyes once again to the floor. Kyte sat silent, poised, ready to pounce.

'Alex,' he repeated once more, '. . . what are "squiggles"?'

Alex said nothing. The room was silent.

'Tell me what it means,' Kyte spat.

Alex looked up, his eyes glinting. 'It doesn't mean anything.'

The policemen looked at each other. Kyte paused for a moment, before suddenly snapping up, his entire body bristling with fury.

'Right,' he barked. 'Have it your way. Officers, take Alex to the car. We'll see if he's prepared to talk more once he's at the Cusp.'

Matthew made to stand up again. 'Now, hang on one second . . .' he said nervously.

'I suggest you keep your mouth shut, Mr Price,' said Kyte, throwing Matthew a furious look. 'Unless you want to join him, too.' He turned to the police. 'Get the boy's things. We leave now.'

Matthew slowly sat back down. The police got to their feet, and grabbed Alex.

'No!' Alex cried, thrashing desperately in their grip. 'You . . . you can't do this!'

'I can, Alex,' said Kyte. 'I have the power to do whatever I have to do.'

'Not without consent, you don't!' Alex cried, his eyes lighting up. 'I'm only eleven – you can't take me anywhere without permission from my family! Call my mother – she'll never let you take me, she knows what you're like, and how much you've always hated us . . .'

'We've already spoken to your mother,' Kyte said. 'And she says it's fine.'

Alex stopped struggling. '. . . She what?'

Kyte nodded. Alex stared back at him.

'No,' he said quietly. 'She wouldn't.'

Kyte smiled. 'She did.'

Alex turned to face the policemen holding him. They nodded.

'No,' said Alex, his voice broken.

Kyte rolled his eyes. 'Get him out of here,' he snapped. 'And don't let anyone see you do it.'

The police wrenched Alex off the chair. Matthew suddenly felt a hand grab his own. He looked down. Alex was clutching his fingers across the table.

'Mr Price,' he said. 'Please.'

The Headmaster looked up at Davidus Kyte, tidily arranging his cuffs across the table.

'Alex,' Matthew said quietly, turning back to the boy. 'I'm so sorry. There's . . . there's nothing I can do.'

Alex continued to look at Matthew. Then, slowly, he relaxed his grip, and let go of his hand. The policemen dragged him out of the room.

'I'll take my leave now, Mr Price,' said Kyte, picking up the helmet in both hands. 'I have a rehearsal to attend. And if I'm not mistaken, I believe you have a school to run.'

He placed the helmet back on his head and strode out after them.

And with that, it was as if no one had ever been there at all.

4

The policemen marched Alex down the corridor, their hands firmly on his shoulders. Alex stared ahead glumly. There was no one around to see him led away. He doubted anyone would have helped if there had been.

'Take this,' grunted Officer Duncan.

He slammed Jeremy's horn case into his chest, knocking the breath out of him. Alex clutched it feebly.

'Which way to the dorms?' barked Officer Mike.

Alex let out a feeble wheeze. Officer Duncan gripped his wrist.

'You'd better answer him,' he threatened.

Alex waved his arm down the empty walkway ahead of them. Officer Duncan looked back at him suspiciously.

'You're sure?'

Alex nodded.

'Good,' said Officer Mike, tightening his grip on Alex's

shoulder. 'Now, don't try anything stupid.'

Alex nodded miserably, and started walking along the silent corridor. His eyes flickered across the doors lining the walls. They'd be passing the PE hall any moment. It had fire escapes at the back. They led out onto the playing fields. He could be out the school and into the fields in a matter of seconds . . .

Then Alex's heart sank. Outrun the policemen? He could barely run the length of the hall before he had to stop for breath. This was the signal for Mr Braker to stand Alex up in front of the others, and carefully explain that one length of the hall was two hundred feet exactly, and that was not very far for a boy Alex's age. A boy his age, he would say, should be able to run farther than a dog running into the woods.

'And how far can a dog run into the woods, Jennings?'

The other children would snigger and nudge each other. They all knew that the wrong answer meant doing Mr Braker's weekly underwear wash. No one knew what saying the right answer meant. Nobody had got it right yet.

'A mile?' Alex would guess. Or something like it.

A hush of silence. Mr Braker would stare down at him. Like all PE teachers, he was an expert of the sadistic pause.

'*WRONG!*' he would suddenly bellow. The class would

collapse into howls of laughter. 'Wrong again, Jennings! Wrong again!'

Alex looked gloomily down the corridor. He didn't know how far two hundred feet got him from here, but it certainly wasn't far enough to escape the two policemen. He signalled wearily up a spiralling stairwell beside him.

'This way,' he said.

The three of them filed slowly up the stone stairs. The dormitories lay either side of another long corridor at the top. Officer Mike gave Alex a nudge.

'Which one's yours?' he said.

Alex pointed to the nearest door. From behind it came the blaring of extremely loud guitar music. Jeremy was obviously still inside. He had already found the time to vandalise their new door plaque with Tipp-Ex.

DORM 051
JEREMY BUTTERWORTH
mary ALEXANDER JENNINGS is a div

'Someone in there?' said Officer Mike.

'My roommate,' said Alex drily, pointing at the name on the door. 'You'll have to excuse him. He's a moron.'

The policemen looked at each other nervously.

'What do we do?' said Officer Duncan in what he

imagined was a whisper. 'You heard what Kyte said. We can't be seen by anyone.'

Mike's moustache bristled. He turned back to Alex.

'There another exit in there?' he said, jabbing a finger at the door.

Alex shook his head.

'No other doors?' said Mike. 'Windows?'

Alex snorted. 'What kind of bedroom wouldn't have a window?'

Mike's eyes thinned. He grabbed Alex by the collar. 'Listen here, squirt,' he snarled. 'You've got one minute to get in there and get out. One *peep* to your friend in there, and we'll make sure your ride to the Cusp is a long and unpleasant one. Understand?'

Alex nodded nervously.

'Good,' snapped Officer Duncan, leaning forward and grabbing the black case out of his hands. 'Now get inside.'

'Hey!' said Alex. 'I need that!'

The policemen stared at him. Alex pointed at the black case.

'The horn,' he said. 'I need to give it to Jeremy.'

'Is there something wrong with your head?' Mike snapped. 'Get in there now before I pull your arms off!'

Alex bristled.

'Well, officer,' he said carefully, 'if I *don't* give him the French horn then he'll spend the next hour beating me to a pulp. You'll have to wait here while he does. And who *knows* who might walk past here in that time?'

The policemen stared at him.

'And furthermore . . .' said Alex.

'He's messing with our minds, Mike,' said Officer Duncan nervously.

'Give him the bleeding horn,' Officer Mike gasped. He glared at Alex. 'But listen closely, midget. Every *minute* extra you're in there, I'll take off one of your fingers. After that, I'll move on to your little toes. And just in case you even *think* of escaping, don't forget – you're twenty miles away from the nearest town. We'll catch you. And when we do, you can forget about ever running *anywhere* ever again. Get it?'

Alex nodded, grabbed the case and stepped through the door. The room was much the same as he had left it. As usual, the air smelled of unwashed T-shirts, and as usual the curtains were closed. Jeremy was lying on his bed, as usual, listening to a band called Pig Destroyer while kicking the radiator, as usual. He appeared to have already worked his way through a family-sized multipack of NikNaks. As usual. He didn't seem to have noticed Alex come in.

Alex silently lowered the case to the floor, and tiptoed to his wardrobe. Jeremy had apparently also spent the morning vandalising Alex's 'Best of Crufts' poster. Alex ignored it, and with careful hands inched open the doors.

A tidal wave of dog books and magazines crashed to the floor. Alex silently cursed. Jeremy immediately sat up.

'*Hey!*' he bellowed. 'Where do you think *you've* been, Mary?'

He thundered towards Alex in a tornado of empty crisp packets and NikNak crumbs.

'Jeremy!' said Alex nervously. 'Er . . . how are you?'

'The bus is outside, you plank!' Jeremy cried.

He jabbed his finger out the window. A bus was parked outside the school gates. The side of it was emblazoned with the words *Conduct Yourselves*, written across waves of rainbow-coloured sheet music.

'They've been waiting for twenty minutes!' Jeremy bellowed. 'I'm supposed to be on the way to the concert *right now* to entertain my adoring fans, and here I am, waiting for some *amateur* to bring me my horn!'

Alex pointed calmly at the case beside them.

'It's on the floor,' he said. 'I . . . had to talk to some people. Sorry it took so long.'

Alex turned away, and started quietly picking up the dog books from the floor. Jeremy's watery pig-eyes darted around, struggling to take it all in.

'Going somewhere, Mary?' he grunted.

Alex kept tidying. 'I'm going home, Jeremy.'

'No you're not,' said Jeremy bluntly.

Alex stopped, and looked over his shoulder.

'I'm sorry?' he said.

'You've made me late for my concert,' Jeremy muttered menacingly. 'And I'm going to make you pay for it.'

Jeremy was significantly bigger than Alex in pretty much every aspect. Alex sighed. Normally, he'd just let this happen. Any kind of protest just made the consequences even more prolonged and even more humiliating. But quite frankly, he had two bigger things to worry about waiting outside the bedroom door, and ten little things on his hands and feet that he felt strongly attached to. He calmly pushed Jeremy's hand away. The boy's face fell in disbelief. Alex looked up.

'Sorry, Jeremy,' he said sternly. 'I'm afraid that's not going to happen.'

Within seconds Jeremy had him dangling up against the wardrobe by his tie.

'You trying to be funny, *Mary*?' he growled, bearing in on him. His breath stank of spicy crisps. 'Don't you know how many beatings answering back gets you? And what's *this*?'

Jeremy suddenly stuffed his hand into Alex's pocket and brought out the muffin, squashed to a patty inside the clingfilm. He held it up to Alex's face.

'Keeping treats from me!' he guffawed. 'Well, we can't have that! Looks like I'm going to have to beat you up even harder, *and* eat your muffin while I do it!'

Alex struggled against his grip, his eyes darting to the closed door. 'Jeremy, please,' he gasped. 'I have to go! It's urgent!'

Jeremy snorted. 'Urgent? Going back to see your mental dad, are you?'

Alex froze against the wardrobe.

'What did you say?' he whispered.

Jeremy sneered.

'Yeah, that's right,' he said, holding him even closer. 'My dad told me all about your dad. Said he thought he was really big business back in the day – Alex J. Jennings, Mr Head of Expeditions, bragging on how he'd be the first to find out what was in the middle of the Forbidden Land. Not so big *now*, is he?'

He sniggered, and started peeling the clingfilm off the muffin.

'Makes sense,' he said. 'Only you could have such a loser for a dad. Is it true he thinks he's a dog?'

'Don't you dare', Alex seethed, his eyes flashing with rage, 'talk about my father with your fat, dirty mouth.'

Jeremy's grin dropped. He looked like someone had just shot him. Then his lip started trembling, and his eyes thinned to slits. He heaved Alex off the wardrobe, and thrust him towards the hatch door that lay on the wall between the beds.

'No!' Alex cried desperately. 'Not the rubbish chute!'

The chutes led from each dorm to the skips below, where rumour had it the rubbish was collected by the cooks every night and made into the next day's lunch-time carbonara. Alex knew this was only a rumour as Jeremy had thrown him down the rubbish chute twice now, and no one had turned up till the morning except for a family of wild foxes.

'Bad idea, Mary!' Jeremy wailed, flinging open the hatch door. From inside came the stench of rotting garbage. 'I hope you enjoy your day in the skip! You might as well consider it your new bedroom. Because from now on I'm going to make sure that not one day passes in Cloisters without you getting beaten to a pulp by every boy in school!'

'Jeremy, no!'

But there was no stopping him. In one move Jeremy had shovelled the entire muffin into his mouth, and raised Alex above his head, ready to thrust him down the stinking hatch.

'So long, Mary!' he cried in a spray of seedy crumbs. 'Enjoy your new life!'

Alex screwed his eyes shut and prepared himself for the drop.

Nothing happened.

Alex looked down nervously. Jeremy was standing

stock still, holding him up. His throat was making a sound like a sink gurgling.

'Jeremy?' he asked.

Then Jeremy's arms began to tremble. They trembled more and more, until all of a sudden they wilted completely and he dropped Alex to the floor. Alex gazed on in shock. Jeremy was staggering backwards, clutching at his throat. His face was turning bright red.

'Oh crikey,' Alex muttered.

'The muffin!' Jeremy squealed, his face getting redder and redder. 'It doesn't have linseeds in it, does it?'

'What's linseed?' said Alex.

'*I'm allergic to linseeds!*' Jeremy cried. 'Quick! I need injections!'

Jeremy's head had now swelled to the size of a football, and his tongue was dangling out his mouth like a packet of raw bacon. Hives were bubbling up across his face and arms and legs. He swayed briefly on his feet, his eyes rolling around in his head, until he keeled over backwards and hit the floor like a cow. Alex leaped up and ran to the bedroom door.

'Wait there!' he cried. 'I'll get the . . .'

He suddenly stopped, and pricked up his ears. A car horn was repeatedly honking outside. Alex turned round. Out the window, he could still make out the bus in the distance. It was waiting for Jeremy.

Alex looked down at Jeremy. He looked at the bus outside. He looked at the battered French horn case. Then he looked at the rubbish chute.

He smiled.

He turned back to the bedroom door.

He locked it.

■ ■ ■

By the time the Headmaster had arrived with the keys the policemen had already started booting the door in.

'Stop it!' Matthew gasped. 'There's no need for that, I've got the keys . . .'

'No time!' cried Officer Mike. 'I'm going to barge in!'

He stepped back and took a deep breath.

'Please don't do that,' said Matthew desperately.

'This is your last chance, Alex!' Officer Mike shouted, ignoring him. 'Open the door right now!'

There was no response. Officer Mike steadied himself on the wall.

'Very well!' he cried. 'If you're behind the door, I suggest you move!'

Matthew stepped forward. 'Officers, please . . .'

The policeman charged. In a great crack of wood the door was ripped clean off its hinges, and Officer Mike tumbled inside. Officer Duncan flew in after him. Matthew sighed and followed them in.

Officer Mike was lying on top of the door, groaning in pain. Officer Duncan stood assessing the situation. Neither Alex nor the horn case was anywhere to be seen. Jeremy Butterworth was flubbering around on the floor like the queen of all maggots. The rubbish hatch was open. Out the window, a distant bus could be seen shutting its doors and pulling away from the school. Officer Duncan's eyes moved from Jeremy to the window, to the rubbish hatch, to Jeremy, to the window again, to the rubbish hatch, and finally settled back on Jeremy, his fat tongue slumping and slobbering on the carpet. Officer Duncan's eyes widened with horror.

'My God,' he said. 'He ate him.'

5

The rubber doors of the bus closed with a hiss. Alex stood on the stairwell beside the driver, gasping for breath, smeared with baked-bean juice and bits of orange peel. The bus lurched forwards, and they drove off. Alex stared outside as the school gates slowly slipped away. He laughed. He had made it.

'*Hey!*' someone suddenly shouted behind him.

Alex flipped round. The bus was filled with what seemed like a hundred screaming children and as many instruments, all of which were being practised on at the same time. A young woman was pushing her way through the mob to the front of the bus, waving her clipboard at him. Even in the din of trumpets and cellos and bass drums and bagpipes, her voice stood out like an air-raid siren.

'*Where have you been?*' she shrieked, her eyes pained

with stress. 'You were supposed to be at the gates twenty minutes ago!'

Alex panicked. 'Er . . . I . . . er . . .'

'Butterworth,' she sighed miserably, running through the list in front of her. She had the look of someone flinging sea water out of a sinking boat with both hands. 'Here we are – Butterworth, Jeremy Mary. Is that right?'

'Yes,' said Alex, nodding furiously. He did a double take. 'I'm sorry, did you say Jeremy *Mary* Butterworth?'

'Yes,' said the woman. 'That's your name, isn't it?'

'Er . . . yes,' said Alex, dumbfounded. 'Yes, I guess it is.'

She glowered at him. 'Well, Jeremy Mary Butterworth, we'll be lucky to make it in time now you've made us twenty minutes late . . .'

Alex fumbled. 'I'm really sorry. I, er . . . I couldn't find my trumpet.'

'Your *trumpet*?' the woman said.

Alex held up the battered case in his hands.

'You told us you play French horn,' said the woman.

'That's what I meant,' said Alex quickly, dropping the case. 'The French horn-trumpet. That's what we call it here.'

'And what's that *smell* . . .?' she asked, screwing up her nose suspiciously.

'No idea,' Alex muttered.

'What's that?'

She pointed at his jumper. Alex looked down. Half an old grapefruit was squashed flat on his chest. The woman stared at him.

'. . . Are you covered in old food?' she said.

Alex thought about the best possible answer.

'Yes,' he said.

The woman was silent for a moment. It was as if she was trying to read his face. Suddenly her eyes softened.

'Of course,' she said soothingly, kneeling down to him. 'Of course you are. Hey, I'm not here to tell you what you should or shouldn't do. You go right ahead and cover yourself in food scraps if you want.'

'What?' said Alex.

The woman smiled, and offered her hand.

'I'm Steph,' she said warmly. 'I organise the concerts held by Conduct Yourselves for extremely sensitive and psychopathically violent children just like you.'

'Sensitive?' said Alex. 'Violent?'

'Yes,' she said, pointing at the rioting bus behind them. 'All the children here have an addiction to violent behaviour. But they're really good kids, just like you, and use classical music as an outlet for their violent emotions. Here, have a T-shirt.'

She thrust a T-shirt into his hands. Alex looked at it in dismay. The logo was a boy squashing a smaller boy's head between a giant pair of cymbals. Underneath it read

Conduct Yourselves: Don't Fly Off The Handel.

'Welcome to the family, Jeremy,' said Steph. 'We really appreciate you stepping in at the last minute. Some idiot ran over our regular performer with a bicycle this morning.'

'Thanks,' said Alex, his eyes darting out the windows. 'Er, where exactly is this bus going to . . . ?'

'Come on!' Steph said, grabbing his hand. 'Let me introduce you to Noah. He's going to be your Bus Buddy for this trip.'

She turned to a boy sitting on his own by the window, a triangle clutched in his hands. He had 'Noah' shaved into both eyebrows.

'Noah had a hard time fitting in when he first joined us,' said Steph gently. 'But he's really opened up since finding his new place as Second Triangle.' She pushed Alex forward. 'Noah, this is your new Bus Buddy! What do we say to new friends?'

'Touch my triangle and I'll kill you!' cried Noah.

'Noah!' Steph snapped. 'For the last time, no one wants to take your triangle. Don't worry about him, Jeremy. Noah's really a big softie. Aren't you, Noah?'

'I don't think Noah wants me to sit next to him,' Alex whispered. Noah was now punching his own hands.

'Nonsense!' Steph laughed, ripping a nametag off her clipboard and slapping it on Alex's chest. 'Be nice, you two!'

She dashed away before Alex had a chance to protest any further. Alex stood in the aisle, his heart thumping. He looked back at Noah, still punching his own hands. There was no way he was staying here any longer. He stole a glance out the window. The police were nowhere to be seen. Empty fields stretched out either side of the bus. Now was his chance. He had to get out of here, before it was too late, and go . . .

Alex stopped. Go *where?*

Well, he wasn't going home, that was for sure. Not now his own mother was prepared to hand him over to Kyte and the policemen. He couldn't go back to the school. And he couldn't stay with his friends, because Alex didn't have any. Except for the dogs, of course, but then they weren't even his. And dogs wouldn't be much help to him now. Alex was completely alone. There was only one other person he knew in the whole entire world who wasn't a dog, and who didn't hate him, and who wouldn't betray him, and that was . . .

'Dad,' said Alex quietly.

His heart sank. It had been almost two years since he had last seen his father in the hospital. They hadn't spoken since. And now he was finally out of the coma, he had walked straight back into the hands of Kyte, who was going to do who knows what to him. And there was nothing Alex could do about it.

Alex fought against the desire to cry, and turned back round to the bus. There *was* something he could do about it. He could make sure that he got away, even if his father couldn't. All he had to do was keep his head low – try and fit in. So long as he didn't stand out, he could be off the bus and ten miles away before anyone even knew he had gone. He turned back to Noah and put his hands in his pockets. He had been bullied by enough kids to know how they were supposed to act.

'So Noah, bro,' he said. 'We're Bus Buddies. That's, like, really cool.'

'You're looking at my triangle,' growled Noah.

'Totally,' said Alex, nodding. 'I really get that.'

'Red dots,' said Noah quietly. 'I'm seeing the red dots again.'

'No way!' said Alex. 'That's so cool. Well, see you at rehearsals!'

He scampered off to the back of the bus and threw himself down onto an empty seat, closed his eyes and breathed a sigh of relief. It had been a total success. Being cool was really easy.

'That's quite a jumper you have there,' came a voice.

Alex opened his eyes and looked up. A girl was leaning over the headrest in front of him.

Quick, Alex, said a voice in his head. *Say something cool.*

'My mum made it,' said Alex.

Great work, Alex, said the voice.

The girl was undeterred. 'Is your middle name really Mary?'

'Er . . . pardon?'

'It says Mary on your nametag.'

She pointed to his chest. Alex nodded.

'Yes it is. I mean, yeah.'

'Mary is a girl's name,' she said.

'Yeah, totally.'

'And you're covered in bits of old food.'

'Yeah,' said Alex. 'Totally.'

They looked at each other for a moment. The girl scrambled over the headrest and dropped into the seat next to him.

'I'm Martha,' she said. 'I play French horn.'

'Er, me too,' said Alex. 'Bro.'

Martha beamed. 'Hey! You're the one they got to replace Tania! I'm Second Horn.'

'Great!' said Alex, nodding. 'So cool!'

The girl looked at him incredulously.

'Er, not really,' she said. 'I *used* to be Second Horn, until Tania came along. And now I'm playing all the bits under you, even though you've never played with us before. Didn't you know that?'

'Er . . . yeah,' said Alex.

'Then that was a really insensitive thing to say,' she said.

'Yeah!' Alex shouted, nodding helplessly. 'Totally!'

Martha turned to face the window absent-mindedly. She didn't seem to be bothered by how much Alex was sweating.

'Actually I don't mind being Second Horn,' she said. 'I still get some good bits, and there's less pressure. Plus it means I don't have to sit behind Trent Davis. He plays piccolo. He's a reprobate and he stinks of farts.'

A head popped up from across the aisle. 'Shut up, Martha.'

Martha ignored him and turned back to Alex. 'So why are you in Conduct Yourselves?'

Alex thought fast. 'Me? I just, like, love beating people up,' he said. 'It's brilliant.'

Martha shrugged. 'Yeah, the other kids here are like that too. Not me though. I just keep getting into fights. My parents think I do it on purpose.'

'Cool!' said Alex.

'It's not cool!' Martha snapped. 'I don't want to be here. I'm no bully. I'm just sick of bigger kids thinking they can boss me about.'

Alex sighed. 'Yeah,' he said. 'I know what you mean.'

'I stick up for myself, that's all,' she said. 'If I went around picking fights I'd be no better than Trent Davis, and he's a reprobate who stinks of farts.'

The head popped up again. 'Shut *up*, Martha!'

'You shut up, Trent!' she snapped back.

'Then stop saying I stink of farts!' Trent shouted.

'I'll say whatever I damn well please!' Martha shouted back, standing up in her seat. 'Got a *problem* with that and I'll punch your lights out!'

Alex tugged at her socks nervously. 'Er, Martha, I don't think . . .'

'Sit *down*, Martha!' someone shouted wearily.

'Yeah, sit down, Martha,' Trent sneered. 'And stop shouting so much . . . don't want your *false teeth* to fall out, do we?'

Everyone howled with laughter. Martha's face turned beetroot red, and she quickly sat down again. Alex looked at her with confusion. She was making a concerted effort not to meet anyone's gaze. Trent sensed his moment and leaped across the aisle, snatching a rucksack from the luggage rack.

'*Don't!*' Martha cried furiously, tugging it back. But she was too late. Trent had ripped open the top and grabbed something from inside, and was now waving it above his head for all to see. The bus howled with laughter. Alex looked up. It was a small carton of soup. A single plastic spoon had been carefully Sellotaped to its side. Trent leaned down and waved it in front of Martha's face.

'More soup, Grandma?'

Her response was so quick that Alex barely saw it happening. In a moment Martha had swung out her leg and stamped the carton against Trent's chest, bursting it open and spraying the surrounding eight rows in an enormous sloppy geyser of carrot and coriander. Everyone screamed and leaped out of their seats.

'You idiot, Martha!'

'You're dead!'

'Get her!'

'*Wait!*' someone shouted.

Everyone stopped. A few seats ahead, an older girl was standing up, holding her arms out over the crowd.

'We're stopping,' she murmured. 'The bus. It's stopping.'

Everyone froze. Alex's hair stood on end. She was right – the bus was slowing down.

'What's going on?' said Martha.

The bus ground to a halt. The children began muttering with confusion, piling over each other and wiping the soup off the windows to look outside. Either side of the bus were empty fields. They were in the middle of nowhere.

'Where are we?' someone said. 'This isn't the Baboon Sanctuary.'

Everyone suddenly started talking at once. Alex's face drained of all colour, and he sank into his chair, his heart racing. They had stopped the bus. They'd found him.

'Oh crikey,' he whimpered.

A wail of feedback suddenly came out over the bus speakers, silencing the crowd of muttering children. Steph was standing at the front with a microphone.

'Settle down, everyone!' she announced, waving her hands. 'In your seats, everyone! I need quiet. I have a very important – *Oliver I said quiet!* – a very important announcement to tell you all.'

A hush finally descended on the bus. Steph paused for a moment, brushing her hair behind her ears.

'First of all,' she said, 'I'd like to reassure you that I've just spoken to Tania's mother at the hospital and she says she's going to be fine. They're cutting her hair out of the bike wheels this afternoon.'

There was a polite round of applause.

'But more importantly,' she continued, 'I have some news that you may find shocking.' She paused to take a breath. 'We will not be performing at the Howler Woods Baboon Day Celebrations this afternoon.'

A series of dramatic chords came swelling from a huge organ at the front of the bus. Steph sighed and rubbed her temples.

'Clarissa, was that entirely necessary?'

'Sorry,' came a quiet voice.

She pointed angrily down the aisle. 'Go and sit with Noah.'

A young girl with glasses got up and slumped reluctantly down the gangway. Steph turned back to the bus.

'I repeat,' she said. 'We are not going to be performing at Howler Woods Baboon Sanctuary.'

'But we've been learning our parts for months!' someone cried at the front. Everyone muttered in agreement.

'*We won't be performing at Howler Woods*,' Steph said carefully, waving them quiet, 'because, in fact, we've been booked to play another concert all along. A top-secret one.'

A mutter of intrigue fluttered over the seats. Steph smiled.

'The Howler Woods concert was a cover-up,' she said breathlessly, 'for something far more important. Something so important that we had to keep the fact a complete secret . . . even from you. Even I didn't know the whole truth – I only found out the location this morning.'

Steph took the opportunity for another dramatic pause. There was total silence.

'We have been asked', she said slowly, a smile stealing across her face, 'to perform for none other than Davidus Kyte!'

The bus gasped with excitement. Alex's stomach flipped.

'. . . Davidus Kyte?' he said.

'Davidus Kyte!' cried Martha.

'Why?' came a shout from the front.

'Conduct Yourselves orchestra', said Steph, waving her quiet, 'have been asked to perform at the grounds of the Grand Expedition Centre the day after tomorrow.'

There were a handful of gasps across the bus.

'The Grand Expedition Centre!' someone shouted. 'Does that mean . . . ?'

'That's right,' Stephanie laughed. 'You're all going to the *Cusp*!'

The bus went wild. In one moment everyone had leaped from their seats, shaking their neighbour in disbelief. The Cusp! They were going to see the Cusp! Everyone knew someone who knew someone who had once talked to a person who had been inside the Cusp, but to see it with *their own eyes* . . . to pass the rows of security fences and enter the top-secret base, and stand within a stone's throw of the Forbidden Land itself? It was a once-in-a-lifetime opportunity. Within seconds the whole bus had taken the opportunity to grab whatever instruments were to hand, and were playing out a glorious, rambling celebration march that shook the windows of the bus and made Steph's microphone send out another earsplitting wail of feedback. The incident with the soup was forgotten. No one wanted to fight now. They were going to the Cusp. They were the luckiest children in the world.

With one exception.

'Oh crikey,' Alex muttered, as the bus pulled off and made its way down the barren road ahead.

Part Two

The Cusp

6

'What do you mean, they're not here?!'

Matthew the Headmaster stared in horror at the giant baboon across the counter. It was wearing a shirt and tie. The shirt had a label on the chest pocket that said 'Information'. The tie had bananas on it. The baboon mumbled something apologetic.

'For the last time, I can't hear you with that stupid thing on!' Matthew snapped.

The baboon sighed and pulled its head off. Underneath was a much smaller head, belonging to a middle-aged man. His glasses were steamed up. He took them off and wiped them with a tissue.

'I said,' the man repeated, 'there's no orchestra here. Period.'

'There must be,' Matthew begged.

'Check if you want!' the man snorted, jerking his

thumb behind him. Matthew looked over his shoulder. Howler Woods Baboon Sanctuary was a handful of cages surrounding an empty stage. If there was an orchestra inside, then it was very well hidden. Officer Mike shoved Matthew aside.

'Let me explain,' he said, leaning over the counter. 'One of this man's pupils was supposed to be playing in a concert here today. He's with a youth orchestra, something to do with behavioural issues . . .'

The man in the baboon suit shook his head. 'Never heard of them. There's never been a booking for an orchestra here.'

Officer Duncan's head popped up from behind Mike's shoulder.

'So if they're not here,' he asked meekly, 'then . . . where have they gone?'

The man in the baboon suit shrugged. 'Beats me.'

All four men stood in silence. The only sound was the occasional sad honk of a baboon in the distance. A drizzle started falling.

'Mike,' said Officer Duncan. 'We are in so much trouble.'

'Shut up, Duncan,' Mike snapped.

Matthew turned away and put his head in his hands. The last hour had passed like a terrible nightmare. Once they'd injected Jeremy's backside with enough adrenalin to stop the allergic reaction – and he'd finished crying – he'd explained about Alex stealing the horn and taking his place on the bus for the Howler Woods Baboon Day Concert. They'd all shot to the police car only to find that the locks had been glued in – another new addition to the ever-growing list of First Day pranks, apparently. Matthew had dragged Laurence Davy out of detention and told him he'd be expelled if he didn't break into the car for them.

Matthew looked up at the darkening clouds above him. It was his first day as a headmaster. He'd already turned up late, hospitalised a child with a bike, sent another into anaphylactic shock, forced one to commit an arrestable crime and sent another on a run from the law . . .

And yet all he could think about was the look in Alex's eyes as he'd been dragged away.

At that moment, his phone started ringing. Matthew took it out of his pocket and looked at the screen. He gulped.

'Oh no,' he said, turning to the policemen. 'It's the school.'

The policemen winced. Matthew stared at the phone like it was a knife he had decided to stab himself with. He answered it with gritted teeth.

'. . . Hello?'

'*Matthew!*' It was Mrs Beaumont. She sounded furious.

'Where on earth have you gone?!'

'Ah, Mrs Beaumont,' Matthew said, wrapping himself against the drizzle and stepping away from the policemen. '. . . How are you?'

'How am I?' she spluttered. *'Matthew, you're supposed to be here dealing with troublemakers – the whole place is in chaos! Where have you gone?'*

'Where have I gone?' Matthew repeated nervously, looking around him. 'I'm, er . . . I'm at Howler Woods.'

There was a heavy silence.

'. . . Howler Woods, the Baboon Sanctuary?'

'Yes,' said Matthew.

There was a pause.

'Why, Matthew?'

'We've, er . . .' Matthew took a glance back at the policemen. They seemed to be having a heated argument. 'Well, we've lost Alex Jennings, Mrs Beaumont.'

He was met with silence.

'. . . You what?'

'We've lost Alex Jennings,' he repeated. His heart sank. It made it sound even more real to say it again. 'He ran away. And no one knows where he is.'

Mrs Beaumont was silent. Matthew stood in the drizzle. His blazer was slowly soaking through.

'Matthew,' she began again. Her voice was wound like an iron spring. *'This is a matter for the police, not for you.*

Let them get on with their job and come back here at once.'

Matthew glanced around at the policemen. They were still arguing in the rain behind him.

'You don't understand, Mrs Beaumont,' said Matthew. 'The way he looked at me when they took him away . . . it was like I'd failed him. And now he's out there, frightened, with nowhere to go . . .'

'*Headmaster*,' she interrupted furiously, '*I can't listen to this for a moment more! Get back to your school this instant and . . .'*

Someone tapped Matthew on the shoulder. He turned around. The policemen were standing nervously, waiting for him to finish.

'I have to go, Mrs Beaumont,' said Matthew. 'I'll speak to you later.'

'*Matthew! . . .'*

Matthew cut the phone off and turned back to the policemen. They both seemed extremely tense.

'Mr Price,' said Officer Mike, 'we really have to get going.'

Matthew nodded. 'Yes, of course we do,' he said. 'Where do you suggest we go now? The police station?'

Officer Mike shifted uncomfortably. Behind him, Officer Duncan was beginning to squirm.

'We really don't need your help any more, Mr Price,' said Officer Mike. 'But thanks for the offer. We'll drop you back at the school now if you don't mind.'

Matthew sighed. The rain was falling heavier now. He would have to fill out all the paperwork on Alex's disappearance.

'Yes,' he said sadly. 'I suppose you're right. I guess I should really get back to w—'

'*We're not really police officers!*' Officer Duncan suddenly cried out.

Officer Mike looked as if he'd had his legs kicked out from under him. Matthew did a double take.

'Er . . . pardon?'

'Nothing!' Mike quickly shouted.

'. . . Did you just say you're not police officers?' said Matthew suspiciously.

'No, no!' Mike laughed, gripping Duncan's arm a little too tightly. 'My colleague here is just a little confused, *aren't you Officer Duncan . . .*'

'I'm not Officer Duncan!' he cried, throwing himself forward and grabbing Matthew by the lapels. 'I'm just Duncan! *Duncan!* I'm not a police officer, and neither is he!'

'Shut up, you idiot!' Mike hissed, dragging him off Matthew. 'Don't you realise what you're saying?'

'I can't take the lies any more, Mike!' Duncan cried. 'I thought I could, but I can't! They're just confusing my head!'

'So . . .' said Matthew slowly. 'You're *not* policemen . . .'

'No!' said Duncan. 'It's all lies! We stole the outfits and the car!'

Matthew's jaw dropped. '. . . You *what?*' he said.

'We work for Davidus Kyte!' Duncan wailed.

'You *idiot!*' Mike roared, shoving Duncan aside. 'Shut up before you make it any worse!'

'It can't get any worse, Mike!' cried Duncan, shoving him back. 'We've lost the boy! There's no way we can get him to the Cusp before tomorrow night . . . Davidus is going to kill us, Mike! Kill us!'

The man fell to his knees in the car park, burying his face in his hands. Mike looked like he was strongly considering punching him, but managed to contain it. Matthew stared at them both in disbelief.

'So then Alex's father . . .' he said quietly.

'He's disappeared!' Duncan wailed from behind his hands. 'When he broke into the base the other night, they lost him – nobody has a clue where he is! He could be anywhere!'

Mike shook him with fury. '*Shut up, you moron!*'

'It was all Kyte's idea,' Duncan continued, undeterred. 'He thought that if he had the boy, then he could use him to get Jennings back without anyone finding out he'd messed up!'

'*Shut up, Duncan!*'

Matthew started trembling. 'But the letter from the Grand High Pooh-Bah . . .'

'It's a fake!' cried Duncan. 'Just a telephone bill! That I haven't paid!'

'And Alex's mother . . . ?' said Matthew quietly.

'Duncan!' Mike warned.

'She has no idea!' Duncan wailed.

Mike slapped himself with despair and rolled his eyes.

Matthew's eyes widened. 'You were . . . *kidnapping* him?'

'Great!' Mike snapped, throwing Duncan to the ground. 'Nice going, Officer Dipstick. Now we have to kidnap *him*, too.'

Matthew started. 'What? Kidnap me?'

'Yep,' said Mike, shaking his head. 'Thanks to Constable Blabbermouth here. Duncan, give me the handcuffs.'

'Y-you don't have to kidnap me,' Matthew stammered, his eyes darting about the car park. 'I didn't hear anything. Honest. Just let me go and I won't say a thing.'

Mike snorted. 'Yeah, right. Duncan, give me the handcuffs already. We can keep him in the boot of the car.'

'I don't have them,' said Duncan, standing up and wiping his eyes. Mike bristled.

'Yes you do.'

'I don't!'

'I gave you the handcuffs this morning.'

'Yeah, they're in my coat pocket.'

'Where's your coat?'

'In the car.'

Mike sighed. 'What did you leave it in the car for?'

'I forgot.'

'What have I told you about leaving the handcuffs in the car?' Mike snapped. 'Anything could happen. For Pete's sake, let's just get them and kidnap him now before anything else goes wro—'

Mike froze. The man in the baboon suit was strolling towards them. They all stared silently as he came to a stop beside them and rocked on his heels, leisurely eating a microwave pasty.

'Everything OK, officers?' he asked, munching at the pasty. Mike and Duncan shared a glance.

'Everything's fine, sir,' said Mike calmly.

'Oh, right,' said the man. 'Thought I'd check. I could swear I heard a little girl crying down here a moment ago.'

Mike stared at Duncan with fury. 'We've seen nothing,' he said through gritted teeth. 'We were just about to get on our way, actually – weren't we, Mr Price?'

He put a hand on Matthew's shoulder and clenched threateningly. All three of them grinned at exactly the same time.

'That's right!' said Matthew.

'Right ho,' said the man cheerily. 'Well, just so you know, there's been an announcement on TV. Apparently

Davidus Kyte's holding a big press conference at the Cusp tomorrow morning. Exciting stuff, eh?'

'Yes,' said Mike darkly. 'Very exciting.'

'Mmm,' said the man. 'Thought that might be where your orchestra have gone to.'

He took another bite of his pasty and chewed on it thoughtfully. The other three stared at him.

'. . . Pardon?' said Mike.

The man swallowed. 'Well, if it's a *really* big announcement then they might need an orchestra. To perform for the ceremony and that. And of course, they'd have had to lie about where they were going, seeing as it's the Cusp. To cover themselves up. So maybe that's where they were really going all along.'

The man rocked on his heels. Mike's face broke into a smile.

'Of course,' he beamed. 'For the ceremony the day after tomorrow . . . they're at the Cusp!'

The man popped the last piece of pasty in his mouth and brushed the crumbs off his hands, and turned away.

'Well, glad I could help, officers,' he said with a wave. 'Good luck wi—'

'*We're not really police officers!*' Duncan screamed, bursting into tears.

The man stopped. 'Come again?'

Mike flipped round. '*Shut up, Duncan!*'

'And we're going to kidnap him!' he wailed, pointing to Matthew. Matthew waved. Mike punched Duncan in the head.

'Great!' he bellowed. 'Now we have to kidnap *him* as well!'

'What?' said the man.

'Who?' said Duncan.

'The gorilla!' said Mike.

'I'm supposed to be a baboon,' said the man.

'I don't want to kidnap anyone!' sobbed Duncan.

'You haven't left us much choice!' Mike roared.

'Can't we just let them go?' cried Duncan.

'No we can't!' Mike screamed.

'I don't want you to kidnap me,' said the man in the suit.

'Why can't you keep your mouth shut?!' Mike spluttered.

'I'm sorry!' wailed Duncan.

'This is probably the tenth time you've done this!'

'I said I'm sorry!'

'You have to get some self-control!'

'I'm trying.'

'It's just getting ridiculous now.'

'I am trying.'

'I know you're trying, mate.'

'I really am.'

'I know.'

'I'm sorry I ruined it, Mike.'

'No, I'm sorry. I don't mean to be down on you all the time.'

'Thanks, Mike.'

The two men gave each other a pat on the back and smiled.

'Right, let's just kidnap them and get it over with,' said Mike, sighing with relief.

'What, both of us?' said the man in the baboon suit.

The policemen nodded.

'Good luck,' said the man. 'He ran off ages ago.'

Mike and Duncan swung round. Matthew was gone. So was the police car. All that was left was a set of tyre marks speeding across the wet gravel and off down the road.

'Ah,' said Mike.

They stood in the rain for some time.

'So what do we do now?' said Duncan.

The man in the baboon suit shrugged.

'You could call the police,' he suggested.

7

By the time the bus had been waved through the last level of security, and all of Alex's chances of escape were erased completely, night was falling. The children sat up frantically, exhausted and breathless with excitement.

'Jeremy, we're moving!' Martha cried, bouncing on her seat. 'We're finally here!'

'Mmm,' said Alex.

Everyone fought to be the first to press themselves up against the windows and see the Cusp with their own eyes. They gasped. The setting sun stretched across the endless concrete before them, bathing the base in a golden light. Cast against the reddening horizon were row upon row of enormous warehouses. Hundreds of men were running around, stopping and starting, clambering over piles of sandbags, screaming into walkie-talkies, herding lorries and cranes across the runways. The air was thick with shouting and drilling. It was chaos.

'Come on Jeremy, you're not going to see *anything* down there,' Martha sighed, prodding him with her foot. 'Just look out of the window.'

'I can't!' Alex protested. 'I'm feeling carsick! I told you . . .'

'I don't think hiding under your seat cures carsickness, Jeremy,' she said sarcastically. She dragged him off the floor and plonked him back onto his seat.

Alex hid himself from view and peeked carefully out the window. Everywhere he looked people were charging about, carrying big metal cages in and out of the warehouses. A speeding truck careered past them, missing the bus by inches and screeching to a stop at the nearest warehouse doorway. At once a dozen men ran up and threw open the back doors. Alex sat up in amazement. The inside of the truck was stacked up with cage after cage of barking dogs.

'Look at that!' he said, shaking Martha. 'Dogs! Loads of them!'

The dogs were all spinning around inside their cages and wagging their tails, barking and whining in fear and excitement. Their cages were carted off the back of the truck as quickly as they had arrived, and carried into the darkness of the warehouse behind them. The truck sped off and was immediately replaced by another. Alex turned to Martha, beaming.

'They had beagles!' he said. 'At least ten of them. They're my favourite dog. Actually probably more like third favourite. Definitely my favourite of the hound category anyway.'

Martha gave him a bemused look.

'I mean, dogs are for losers,' Alex quickly corrected himself. 'Yeah, I totally beat people up who like dogs.'

'Really,' she smirked. 'Well, there's plenty more where they came from.'

She nodded out the back window. Alex looked up. The line of honking lorries stretched all the way out of the base. He turned back to her in disbelief.

'What do they need so many dogs for?' he said.

The bus came to a sudden stop. Everyone jumped up, stretching their legs and pushing each other irritably. Steph leaped into action with her microphone and blocked them all from escaping.

'Sit down everyone!' she shouted, waving her arms. 'I know we're all very excited. I am too. A few words while we wait for our guide. We've got less than two days to prepare for the performance of our lives. Now, they still can't tell us what we're actually performing *for* – all I know is that we'll be playing one song. So remember – while you're here, you're representing the orchestra. No running around! No breaking away from the group! *Straight* into rehearsal. Maximum energy, maximum focus!'

Before anyone could protest the rubber doors hissed open and a man stepped onto the bus. Alex gasped. He was wearing a black tie and tails and had an enormous metal helmet on his head. Alex instantly flew back under his seat.

'What's wrong with you?' Martha said, punching him on the shoulder. 'How can you be carsick when the bus isn't even moving?'

'*Shh!*' Alex hissed desperately. 'That man! He . . .' He stopped himself. The man who had just stepped onto the bus was not Davidus Kyte. He was a rather gentle-looking man in the exact same clothes, with a clipboard not unlike Steph's in his hands. Alex blushed and pulled himself back onto the seat.

'Conduct Yourselves orchestra?' the man said, flipping through his ream of papers. 'We were expecting you twenty minutes ago.'

Steph smiled apologetically. 'Yes, we are late, sorry about that,' she laughed. 'If it's fine by you, we'll just get straight to the concert hall and . . .'

'No chance,' said the man, shaking his head sadly. 'You've missed your slot. Concert hall's booked.'

Steph's face fell. 'What? But – but we're playing the day after tomorrow, we have to rehearse and . . .'

'You'll have to book another slot for tomorrow morning,' the man said, shaking his head. 'Right now the hall's being used to store dogs. Things run on a fairly tight schedule around here. They have to. That's why we have the Rota.'

He held up the clipboard, admiring it like a precious stone.

'I suggest you get to your rooms for now,' he said. 'We'll bring you over some dinner. Where are you booked?'

'Er . . .' Steph rifled through her clipboard in a panic. '. . . B Block.'

'Not any more you're not,' said the man, scanning the Rota. 'B Block's being used to store dogs.'

Steph threw up her arms.

'So what are we supposed to do?' she snapped. 'Sleep outside? Or is *that* being used to store dogs too?'

The man looked at her without blinking. 'Ha ha,' he said blithely. He turned round. 'Come with me, I'll take you down to T Block. You can sleep there for tonight. Better bring all your luggage now, it's quite a walk.'

Steph furrowed her brow. 'Walk?' she called after him. 'Can't we just drive? The children all have instruments, some of which are very heavy and . . .'

'Miss,' the man interrupted. 'You don't understand. We'll be walking right along the boundary. Engines don't work around it.'

Steph pressed on her temples and turned back to the bus.

'Change of plan!' she shrieked. 'No rehearsal! Get your instruments and wait outside the bus!'

The children fought tooth and nail to be the first outside. Soon they were all standing out on the runway, chattering excitedly and staring at the chaos that surrounded them. Despite Alex's best efforts to stay hidden under his seat he was dragged off by Martha and thrust out onto the concrete. She stepped down after him, shaking her legs, and suddenly started hopping up and down.

'Ow!' she said. 'Aaargh! Can you feel that?'

Alex looked blank. 'Feel what?'

'In your feet!' she said, hopping away. Alex looked around. The others were all doing it too. He shrugged.

'Not really,' he said, looking down at his feet. He couldn't feel anything.

'Like pins and needles?' Martha said, shuffling uncomfortably. 'It's agony! Ooh! That's the last time I sit on a stupid bus for eight hours.'

The man with the clipboard stepped forward.

'Right, hello everyone!' he called. 'My name's Greg. I'm going to show you how things work around here.'

'Why are you dressed like a knob?' someone shouted.

'*Oliver!*' Steph screamed.

'Rehearsal costume, Oliver,' Greg replied politely, not

missing a beat. 'Now listen up! As you can see we're going to be walking across a very busy base. It's very easy to get lost here. If in doubt, always head for the statue.'

He pointed behind them, and they all turned round. Jutting above the chaos of the base was an enormous brass statue. It was of a man in a metal diving suit, his helmet topped by a great plume of feathers. In one great hand he held up a flaming torch. In the other he held out a pointed sword. Before they had a chance to admire it for too long Greg had already shot off down the runway. The children didn't need any more reminding. They charged after him, their instruments clattering on the ground and bashing against each other. Alex tried to subtly sidestep away, but Martha grabbed him by the arm.

'Come on!' she shouted, dragging him along. 'Why do you keep *doing* that?'

'First things first,' Greg called out behind him. 'We are no longer in the Outskirts: we are in the Cusp, closer to the Forbidden Land than most people get to be in their entire lifetimes. First rule of the Cusp: things act differently here. No one really knows why. It's just one of the many mysteries of the Cusp. As you've already heard me say, engines stop working once you get near it. That's why they can't send planes or cars over the boundary, and why we can't have lorries going any farther than F Block.'

He indicated the enormous set of barracks beside him.

Alex peered through the windows as they raced past. It was filled with barking dogs.

'You're probably exhausted already,' said Greg sympathetically. 'And quite homesick. Am I right?'

Everyone muttered in agreement.

'Yes, being near the Forbidden Land does that too. Anyone have an itching in their feet yet?'

Everyone around Alex nodded in amazement. He looked down at his feet again. He still felt nothing.

'That's the Forbidden Land again,' Greg smiled. 'Just something it does to us humans. For now it's nothing extra socks won't cure, but it gets even worse when you cross the boundary apparently. And speaking of which . . .'

Greg stopped sharply, forcing the children to slam to a halt. One by one they looked up. Somebody dropped a glockenspiel.

'Whoa,' said Steph.

'I don't believe it,' said Martha.

'Oh crikey,' said Alex.

'Ladies and gentlemen,' said Greg with a grin, holding up his arm, '. . . the Forbidden Land.'

The concrete walkway ahead of them suddenly ended. Immediately beyond it was grassland, the lushest and greenest grassland one could possibly imagine. It was the green of a grass that has never been set foot on. It stretched out ahead of them as flat and perfect and round as a lake in the morning. At its very centre – like some distant continent – stood a vast forest, each tree a hundred metres tall. The children stood in silence, awestruck. They were looking at the Forbidden Land.

'The Cusp runs, as you can see, in a perfect circle,' said Greg, indicating the faultless line. 'It's mathematically perfect. As is the boundary; as is the Forbidden Land; as is the forest in the centre, which stops us from seeing what might actually lie within the centre. It's one of the reasons for the statue.'

Greg turned round to face the enormous brass diver again.

'The statue is like a lighthouse,' he said, his face glowing. 'Built for the Jennings Expedition. There's a bulb inside the helmet to guide anyone back here who gets lost. You can see the light from the Order's second base, right across the other side of the Outskirts.'

There was a dark mutter across the group. Everyone had heard stories about the other base. Greg looked nervously around and quickly regained himself.

'And speaking of the boundary,' he warned, 'here's the second rule of the Cusp: whatever you do, *don't step across it*. Don't even pretend to as a joke. I mean it! No matter how much you might want to try and walk into the Forbidden Land, stay right away. Does anyone here know what happens once you step over the boundary?'

The group was silent. A girl put her hand up.

'You . . . you run away,' she said quietly.

Greg snapped his fingers. 'Precisely. Something takes over your body, and there's nothing you can do about it. You'll find yourself running all the way home, and you won't stop till you get there. Not for sleep, food . . . nothing. And when I say straight home, I mean straight home! And that's even if you make it past the barbed-wire fences, which most don't. Not a pretty sight. And even if you do make it we have to run alongside you with a drip so you don't pass out. Don't even *ask* what happens if you live overseas. Come on!'

Greg suddenly turned and marched swiftly along the runway, skirting the great curve of the line where concrete met grass. The children followed with their eyes fixed on the Forbidden Land, hypnotised.

'What's with the diving suit?' said Martha, nodding back at the statue.

Alex tried to appear nonchalant.

'Oh, that,' he said. 'The Head of Expeditions wore it on the last Expedition. Jennings, I think his name was.'

'Why?' said Martha.

Alex shrugged. 'Well, even if you're not stepping directly on the grass, once you cross the boundary the Forbidden Land tries to push you out. To try and make sure you can't get to the centre. It even gets harder to breathe, apparently. So they hooked him up to a pipeline for air. It's how they reeled him back in.'

'Wow,' said Martha in amazement. 'How do you know all that?'

Alex's face flushed, and he fell silent.

'And here', said Greg, coming to another stop, 'is where your group sleeps tonight. T Block.'

Everyone gasped with relief and threw down their instruments. Greg ticked away at his Rota with a flourish.

'I'm booking you into the concert hall for seven o'clock tomorrow morning,' he said, turning to Steph. 'It's the same time as the press conference, so nobody else will be using it. Don't be late.'

'We won't,' said Steph breathlessly. 'Any chance you can tell us what it *is* we're performing for now . . . ?'

'No,' said Greg, snapping his Rota shut. 'Now if you don't mind, I'm needed at dress rehearsal.'

He dashed off and was gone. Steph muttered darkly and turned to the group.

'Well, you heard him, guys!' she said. 'We've got *one* practice before the big performance. Everyone ready to give it everything they've got?'

Everyone cheered weakly.

'And maybe, if there's time at the end of rehearsal,' Steph said, suddenly turning to Alex, 'our new stand-in

Jeremy can entertain us with a solo performance.'

Alex gulped. 'Er . . . pardon?'

Steph turned to the group. 'What Jeremy here has been too modest to mention is that he's considered the best French horn player his age in the country. He's proof that children with behavioural issues can overcome their violent urges and show people their sensitive side. And I'm sure everyone will agree, we're all extremely grateful that he's chosen to bless our group with his extraordinary talent.'

Alex looked around in horror. Some of the other children were actually nodding.

'Come on, Jeremy!' said one. 'Do it!'

'Please!' said another.

'You're an inspiration to us all,' said Trent Davis, wiping away tears from the corners of his eyes. Alex looked around and took a deep breath.

'Cool,' he said emptily. 'That's totally cool.'

'Great!' Steph beamed.

Everyone applauded and patted Alex on the back. Alex gave a thumbs-up, his face crumpling with misery. He had no idea being popular was so awful.

'Well, come on everyone!' Steph shouted, running up the stairs. 'Let's get some well-earned rest for our big day tomorrow!'

Everyone grabbed their instruments and ran up the

stairs, piling in through the door. Alex sighed desperately and trudged after them.

'I didn't know you were good,' said Martha. 'You don't look it.'

'Oh yeah!' said Alex. 'I'm like, totally the best at horn playing there is!'

'What are you going to play us?' she asked.

'Oh, you know, whatever!' Alex laughed, looking away. 'Like, an opera, or whatever.'

'You're going to play a whole opera?' said Martha suspiciously.

'Awesome!' said Alex, fighting through the crowd to get away from her. But everyone had stopped and had started all shouting at once. Over the top of their voices, Steph's air-raid siren could be heard screaming with frustration. Alex pushed to the front and looked into their barracks. The room ahead of him was filled with hundreds of barking dogs.

8

The night watchman rubbed the stubble on his cheeks with a tea-stained hand and looked with apprehension at the young man standing in front of him. In all his years working as a security guard at the Cusp he hadn't seen much. He'd certainly never seen anyone quite like this.

'Please,' said the young man, clawing at the edge of the desk. 'I'm begging you.'

The night watchman glanced down nervously, shifted his half-eaten slice of cake a little closer and looked back up.

'Look,' he said wearily. 'I've already told you: there's nothing I can do. The bus got inside the perimeter a few hours ago. That's all I can say. Firstly, it's against base regulations to tell you anything else. Secondly, even if I *could* tell you, I wouldn't know who was on that bus.'

He punctuated the statement by taking a mouthful of cake.

'But it's an emergency,' said the man.

'So you keep saying,' said the night watchman through the cake, spraying crumbs across his front and a wide spread of the table. 'But that's just how things work around here.'

The young man groaned. The night watchman finished the cake and had a good long look at him. He wasn't certain, but he could almost swear the man was wearing a school blazer two sizes too big for him.

'Please,' the young man repeated. 'I'm desperate.'

'I can see that,' said the night watchman. 'But there's nothing I can do. Now if you don't mind, I'll have to ask you to leave. I'm extremely busy.'

He leaned back in his chair and folded his arms. The young man didn't move. The night watchman sat with arms crossed for a bit. Then he took a flapjack from his pocket and started eating it.

'You're not busy,' said the young man angrily. 'You're not doing anything!'

'I'm doing paperwork,' said the night watchman, nodding at the stack of papers on the desk in front of him. The young man grabbed the top sheet and looked at it.

'This is a script,' the young man said. 'For a local production of *HMS Pinafore*.'

'Give that back!' the night watchman yelled, snatching it out the young man's hands. 'All right, fine, I'm not busy. But I already told you, there's nothing I can do. Have you taken a look over there?'

He nodded at the vans piling up at the main gates in the distance, honking and flashing their headlights. People were jumping out, carting enormous television cameras and microphone booms up to the barbed-wire fence, vying for a good shot of the floodlit base in the distance.

'It's chaos,' said the night watchman. 'Vans coming in, vans coming out, everything's behind schedule . . . By tomorrow morning every news station in the world's going to be inside, too!'

'For the press conference?' said the man.

'Yep,' the night watchman nodded. 'There's going to be a big announcement. *Really* big.'

'Do you know what it is?'

The night watchman blinked.

'Er, no,' he said. 'They don't tell me stuff like that. It's top secret. But quite frankly our last concern is whether or not the wrong child is playing First French Horn in the orchestra.'

'Then let *me* in,' said the young man. 'Let me sort it out.'

The night watchman stared at him like he was

completely mad.

'Listen,' he sighed, picking up his phone. 'I'll do you a favour, seeing as I feel sorry for you. I'll send a message to the people at the boundary about your boy. How about that?'

The young man's face suddenly flooded with horror.

'No!' he cried, throwing himself over the counter and slamming his hand down onto the phone. 'Don't phone anyone!'

The night watchman leaped back a foot. 'What do you think you're doing?!' he bellowed. 'This is a security booth!'

The young man slithered over the counter and landed on the floor beside him, clutching the phone. The night watchman trembled with indignation.

'That's it!' he cried. 'Get out! I'm in a whole lot of trouble at the moment, believe you me, this is more than my job's worth!'

'Trouble?' said the young man.

'Yes, trouble!' the night watchman shouted, shoving the young man out the door.

'Is it to do with Alex J. Jennings the explorer?' said the young man quickly. 'And how he broke into the Cusp last night?'

The night watchman started and glared at him in horror.

'. . . You know about that?' he muttered.

The young man nodded. The night watchman dragged him back inside the booth, slamming the door behind him.

'Who told you?' he hissed, prodding him. 'Was it Steve?'

'Er . . .' said the young man.

'That's top-secret information!' the night watchman growled. 'No one's supposed to know about it! It was Steve, wasn't it? I bet it was Steve.'

'Er . . . yep,' the young man nodded.

The night watchman trembled with anger.

'That damn loudmouth! I'll kill him!'

'Is that why the announcement's been so sudden?' said the young man.

The night watchman's eyes widened with worry.

'It wasn't supposed to be announced for *months* yet,' he said. 'But ever since the break-in the whole place has gone crazy. Kyte's really spooked by it. I mean, I only turned my back for one second . . . how was I to know that nutjob was hiding outside my booth?'

'Alex J. Jennings?' said the young man. 'He just snuck past you?'

The night watchman sighed with humiliation. 'Worse. He waited until I went to the toilet and barricaded me inside with a chair. There's no windows in there or anything! And I'd left my walkie-talkie on the desk, so I couldn't call the other perimeters . . .'

'That's not your fault,' said the young man. 'It's a simple mistake. Anyone could have made it.'

'Exactly!' said the night watchman. 'But try telling that to management. "Gross negligence", they said! "Inadequacy"!'

'What, and it's *your* fault that you've been provided with improper facilities?' the young man said furiously. 'Without a panic alarm in the toilets? You're a security guard, for heaven's sake! You're risking your life every night! It's a disgrace!'

'You think?' said the night watchman.

'Without a doubt!' said the young man. 'Where's your toilet?'

'Here,' said the night watchman, opening a door at the back of the booth. The young man looked in and shook his head in disbelief.

'Barely even enough room to turn around,' he muttered. 'How long did you say you were stuck in there?'

'All night,' said the night watchman pitifully. 'I got terrible cramp.'

'Unbelievable!' the young man cried. 'And just look at how easy it is for me to lock you in here!'

He pushed the night watchman into the toilet.

'Yeah, you see?' said the night watchman. 'We should take some pictures and send them to the press! That'd show them!'

The young man closed the door. There was the sound of a chair being jammed under the handle. The night watchman pushed against the door.

'Yep, doesn't move an inch. Just goes to show, eh? Ridiculous.'

'Absolutely,' said the young man. From behind the door came the sound of a filing cabinet being dragged across the floor.

'No need for that, mate,' the night watchman shouted. 'The chair's all we need to prove it.'

'Great!' There was a smash, not unlike the sound a computer screen would make hitting the floor as the desk was overturned and placed against the door.

'You can let me out now,' said the night watchman.

There was no reply. The night watchman swore he could hear his locker being opened and his spare uniform being zipped up.

'Mate?' he said nervously.

And the sound of the booth door being slammed shut.

'Mate?'

Silence. The night watchman pushed against the door. It was stuck fast. He grabbed in his pocket for his walkie-talkie. He pulled out his half-eaten flapjack.

'Oh dear,' he said.

9

Alex peered out from under the blanket. The barracks were still and silent. Outside, dawn was breaking. The only sounds around him were the gentle snores of children and dogs lying side by side. The air was thick and warm with the smell of the sleeping dogs.

Now, Alex, said a voice in his head. *Now's your chance*.

Alex sat up and started. Something was brushing up against his leg. He looked down. At his side, a friendly-looking terrier was gazing up at him. It wore a black patch over one eye and was wagging his tail sleepily.

'Hello, friend,' whispered Alex.

The dog wagged his tail harder and made to lick Alex's face.

'*Shh!*' Alex said, pushing him gently away. 'Not now. Go back to sleep.'

The dog grumbled and fell drowsily back to the floor.

His chest was soon once again rising and falling and his legs gently kicking, dreaming his dog dreams.

Alex picked himself up and looked around the barracks. No one else was awake. Most were curled up on their bunk beds with a handful of snoozing schnauzers, or on the floor using fluffy poodles as makeshift pillows. Trent Davis was cuddling up to a snoring Dobermann. Only Martha lay alone against the wall, her back to the room. She was trying to hide her face, so no one could see she'd taken her teeth out for the night.

Alex tiptoed silently between the sleeping bodies and came to the door. His exit was blocked by Steph, sleeping surrounded by a collection of long-haired Labradoodles. Her arms were wrapped protectively around her clipboard.

'It's such an honour to receive this award,' she murmured groggily.

Alex took a silent breath and lifted up one leg. He stretched it over the mound of sleeping dogs, until in one giant step he had finally placed his foot on the other side. He held himself for a moment, legs akimbo. Then, in a flash, he whipped his other leg across and fell unsteadily against the door. No one stirred. Alex exhaled. He opened the door, fraction by fraction, and squeezed himself through the frame.

He stood outside in the early morning sun. In front of him stood the Unfinished Pier, a great broken mess of wooden boards and steel rivets jutting out from the boundary. The Forbidden Land lay stretching out before him, its waves of grass swelling with the breeze that seemed to blow endlessly across it.

'The Forbidden Land,' said Alex quietly.

He peered at the trees just visible on the horizon.

That's the forest, said the voice in his head. *The one he told you about*.

Alex stood and stared. Far away, the treetops leaned and swayed in the wind.

Do you remember the stories he used to tell you, before he got sick?

Alex's stomach tied itself in knots.

'Stupid,' he said out loud.

He crept down the runway, back towards the main part of the base. Work was still going on at a feverish pace under the glow of floodlights. Three more enormous warehouses had been put up, their curved steel roofs now alive with the flickering blowtorches of a hundred frantic welders. Alex leaned against the side of one of the buildings and peered around the edge. The perimeter fence was now in sight. Trucks were still pouring in, weaving through the bustling crowd of reporters and cameramen that clogged the runways.

'Perfect,' said Alex. All he had to do was hide in the crowds, and he'd be able to sneak back through the security fences without being noticed . . .

Only once you leave, said the voice, *you won't be able to come back*.

Alex started. 'Why would I want to come back?'

Deep down, Alex already knew the answer. His stomach tied itself in knots again.

'I already said,' he muttered. 'I can't save him. They'll find me, and lock me up too. And what good is that?'

You're just going to . . . leave him here?

'Why not?' said Alex bitterly. 'He left me too. He left me more than anyone else.'

You would rather run away, said the voice, *and live alone in the Outskirts?*

Alex turned back to the forest, a solitary island on the horizon.

'I'm alone already,' he said quietly.

'*WATCH OUT!*'

A speeding truck suddenly screeched to a stop, narrowly missing him. Alex swung round. The driver furiously leaned out the window.

'You idiot!' he cried. 'Are you trying to get yourself killed?'

Alex panicked. 'I . . . er . . .'

The worker shook his head and picked up a walkie-talkie. 'Kids! Hang on. What's your name?'

Alex didn't think. In one second he had spun on his

heel and flung himself into the darkness of the nearest warehouse.

'*Hey!*' cried the worker. '*Hey, come back!*'

Alex ran as fast as he could without looking back, his eyes desperately searching the darkness for a way out. All around him were cages, hundreds of cages lining the walls on every side, stacked right up to the ceiling. There was no way out. The air was filled with the echoes of barking dogs and the clanging of their metal doors as they tried to escape. He came to a far wall, and there it was – a metal door in the corner. He threw it open and fell into the dimly lit corridor that lay behind it. It was empty. Alex ran on, glancing fearfully over his shoulders. In the darkness it was impossible to tell if the man was following him or not. He had to keep running.

He turned a corner, skidding on his heels. At the end of the corridor was a shabby-looking curtain. He breathed a sigh of relief and flew inside. Alex stopped dead. He was on a stage. He was in front of an enormous crowd of people.

'Oh crikey,' he said.

He caught sight of a great long table in the centre of the stage beside him. Without another moment's pause he flung himself underneath it and covered his head with his hands. The auditorium was bustling and noisy. Nobody seemed to have noticed him come in. He carefully lifted the side of the tablecloth with a finger. The place was filled with hundreds upon hundreds of reporters, chatting animatedly to each other.

'Oh crikey,' Alex said again.

There was a wail of microphone feedback. Everyone turned excitedly to face the stage, and at once the air was filled with shouts and cries and the sounds of photographs being taken. Alex's eyes were suddenly blinded by a thousand camera flashes.

'Ladies and gentlemen,' came a voice over the speakers, 'thank you for your patience and co-operation this evening. The press conference is finally ready to begin. May I introduce the Official Head of Expeditions . . . Mr Davidus Kyte.'

Alex's stomach dropped. He crawled back as fast as he could to the edge of the table, but a pair of shoes immediately shot under the red tablecloth, missing his fingers by inches. The raised heels of Davidus Kyte were unmistakable. Alex fell backwards again, his heart racing.

He was trapped.

The applause died down. Kyte's reedy breath seethed out of the speakers around him.

'Good evening.'

The reporters fell silent. Kyte took the opportunity for a dramatic pause.

'For over a thousand years,' he began, 'the Order has

struggled in vain to discover what lies at the centre of the land beyond the boundary.'

He took another pause. You could have heard a pin drop.

'Tomorrow morning', he continued, 'will mark an historic moment in its relationship with that struggle. For too long the land past the boundary has been left unexplored, unknowable, undiscovered. But after tomorrow, our children will no longer think of the Cusp as the extent of man's knowledge.'

There was a growing murmur of excitement throughout the audience. The flashing of cameras reached a fever pitch.

'Because tomorrow,' Davidus announced, 'a new Expedition will set out across the boundary. And this time the Expedition shall succeed.'

The room exploded. Everyone started shouting at once. Alex lay on the carpet, his heart pounding.

'Quiet, please!' came a voice over the speakers. 'Mr Kyte will now take several questions from the audience.'

Alex peered carefully under the tablecloth. The reporters in front of him were now on their feet, waving their hands in the air.

'You,' came Davidus's voice, 'at the front.'

'Thank you, Mr Kyte,' said a woman in the front row. 'If you don't mind, would you please shed further light on *exactly* what's going to happen tomorrow? Are you going to journey into the Forbidden Land?'

Everyone nodded eagerly.

'Well, actually I *do* mind,' said Kyte testily. 'I mind because I cannot stand to hear what lies beyond the boundary referred to as the "Forbidden Land". It is idiotic to suggest that we've been "forbidden" from there, by any*one* or any*thing*. The land beyond the boundary is there to be discovered, just like everything else. And we will discover it.'

'But how do you intend to get to the centre of it?' said the woman. 'How exactly will you . . .'

'That's a secret,' Davidus snapped. 'Next question.'

The room burst into life again. The journalists all jumped to their feet and started leaping around, stretching their hands up as far as they could.

'You, second row, bad tie,' said Davidus.

'Thank you, Mr Kyte,' said the man, blushing. 'What exactly is the aim of this new Expedition?'

'What's that supposed to mean?' Davidus snapped. 'You heard me – we're going to discover what's at the centre.'

'Well, what if you do?' said the journalist. 'What do you plan to do with it once . . . or rather, *if* you've succeeded?'

Kyte sighed. 'There is no "if" here,' he said tersely. 'This Expedition combines established understanding of the so-called "Forbidden Land" with the most cutting-edge technology available. We cannot fail.'

'Well, excuse me for saying so, Mr Kyte,' said the reporter, 'but they've always said that.'

There was a collective gasp of astonishment, followed by total silence. Alex guessed by the way the journalists trembled that Kyte would be glaring at them.

'I mean,' said the man nervously, nervously rifling through a wad of notes in front of him, 'when the Order first set out to discover the centre, they were certain they would make it. They didn't. So did the Twenty-fourth Head of Expeditions, when he glued bird wings to his arms and threw himself off an enormous wooden diving board. He didn't. And when the One Hundred and Sixty-seventh Head of Expeditions used an enormous catapult to fling himself over the trees, and when the Three Hundred and Third Head of Expeditions ordered the building of the great Unfinished Pier to the centre . . .'

'Get to the point,' snapped Davidus.

'. . . Well, I guess what I'm saying', the man continued shakily, 'is that even on the last Expedition, the great explorer Alex J. Jennings assured us absolute success. What makes your Expedition any different?'

There was a dreadful silence. Someone took a photograph.

Kyte snorted. 'Well, let me start by saying that I greatly resent having my Expedition compared to *that* disaster,' he said. 'The last Expedition failed for one reason and one reason alone – Alex J. Jennings.'

Under the table, the young Alex's face burned.

'His poor decisions – his arrogance – his *inability* as Head of Expeditions,' Kyte continued, 'all doomed his attempt from the word go. You only have to look at the state of him now to see that he was never capable of leading an Expedition in the first place.'

Some of the journalists in the audience sniggered. Their papers had made a lot of money writing about Alex's father over the last few years. Alex clenched his fists and fought the urge to leap out and beat all of them senseless.

'In short,' said Kyte, 'I don't plan on making the same mistakes as him. Next questi—'

'But aren't you forgetting what Jennings said he saw in there?' someone interrupted. 'Surely what he says can't just be . . . disregarded?'

This was met by laughter from the audience. Davidus snorted into his microphone.

'What, about there being "nothing in the centre"?' he scoffed. 'Jennings said a lot of things. Let's not forget he said he was a dog, too.'

The audience burst into laughter. Alex watched them slap each other's backs, wiping tears from their eyes that weren't really there, and he trembled with silent rage. Davidus Kyte got to his feet and pushed himself away from the table.

'The launching ceremony is tomorrow morning at nine,' said Davidus. 'No further questions.'

Everyone groaned. Without further ado Kyte's shoes disappeared from beneath the tablecloth, and the journalists leaped to their feet and flew outside after him, grabbing phones and shouting orders to cameramen. Soon, silence had once again fallen over the room.

Alex lay on the carpet beneath the table, his heart thumping, his eyes brinking with furious tears. It had never been easy hearing people talk like that about his father. It stung just as hard every time. His mother still cried every time someone made a joke about his father in the street, or in the papers, or on the news.

Alex screwed his eyes shut.

His mother.

She had cried a lot over the past few years. Alex had learned that it usually helped to hug her when she did. Usually. Sometimes she shut herself in her room because she didn't want Alex to know she was crying. He could still hear her though. He would wait until she had stopped, and then pretend he was playing when she finally came out.

She hadn't always cried so much. It had started when Alex was about four years old. That was when his father first began to change.

He started going out for longer and longer walks. Soon

he was sleeping on top of the duvet, and then curled at the foot of the bed, eating without using his hands. Alex's mother came home one evening to find him pacing the garden, digging holes. She began to realise that he wasn't pretending any more.

Then one night, when Alex was four, his dad ran away to the Cusp. He started trying to step back over the boundary.

The first few times it happened the Order had allowed him to come straight home without pressing any charges. But that all changed when Kyte became Head of Expeditions. They started arresting him. They'd let him back home, when it looked like he wasn't trying to break into the Cusp any more, but he would always run away again the moment they did, and would have to be dragged screaming from the wire fence, crying out loud *Stop it stop it please, can't you see, I'm a dog, I'm a dog.*

He started getting ill. His hair came out in clumps and his breathing became more and more painful. He began to look like a man twice his age. Alex's mother said it was because of the time he had spent on the Expedition. It was making him age faster than normal people.

They stopped trying to send him home. They started keeping him in the hospital. Even then, he kept trying to escape.

Soon people from the Order came round the house to

ask Alex and his mother questions about why he kept doing it, questions that sometimes went on all night. And his mother would cry the next day when all the newspapers would print the same stories about Alex J. Jennings, the failed explorer, the lunatic, the mad dog-man.

What an embarrassment, they would say. *How difficult for his wife. How painful for his son.*

And then they would stand outside all day, taking pictures of the house.

'No,' said Alex out loud. 'Not again. Not this time.'

Alex wiped his eyes and crawled out from under the tablecloth. The room was empty now, and Alex was alone. He looked out over the rows of empty seats ahead of him. He knew what he had to do.

'I won't let you do it,' he said to the room. 'Not to him. Not to me.'

But Alex, said the voice. *There's nothing you can do. You said so yourself.*

'No,' said Alex defiantly. 'There is. I'm going to find him.'

He glared out over the room, across the empty chairs. In his mind it seemed like they were still full of journalists, laughing and pointing at him.

'Laugh all you want,' said Alex. 'I'm going to find him, and I'm going to get us both out of here.'

The journalists were changing now, morphing into the

grinning faces of all the bullies at school. They changed again and again, into the howling face of Mr Braker, the scowls of the policemen, the sneer of Kyte.

'We'll run away,' he said. 'Far away from all of you. You'll never find us again.'

And again they changed. From each of the hundred chairs, his mother looked back at him. Alex's stomach once again tied itself in knots.

'We don't need you,' he said. 'We don't need anyone.'

Suddenly a hand grabbed his shoulder and spun him round. Alex gasped and stared up at the face before him. It was a man in thick, mud-smeared glasses. His cheeks were covered in a patchy five o'clock shadow, and his eyes were crazed. He was wearing vicar's robes. Alex tried to pull himself free, but the man grabbed at him feverishly, his breath coming out in a rabid croak.

'*Alex . . .*'

'Jeremy?' came a voice behind them.

Alex flipped round. Standing at the entrance to the room, waving her French horn, was Martha.

'Where have you *been*?' she gasped. 'You missed the rehearsal!'

'I . . . er . . .' Alex turned back to the man, but he was already sprinting away across the stage. He flung himself through a door and was gone. Martha ran down the aisle towards him.

'So it turns out we're performing at the launch of the Expedition tomorrow,' said Martha. 'How good is that? We couldn't rehearse without you, though. We had to give up the slot to someone else on the Rota. Steph cried and ate a bit of her clipboard. It was brilliant.'

'I . . .'

'It's OK, you don't need to explain,' she said. 'I know why you ran away.'

Alex's eyes widened. 'You do?'

'Yep,' said Martha. 'You don't know a thing about the French horn, do you?'

Alex considered the best answer.

'No,' he said.

'Thought not,' she said. 'And you're not a bully either.'

'No,' said Alex.

'Are you actually Jeremy Butterworth?'

'No,' said Alex.

'Who are you?'

'I'm Alex Jennings,' said Alex.

Martha frowned. 'What, the famous explorer?'

'No, his son. I'm running away from the police because they think my dad's some kind of maniac terrorist and I'm helping him, but I'm not. I just like dogs.'

'I see,' said Martha.

'Only now I've ended up where they were trying to take me in the first place, and so I need to find where they're keeping my dad and help him escape from prison, and then get us both out of here before anybody sees me.'

'Right,' Martha said, nodding calmly. She looked as if she was deciding how best to style his hair.

'Well, first things first,' she sighed, grabbing his hand, 'let's get you back to the barracks. There's no chance of getting out of this place now. The launch ceremony tomorrow morning's your best bet – everyone's going to be too busy watching the Expedition set off. Until then we need to make sure nobody else suspects you're a fraud, so you'd better listen to everything I say.'

She started dragging him out of the hall. Alex smiled.

'Martha . . .' he said.

'Yes, Alex?'

'How did you know?'

'Know what?'

'That I wasn't a bully?'

Martha snorted. 'Let's just say that jumper does you no favours. And no offence but when you try to talk cool you sound like a total idiot.'

'Right.'

'Don't mention it.'

'Thank you, Martha.'

'You're most welcome, Alex,' she said. 'So, who was that weird old man standing next to you?'

10

Matthew stood with his back to the stage door, his heart thundering against his chest. Alex and the girl's voices disappeared into the distance, out the auditorium behind him. He gasped and wiped his brow. He thought he'd blown his cover when the girl arrived, but it looked like they weren't following him. Matthew beamed. He had done it. He had found Alex.

Not that the boy had recognised him. But then, looking down at the state of himself, Matthew wasn't really surprised. He had spent the entire night clambering over barbed-wire fences and being chased by guard dogs. The night watchman's uniform had been caked in mud and ripped to shreds before Matthew had even stepped a foot inside the base. Realising he'd be found out if he didn't get clean clothes quickly, he'd hidden in an alleyway and knocked unconscious the first person who walked past.

Matthew looked down at his cassock in dismay. It wasn't his fault. How was he to have known that there'd be an elderly vicar wandering round a top-secret army base in the middle of the night?

His phone started ringing. It had been ringing all night.

He pulled it out of his pocket, and looked at the screen. It told him that he had 142 missed calls, all from Cloisters School, and that they were trying to phone him once again. Matthew sighed, and answered.

'Mrs Beaumont,' he said.

'*Matthew!*' she cried. '*Where are you?!*'

'. . . Mrs Beaumont?' Matthew repeated. Something didn't sound right. He was sure he could hear some kind of engine revving in the background. 'Is everything OK?'

'*You have to come back, Matthew!*' she cried. '*It's the children! They've taken over the school! They're like animals!*'

'What?' Matthew gasped. 'But how . . .'

'*First Day Festivities!*' she sobbed. '*Laurence Davy went around telling everyone you said it's school rules to break into cars! They've been doing doughnuts over the rugby pitches all night!*'

'Oh no,' said Matthew, putting his head in his hands.

'*And that's not the worst of it!*' she continued. '*They started saying there was no Headmaster any more, and the school was theirs! It's mob rule, Matthew!*'

Matthew's face turned pale. In the background he

could hear cars honking, and what sounded suspiciously like an explosion.

'They've tied the staff to the rugby posts!' Mrs Beaumont cried. *'So far Mr Braker's been keeping them at bay with his splendid aim, but we're running out of shoes to throw – oh heavens, I think they're starting a fire . . .'*

'Ah, *there* you are, Reverend!'

Matthew looked up in horror. A waiter was strolling down the corridor towards him.

'Come on, Reverend!' the waiter smiled obligingly, taking him by the arm. 'Everyone's been looking for you!'

He began steering him down the corridor. Matthew struggled in his grip.

'Please, I, er, I have to . . .'

'Hurry, Matthew!' came Mrs Beaumont's screams down the phone. *'They've started weeing on the sundial!'*

'Everything all right, Reverend?' said the waiter suspiciously.

'Yes, fine, fine,' said Matthew, snapping his phone shut and stuffing it back into his pocket. 'One of my flock.'

The waiter nodded sympathetically and led Matthew through a set of gilded doors at the end of the corridor, past a sign reading *Order of the Sword and Torch: Press Conference Celebratory Luncheon*. The room inside was lavishly decked in drapes and chandeliers, its enormous round tables laden with white tablecloths and silver cutlery. Around each one sat at least a dozen members of the Order, the women nattering away excitedly and the men grunting like walruses. The waiter led Matthew to the largest table in the room, which was surrounded by a group of especially fat diners, the men in black tie and tails and the ladies in full evening dress. They were all wearing metal helmets with enormous feathered plumes. Matthew realised with horror that it was the head table. He made an attempt at escape, but was tugged back into place by the waiter.

'Ladies and gentlemen,' said the waiter. 'May I introduce the Reverend Trebell. He's come all the way from Zanzibar to visit the Cusp for the press conference. Reverend, these are the most esteemed members of the Order of the Sword and Torch.'

The diners nodded obligingly, doffing their helmets. The waiter sat Matthew down a little forcefully and danced off. At once the man sat to Matthew's right belted him on the back like he was trying to knock a pillow into shape. Matthew gagged and started choking.

'Fantastic to have you with us, Reverend!' said the man, leaning over to brush his face with a whiskery moustache. 'All the way from Zanzibar, eh? Some trip I imagine!'

Matthew pointed to his throat and spluttered.

'No, don't try to talk, you must be exhausted,' said

the whiskery man, turning to the table. 'He's come from Zanzibar you know!'

'We all heard him, Major,' sighed a hugely fat man opposite them. He picked indulgently at a roll. 'Well, at least we'll finally have a new face round here. These Order luncheons have been tremendously dull of late.'

'Hear, hear,' said the lady to his left, taking a slug of red wine. She looked like a pickled herring. Matthew finally finished coughing.

'So, what was your take on the conference, Reverend?' asked the Major, leaning back in. 'Pretty interesting stuff, eh?'

Matthew's eyes widened. 'Er . . .'

'Ladies and gentlemen, your entrées.'

A host of waiters swanned up to the table, their arms laden with beautifully arranged bowls of oysters. The diners immediately forgot about Matthew and pulled themselves as close to the table as possible, guts permitting. The fat man picked up an obscene piece of oyster cutlery from the selection in front of him and nodded snootily over his shoulder.

'How interesting,' he muttered. 'I see that the Grand High Pooh-Bah has not joined us this evening. Nor has our, ahem . . . *host*.'

Matthew looked over to where a pair of chairs, slightly larger and grander than the others, stood empty at the opposite side of the table. The lavish namecards read *His Lordship the Grand High Pooh-Bah* and *Davidus Kyte, Official Head of Expeditions*. Matthew gulped.

'And what's *that* supposed to mean, Charles?' the Major snorted. Charles smiled.

'Well, I'm just *saying*', he said, grabbing at the next oyster, 'that I suppose it's no surprise our host cannot join us, given that things aren't looking very well organised in the Cusp at the moment. They're still putting up those warehouses as we speak.'

The diners were all tucking into their oysters, their eyes glazed. Matthew saw his chance to escape. He pushed himself up from the table quietly.

'Er, excuse me, I . . .' he began. Before he could utter another word the Major had delivered another back-breaking wallop to his spine, sending him crashing back to his chair.

'Never you mind this old gossip, Reverend!' the Major bellowed. 'Charles is renowned for having the biggest mouth in the Order!'

Charles rolled his eyes as he guzzled down another oyster. 'It just seems', he mumbled as he chewed, '. . . a little *strange* to bring forward an Expedition when it's clearly not ready.'

'Raspberries, Charles,' said a woman across the table wearing spectacles. 'There's no way that an Official Head of Expeditions would take a chance on something that wasn't properly organised.'

'Hear, hear,' said the pickled herring, taking another gulp of wine.

'You think so?' said Charles. 'Kyte's got a lot to prove on this trip. Remember, he's *hated* that Alex J. Jennings ever since he threw him off his team for the Expedition. And that's to say nothing of the money he owes the Order – hundreds! Thousands! Millions! How do you think all this "cutting-edge technology" has been financed? Let alone these "experiments" everyone talks about, going on at the other base . . . not all of them *savoury*, I've been told.'

'Someone say savouries?' muttered a woman across the table eagerly.

Matthew suddenly found himself sitting in front of a bowl of steaming mulligatawny soup without even having noticed the plates being cleared away. The other diners wiped their lips hungrily and dived in. He made another break for the exit.

'Excuse m—'

He was immediately flattened onto the table.

'Outrageous, Charles!' the Major boomed. 'What *must* our guest think? Look, you've made him go red and choke with embarrassment.'

'Really?' said Charles with a devilish grin. 'Well, if

you're averse to gossip, Reverend, then I suggest you cover your ears . . .'

He glanced around to see if anyone could hear, and leaned with some difficulty over the table. The others all craned their necks forward eagerly, even the Major, their helmets clanging loudly against each other.

'Seems the Cusp had an *intruder* the other night,' Charles whispered. 'And who do you think it was . . . ? Our old friend, Mr Alex J. Jennings!'

'Hmph! No surprises there,' said the bespectacled woman.

There was a general murmur of agreement that Alex J. Jennings was two partridges short of a boating luncheon.

'Well, get this!' whispered Charles. 'Kyte's been going around telling everyone that they caught him and that he's being kept in the cells. Only my sources at the prison say that no one's been brought in for weeks – not a sausage!'

'Well, what's your point, Charles?' snapped the Major.

'Well, *Major*, if you'll kindly let me finish,' Charles hissed back, 'I was about to add that in fact, *no one* knows where old Alex J. Jennings is. Not even Kyte! Apparently they never managed to catch him when he broke over the fences. They've been looking for two days straight. Kyte's going out of his mind with worry! They've turned the Cusp upside down, and there's been no sign of him . . . with *one* exception.'

Charles took another glance over his shoulder. Everyone stretched closer. The table strained.

'The grassland beyond the boundary', Charles hissed, 'was noticed to be *visibly disturbed.*'

He leaned back triumphantly. The others stared at him, blank-faced.

'Well, can't you see?' Charles gasped. 'It was Jennings! Alex J. Jennings escaped over the boundary!'

There was a collective sigh of exasperation. Matthew tried to drag himself from the table, and was immediately pounded back.

'Listen to him, Reverend!' the Major howled, shaking Matthew as he retched into his soup. 'What nonsense! Escaping over the boundary!'

'Laugh if you want, Major,' Charles snapped, his face turning red. 'But answer this: why do you think that lunatic has been trying to break back into the Forbidden Land all these years? Maybe he *did* find something in the centre after all – something that's been covered up. Maybe that's what he's been trying to get back to all this time. And maybe Kyte's terrified he'll now get to it before *he* has a chance to.'

'And how do you propose mad old Jennings is going to make it there, Charles?' cried the Major, hammering the tabletop in hysterics. 'Is he just going to *saunter* across the Forbidden Land?'

'Who knows,' Charles shrugged, slurping loudly at his soup. 'Maybe it doesn't affect him like it does everyone else. Maybe he came back from the Expedition with *special powers . . .*'

'Excuse me.'

Everyone fell silent. Matthew looked up. The diners were staring over his shoulder. Silence fell like a lead weight. Matthew turned round slowly.

Standing behind him was a group of security guards, armed with handcuffs. Two men stood in front of them. They were both in their underwear, and both glaring furiously at Matthew.

'I believe', said the Reverend Trebell through gritted teeth, 'that those are my clothes.'

Matthew opened his mouth, and the Major delivered another crippling wallop on the back.

'I say, Reverend!' he bellowed. 'That man's not wearing any clothes! Bet you don't see that sort of thing in Zanzibar.'

11

The great hour was almost at hand.

The Cusp had changed overnight. Everywhere was full of jostling crowds. They bustled anxiously down the main runway that led from the warehouses to the boundary, their feet itching, a sea of towering helmets and tuxedos boiling over with enraged and sweaty mutters. The Conduct Yourselves youth orchestra squeezed themselves through towards the bandstands lining the runway, panicked and exhausted. The moment of their great performance had almost arrived, and their only chance to practise was as they made their way to the bandstand. They squawked and bashed and howled their way through the packed crowd in single file, Steph at the front waving her clipboard with misery.

The chaos suited Alex perfectly. He peeked out from inside his hooded top, glancing behind him at Martha through the jostling excitement of legs.

'I can see it!' he whispered excitedly. 'We're almost at the bandstand!'

She nodded irritably and kept parping away at her horn. In this madness, no one could tell if Martha was secretly playing all Alex's parts herself, which of course she was. Her plan was simple. Once things kicked off, she said, the orchestra would be the last place any sane person would look. When everyone's attention was diverted, Alex could sneak out the back, find his father and be out of the base before anyone even realised they were gone. As long as he kept his face out of sight until then, it was foolproof.

The line in front suddenly stopped, and he walked smack into the back of Trent Davis. Alex grimaced. He really did stink of farts.

'Watch where you're going!' bellowed Trent.

'Sorry,' said Alex, quickly hiding his face and peering round. 'What's going on?'

Trent nodded to the front. They were blocked off from the bandstand by a velvet rope, behind which stood Greg, scribbling away at his Rota. The bandstand was full of fat, sweaty men on deckchairs, fanning themselves with their feathered plumes and staring at Steph, who was screaming at Greg till she was blue in the face.

'Booked?' she shrieked, grabbing at her hair with

trembling hands. '*The bandstand is booked?!*'

'Esteemed Members of the Order of the Sword and Torch,' said Greg apologetically, nodding at the men. 'Nothing we can do.'

'Then . . . then where are we supposed to perform?' Steph gasped.

Greg shrugged. 'Let me check the Rota.'

'Rota? *Rota?!*' Steph screamed, throwing herself over the velvet rope. 'I'll show you what I think of your Rota!'

Greg leaped back, clutching the clipboard like it was a picture of his mother.

'OK, OK!' he said testily, pushing her back. 'Calm down! There's one place left. Quick!'

He jumped over the velvet rope and flew into the crowd. At once the orchestra followed him, parping and screeching and drumming. Alex looked behind him nervously.

'Er . . . Martha?' he whispered. 'Where are we going?'

Martha shook her head and kept playing. So far she hadn't said a word to him all day. She was quickly shoved forward by the bassoonist and the bandstand was once again lost behind a crowd of people.

'The bandstand!' Alex whimpered. He made to stop, to look for a spot in the crowd to slip out, but the file kept pushing him on, on through the sea of legs. They were heading towards the boundary. He threw his head round frantically. The crowd was at bursting point. The hour had almost arrived. They danced on their itching feet, nudging each other, peering around for the first sign of the great moment. Under his hooded top Alex was dripping with sweat. There was nowhere to go but forward.

He was suddenly heaved out of the crowd, onto the bare tarmac beside the boundary. People everywhere were pointing at the orchestra, muttering with excitement. Alex buried his head deeper into his top and looked around. In front of them lay the vast expanse of the Forbidden Land. Greg flashed a series of passes to the guards and led the orchestra across the baking tarmac and past their barracks, to where the great Unfinished Pier stood on its shaky legs, jutting over the boundary. Steph grabbed him by the shoulder and spun him round.

'No way,' she said firmly. 'There is no way you are sending the children out onto that thing.'

'There's nowhere else!' Greg snapped, pulling a set of keys out of his pocket. 'Once the ceremony starts the main runway will have to be kept clear. We've got one minute left before it starts. Hurry!'

He marched up to the iron gates and started unlocking them. Alex spun round. There was no way back. In the distance, giant cameras on cranes were being lifted up, ready for the ceremony to begin. Alex grabbed Martha's arm.

'*Martha, quick!*' he hissed. 'I'll be on camera! I'll be seen by everyone! The whole base!'

Martha said nothing. Alex shook her arm.

'*Why aren't you saying anything?*' he cried. Trent Davis leaned in with a grin.

'Yeah, what's the matter Martha?' he smirked. 'Cat got your tongue?'

Martha turned to Trent, her eyes glinting with suspicion. Her lips stayed sealed. Trent snickered and reached into his pocket.

'You're . . . not looking for these, are you?' he said, holding something out towards her.

Alex looked down.

It was a set of false teeth.

Martha's eyes flashed.

'Ladies and gentlemen,' a voice suddenly blared out across the Cusp. 'Welcome to the Four Hundred and Thirty seventh Expedition of the Order of the Sword and Torch.'

The crowds broke into a roaring applause. Martha made to grab at the teeth, but in one movement Trent had snapped his hand up, balled in a fist high above his head.

'Not so fast, Grandma!' he shouted. 'I thought we could use them for the castanet solo!'

'*Give them back, Trent!*'

Alex was surprised by the sudden anger in his own voice. Trent stopped pushing forwards and stared back, apparently rather amused.

'Or what, midget?' he asked, raising his eyebrows. 'Your girlfriend going to beat me up for you?'

'Give them back,' Alex said slowly, his breath coming in a hiss, 'or I'll take them back.'

'May we please remind you', the voice continued, 'that we will soon have to ask you all to clear the main runway, for reasons that will become apparent.'

The base had fallen silent, breathless with anticipation for the main event. From across the Forbidden Land, a cooling wind blew strong and steady. Trent grinned and turned slowly back round to the gate.

'Well, good luck with that,' he said calmly.

In one movement he threw the teeth clear over the fence.

The two halves fell apart as they dropped past the legs of the Pier, where they were swallowed up by the grass and instantly lost from sight.

There was a great roar of bending metal at the back of the base, and the crowd suddenly swung round. The warehouses had burst open, their curved roofs splitting straight down the middle and opening up like bear traps in the glinting sun. They came crashing down to the tarmac with an ear-splitting racket. The audience gasped.

'Look!' someone gasped behind Alex. 'I don't believe it!'

From inside each warehouse, a great balloon was rising. They were vast, like black moons, and their shadows left the runway below them in utter darkness. Their sides were emblazoned with a picture of a knight, holding a sword in one hand and a torch in the other. There were dozens of them. From each of their fronts a hundred steel chains dangled down to the tarmac below. Alex's eyes widened.

'I don't believe it,' he muttered.

Great hordes of dogs were emerging from the darkness of the warehouses, their necks chained to the enormous zeppelins above them. They barked and struggled and whined against their steel collars, pulling with all their might against the balloons in a bid to escape, but it was no use. The crowds gasped as the nature of the new Expedition was finally revealed.

'Sixty full-size zeppelins!' Kytc's voice suddenly boomed from the speakers around them. 'Each one pulled by a hundred dogs! Each one capable of journeying to the centre of the land beyond the boundary in less than five days!'

The base was a sea of flashing cameras, pushing and shoving to get a better view of the dogs. The only person who didn't look was Martha. She stood staring at the spot in the grass of the Forbidden Land where her teeth had landed. Trent turned back to her triumphantly.

'Well, I think we're about even now, Grandma,' he smirked. 'Maybe next time you'll think before . . .'

He didn't finish his sentence because Martha had already leaped onto his back and was pummelling him to the ground. Within moments Steph had dragged the two of them apart and was once again screaming at the top of her voice, heaving them out the group.

'*That's it!*' she cried. 'I've had it with you two! You're out of the performance!'

She threw them both to the side. At that moment Greg flung open the gates, and the rest of the orchestra poured inside. Steph grabbed Alex by the shoulders.

'Jeremy,' she stammered, 'we're on in ten seconds. You'll have to open the performance instead of Trent.'

Alex froze in horror.

'. . . What?'

'It's simple,' she snapped, dragging him to the gate. 'You read the sheet music we sent you, right? Just play the first note. The rest of the orchestra comes in after you. And for heaven's sake take off that hoodie.'

In one movement she had ripped the hood off his head, thrust Alex through the gate and slammed it shut after him. Alex took a moment to register what had happened before staring back up at Martha. They shared the same look of faint surprise at how spectacularly wrong the foolproof plan had gone.

'Martha!' he wailed. Steph grabbed her by the arms and started dragging her away from the gate.

'*Jutht play the firtht note!*' she lisped back at him toothlessly, waving her hands like a madwoman.

'*I don't know what the first note is!*' Alex wailed.

'G*!*' she screamed, jabbing her fingers at the horn and waving it above her head. At least, it sounded like 'G'. It could have been 'D'.

'Jeremy, come on!' someone behind him hissed.

Alex spun round. The rest of the orchestra were in their places, waiting for him. Alex looked back up in dismay.

'Did you say "D"?' he cried.

Martha shook her head frantically. '. . . !' she mouthed.

Alex looked desperate. '*E?*'

'Jeremy, come on!

All of a sudden someone grabbed Alex from behind and dragged him into place. He looked up in terror. The zeppelins were waiting for the music to begin. The television cameras in the distance had started filming the orchestra. An audience of several thousand were now gazing at the Unfinished Pier. All eyes were turned to Alex.

The audience waited expectantly. The boards of the Pier groaned beneath him.

'Jeremy!' someone whispered behind him. '*Start playing already!*'

The cellist suddenly stepped forwards and shoved him furiously to the front of the orchestra.

'*Just play the first note, you idiot!*' he seethed.

Alex stumbled across the boards and looked up. Except for the straining of the Pier beneath him, there was total silence. Up ahead, Alex's terrified eyes gazed back at him from the giant television screens that lined the base.

'When all this is over,' said a flautist behind him, 'you are so dead.'

Alex sighed.

Just play anything, Alex, the voice in his head said. *It's already over.*

With a grand flourish Alex brought the horn to his lips, gulped in a great lungful of air, and blew a faultless F sharp.

The sound was lost to the terrible groan of twisting metal that suddenly rang out beneath him, trembling up through his legs and into his stomach. Alex gasped, and dropped the Horn. The orchestra behind him screamed. Ahead, the rotten boards of the walkway were bending into splinters, snapping one by one in front of their very eyes. Slowly, very slowly, the Pier began tilting to one side.

'It's going to fall over!' cried a bassonist. 'It – '

It was too late. All four legs of the Pier suddenly snapped like matchsticks, and before anyone could register what was going on the entire orchestra were flung off the boards to the ground below in a wave of twanging instruments and reams of sheet music. The crowds screamed with horror.

They were going to land on the other side of the boundary.

The cameras spun round to film the devastation.

The crowds jostled for a better view of the monitors.

One by one, the children hit the Forbidden Land. The effect was instantaneous. They sprang to their feet the second they landed, as if bouncing, and were suddenly sprinting as fast as they could back to the boundary, their eyes glazed.

'Quick!' Greg screamed, waving his clipboard at the horrified crowd. 'Clear a path! Clear a path for them, now!'

But there were too many people to clear a path. The packed crowd looked on in horror as the children hurtled towards them. Their feet barely even touched the grass. Greg turned back to the guards.

'*Move the crowds!*' he screamed. '*Move them before we all get crushed!*'

'Look!' a voice cried out suddenly. 'Everyone, look!'

There was a great flutter of confusion. All across the

Cusp, people were pointing and shouting at the monitors. For a moment no one really knew what all the commotion was about. Then slowly, one by one, their eyes all caught the same unbelievable sight, and everyone gasped in shock at what was unfolding before them.

■ ■ ■

Even from his raised position on the bandstand, Davidus Kyte was too short to make out what was going on.

'Why have they all stopped talking?' he roared, throwing down the microphone. 'What's going on?'

The cameraman next to him didn't reply. He was staring down at the monitor in his hands, speechless.

'Give me that!' snapped Kyte, snatching it out of his hands and shoving him straight off the bandstand. He glared down at the screen.

It was an aerial shot of the Unfinished Pier, now lying in ruins across the grassland. Beside it, someone was picking himself up from among the piles of shattered wood and rivets. He got to his feet and fell stumbling onto the grass.

He stayed where he was.

Davidus's mouth dropped.

'I . . . I don't believe it,' he gasped.

■ ■ ■

Across the base, Prisoner #205513 was straining against the bars of his cell.

'Hey!' he called over to the guards. 'Can I at least make my phone call now? Please. I'm a headmaster.'

The guards ignored him. They were all crowded around a TV in the corner of their office, their jaws dropped in silence. Prisoner #205513 craned his neck round to see what was on the TV.

'What's going on?' he whined. 'Why's that person just sta—'

On the television, a boy was standing stock still on the grass of the Forbidden Land, staring at the crowd in front of him.

It was Alex.

'I don't believe it,' Matthew gasped.

■ ■ ■

Several miles away, at school, the newly elected Grand High Chieftain Wizard of Cloisters (formerly known as Laurence Davy) was holding court in the War Room (formerly known as the TV Room) on his plans for world domination with the Wolf-Tiger Fighter Jet Squadron (formerly known as the sixth-form prefects). The framed map from the Headmaster's office was laid on the carpet in front of them, covered with tactically placed toy cars and beef-and-onion crisps.

'We'll take the town tonight,' said the Grand High Chieftain Wizard, moving the model cars down the road with a hockey stick. 'Once we've grown in numbers and resources, we can finally take the Cusp. And with their weaponry at our disposal, the New Age can begin.'

'Hurrah!' cried the other members of the Wolf-Tiger Fighter Jet Squadron.

'Now I grow bored,' sighed the Grand High Chieftain Wizard, flinging aside his hockey stick. 'Bring me my fool.'

Jeremy Butterworth was brought in and rubbed with butter, and they all started poking him with sticks which thankfully they already had to hand.

'Dance, fool, dance!' laughed the Grand High Chieftain Wizard.

'Hey!' cried one of the Wolf-Tiger Fighter Jets from the other side of the room. They all looked up. He was pointing at the TV that played silently in the corner.

'Is that . . . *Alex Jennings?*'

The council all turned to face the television. On the screen, Alex Jennings was slowly walking through the grass of the Forbidden Land.

'I don't believe it,' said the Grand High Chieftain Wizard.

■ ■ ■

Alex stared at the silent crowd in front of him.

The crowd stared back.

Very slowly, he walked across the grass towards them. He started sweeping it with his hands. It was as if he was looking for something.

He stopped and bent down to part the grass. He had found what he was looking for. The cameras zoomed in.

It was a pair of false teeth.

Alex calmly put them in his pocket and started walking back towards the boundary.

He stopped. There was something else in the grass at his feet. He bent down and picked it up.

It was a hospital gown.

Alex looked down at a badge pinned to the fabric.

Alex J. Jennings
Coma Ward
Order of the Sword and Torch Rehabilitation Centre

Dad, Alex mouthed silently.

Alex stood looking at the gown for some time. He looked at the forest that stood on the distant horizon of the Forbidden Land.

He looked back down at the hospital gown.

He looked at his feet. He was clearly giving something a lot of thought.

He turned back and looked at the crowd.

The crowd stared back, dumbfounded.

Alex paused and slowly turned back to face the forest.

He started walking towards the centre of the Forbidden Land.

Then he began to run.

12

The incidents following this strange moment ran exactly as follows.

Everyone on the newly constructed bandstands stood up in surprise.

All the bandstands collapsed.

The youth orchestra hit the tarmac and sprinted uncontrollably towards the crowd, driven by the power of the Forbidden Land.

Those unlucky spectators at the front, having nowhere to go or even to turn to, ducked to protect themselves.

The charging children ran straight up their backs and onto the top of the crowd and then kept on running, using their helmets as stepping stones.

The collective gasp of astonishment from the crowd was so great that it created a substantial drop in air pressure which was picked up by several local weather stations.

In the darkness beneath the zeppelins, one of the many thousands of dogs took advantage of this sudden distraction to look around. It was a wire-haired terrier with a black patch over one eye.

The dog delicately undid the collar round his neck, as one would remove a watch, and scampered over to the master switch on the wall that automatically released all the chains that attached each dog from the front of each zeppelin.

He stood on his hind legs and, quickly pausing to clear his throat, pulled down the switch.

Six thousand barking dogs poured from the warehouses, their chains dragging behind them.

Meanwhile, a security guard aiming a flare gun to call for help was flattened by a charging bassoonist at the precise moment he pulled the trigger.

His vision blinded, he aimed the explosive flare not towards the open sky, as is the custom, but towards the stockpile of celebratory fireworks instead.

At this point, it became difficult to establish what happened next. In truth, lots of different things happened at once.

Six thousand dogs suddenly charged into the back of the crowd.

The pile of fireworks exploded, showering the base with dazzling colours and deafening explosions.

In a bid to escape, many others imagined that they, too, could follow Alex and run across the boundary to freedom. They were of course gravely mistaken. This in fact managed to make the problem significantly worse, although at the time no one could have foreseen that. The second they stepped over the boundary they spun on their heels and charged back through the crowds, taking out security guards like bowling pins.

Martha chased Trent Davis round the barracks three times before soundly beating him unconscious with her horn.

Several security guards rather ill-advisedly tried to stop the dogs by grabbing onto the chains and suddenly found themselves being dragged forward like they were water-skiing.

Some people started stealing the news vans and driving them through the barbed-wire fences.

Across the base a prison guard overcome by a peculiar mixture of emotions silently opened the door of Prisoner #205513's cell and let him out, before walking into the cell himself, locking the door behind him and swallowing the key.

The dogs that could make it through the crowds suddenly burst across the boundary and charged across the grassland, parting the grass beneath them with the furious pace of their legs and dragging the terrified spectators caught in their chains over the Forbidden Land, whereupon they immediately started trying to run back home like the others, and the line between the Cusp and the Forbidden Land slowly began to resemble an enormous tug-of-war between people and dogs.

An elderly member of the Order looked up to see that her ceremonial helmet had somehow started levitating eighty feet into the air. No one else saw it happen, and for the rest of her life no one believed her when she said it did.

Steph marched straight up to Greg, threw the clipboard out of his hands and kissed him passionately on the lips.

A number of the older men, already drunk on champagne, threw off their hats and shirts and started attempting to box some of the larger dogs, with mixed results.

A chandelier of smoking technicolour lights exploded across the base.

All the milk in the fridges went off at exactly the same time.

Several women fell pregnant, for no reason.

Greg pulled away from his passionate embrace and looked along the concrete to where his clipboard had landed.

The Rota was on fire.

Part Three

The Forbidden Land

13

'Dad?'

'Yes, Alex?'

'What was it like in the Forbidden Land?'

Alex's father picked a book from the shelf, a favourite one, and sat down on the edge of Alex's bed. He crossed his arms and, after a moment's thought, crossed his legs too.

'Alex,' he said, 'answer me this. Has that ever worked before?'

'Has what?' said Alex innocently.

His father gave him a look.

'When you ask me to talk about the Forbidden Land.'

Alex lay down and shoved his pillow in front of his face, which is usually what he did when he'd been found out doing something he shouldn't have done.

'Alex,' said his father patiently, 'what did I say to you when you asked me that question last week?'

'I can't remember,' came Alex's muffled voice.

'I'm sure you can't,' said Alex's father. 'Well, I'm fairly certain I said something about it being a very long time ago, and that your mother and I have agreed that four years old is too young to hear those kinds of things.'

'I'm already a week older,' Alex pointed out.

'Quite,' said his father. He looked around the bedroom and quietly closed the door before sitting back down again. 'Well, it's no good, Alex. I can't tell you about what happened to me.'

'B—' Alex began.

'But I can', his father shushed him, 'tell you a story about another man who went into the Forbidden Land.'

Alex grinned. Alex's father looked at him very seriously.

'But I don't want you to think for a moment that this story is about what happened to me,' he said, wagging his finger. 'Certainly not! Understand?'

Alex threw the pillow back and sat up eagerly. His father took a deep breath.

'Where to begin?' he said, scratching at the stubble on his chin. 'Once upon a time, there was a man who journeyed into the Forbidden Land.'

'What was he called?' said Alex.

'It doesn't matter what he was called,' said Alex's father.

Alex snorted. 'How can it not matter what he was called?'

'The name isn't important to the story,' said Alex's dad

irritably. 'His name was . . . Malex. Malex M. Mennings. Satisfied?'

'That's a stupid name,' said Alex.

Alex's father gave him a look that managed to tell his son not to ask any more questions.

'Malex M. Mennings knew', he continued, 'that there was a forest in the Forbidden Land. Everyone did. You could see it from the boundary. He knew that he would have to pass through it if he was going to find the centre. So he set off on his sledge, and his dogs pulled all day long until the Cusp was far behind them and they finally reached the edge of the trees.'

'Was it a scary forest?' said Alex.

'It was, Alex,' said his father, nodding solemnly. 'In truth, when Malex M. Mennings first set off on his adventure he had no idea just how big and how dark the forest really was – not until he was right next to it. The trees stretched up so high they blocked out the sun, and the ground inside was as dead as stone. It was so dark that you couldn't see your own hand in front of your face. Scary enough?'

'Scary,' Alex agreed.

'And remember, Alex,' said Alex's father, 'back then no one had any idea what was inside the forest. No one had travelled far enough across the grassland to even reach it before. There could have been anything lurking in the trees. Malex M. Mennings thought that there might even be monsters inside that slept in the darkness.' He sighed. 'The truth was, even though

Malex M. Mennings had done lots of brave things in his life, he was very frightened of going inside. But he went in anyway.'

'But if it was so dark,' said Alex, 'then how did he know where to go?'

Alex's father smiled.

'Good question, Alex,' he said. 'Well, it was easy. He just closed his eyes.'

Alex snorted. 'But then it's even darker!'

'Maybe so,' said Alex's father. 'But he didn't need to use his eyes any more, not when it was so dark already. How do dogs find their way in the dark, Alex?'

'They use their noses,' said Alex immediately.

His father beamed. He always looked happiest when he talked about his dogs.

'Exactly,' he said. 'They don't need their eyes, and neither did he. And so he screwed his eyes shut, and once he did he noticed the wind on his skin – the wind that was always blowing in the forest. And so he followed it. He ordered his dogs to go on, and he made them pull against the wind until he finally found where it was coming from.'

'So where was it coming from?' said Alex. 'Was there something in the forest?'

Alex's father shook his head. He suddenly looked very sad.

'No,' said Alex's father. 'There was nothing in the forest.'

Alex looked irritated. 'Well, that's boring.'

His father shrugged. 'Maybe so. But if you think about

it, Alex, there weren't any monsters either. In fact, the only monsters were the ones Malex M. Mennings thought were there, in the darkness in his head. And because he wasn't trying to see them any more he passed through the forest safely and came out the other side. And do you know what he found then, Alex?'

'The centre of the Forbidden Land!' Alex shouted triumphantly, leaping out from under the duvet.

Alex's father shushed him, glancing behind him at the closed door.

'Not quite,' he said. 'He found something else.'

'What?' Alex whispered.

Alex's father smiled and pulled the duvet back over him.

'That', he said, 'is a story for another time. Now, if you don't mind I think it's time for us both to go to bed.'

Alex sat up. 'But . . . !'

'No more questions, Alex. I'll tell you the rest next time.'

'. . . But . . . !'

'Good night, Alex,' his father warned. 'Sweet dreams.'

Alex groaned, and lay back down. 'Good night, Dad.'

His father kissed him on the forehead, and tucked his duvet under him, and turned out the light. He made to get up.

'. . . Dad?' Alex said.

Alex's father sighed. 'Yes, Alex?'

'Does Malex M. Mennings ever get to the centre?' asked Alex. 'Does he ever find what he's looking for?'

Alex's father was silent. In the darkness it was impossible to tell what his face was doing.

'Good night, Alex,' he said quietly.

He stood up from the bed and walked away. Alex could hear him step out the room and pause for a moment at the door. Alex knew that he was looking at him, and so he pretended to be asleep already, even though he wasn't. His father stood for a while, looking at him. Then he closed the door and walked back downstairs.

Alex lay awake and listened to the sounds of his father moving through the house. He had taken to staying up late recently, leaving Alex and his mother in bed. Alex had become used to listening to his footsteps. It was no surprise to him when he heard the front door click open and gently close. His father often went out for walks late at night now, long into the next morning.

Lying in bed, Alex didn't realise that his father would not come home that night, or that it would be the first time that he tried to cross back over the boundary. He lay awake until the house fell completely silent.

'Who's Malex M. Mennings?' he whispered.

■ ■ ■

Alex leaned on his knees in the grassland, heaving for breath. His heart was drumming. His face was red. His jumper was damp with sweat. He wrenched it over his head and wiped his face with it, before wrapping it carefully round his waist. Then, slowly, he looked up.

A stone's throw in front of him, the grassland finally stopped. In its place stood enormous trees, the height and width of skyscrapers, jutting from the ground and towering in either direction as far as he could see. There was a wall of absolute darkness inside. A smile crept across his face.

'The forest,' he muttered. 'Just like he said.'

All around him, dogs were charging from the grassland and into the woods. It was as if they were being drawn towards something far in the distance, something that was calling for them beyond the trees. They were immediately swallowed up by the darkness inside, the sound of their paws thundering across the leafblown ground for a moment before fading into silence. Alex stood, staring into the pitch black.

You have to go back, said the voice.

Alex shook his head. 'I'm not going back,' he said calmly.

He turned round. He hadn't stopped running since he left the Cusp that morning. Now the sun was beginning to lower in the sky, and the towering trees were slowly spreading their shadows onto the grassland behind him. He could still make out the base in the distance. It seemed like another world. Only the great brass statue could still be seen clearly, alone on the horizon of floating black zeppelins. From this far away, it was like a child stood in a row of black flowers.

'I'm never going back,' he muttered.

Then where are you going, Alex? said the voice.

Alex smiled. 'Where do you think?'

Another pack of dogs suddenly burst out of the grass beside him and raced on into the darkness of the forest, their chains jangling along the ground behind them. Alex turned back round, watching them disappear into the black.

'To the centre,' he said.

Because . . . said the voice.

'Because that's where he's going,' said Alex. 'Where he's always been trying to get to. And I'm going to find him.'

And once you've found him, said the voice . . . *then what?*

'Then I'll find out what he keeps going back for,' said Alex.

And then what, Alex? said the voice.

Alex didn't answer. He stepped up to the line where the grassland became the trees. Alex stared into it, his eyes searching.

'Then we'll talk,' he said quietly. 'Just him and me. And he'll tell me why he left, and how he had to do it and didn't have a choice. And how happy he is that I followed him.'

Alex's eyes kept scanning the forest. The darkness was unbroken. He couldn't even see the dogs any more. All he could hear was the rattling of their chains echoing through the trees ahead of him.

And then . . . said the voice.

'We'll live on the grassland,' said Alex. 'With the dogs. And we'll walk them every day.'

And then . . .

The darkness met him face on. Alex gulped.

'And then we'll finally be safe,' he said. 'Just him and me, where no one else can reach us. No one.'

And then . . .

Alex kept staring into the darkness. He saw nothing.

'And then,' said Alex emptily, 'everything will be OK again.'

And all at once, a light appeared.

Alex froze. It was a piercing beam of green light, and it came from far behind him. He spun round.

Back at the base, the helmet of the great statue had been switched on. The shadows of the grassland were immediately lit up with a vivid green that stretched in every direction, over the treetops and far, far beyond.

Alex turned slowly back to the forest. Down through the high branches, a gentle glowing path was now cast onto the forest floor ahead of him. The darkness was slowly coming into view. All around him hundreds of dogs charged onwards, weaving through the trees like channels of water.

Alex looked down and started.

Cast in the green glow directly ahead of him, its hair flickering in the breeze, was a small dog. It was staring at him. It was almost as if it was more surprised to see Alex than Alex was to see it. It was the terrier, with a black patch over one of its eyes, from the night in the barracks. Alex smiled.

'Hello, friend!' he said. 'Remember me?'

Alex stepped carefully over the line where the grassland became the forest and walked over to the dog. He gently held out his hand for him. The dog gaped at him for a moment more, and then slowly sniffed it. Alex looked it over and placed a hand under its chin.

'Mmm,' he said. 'You're male, maybe . . . eleven or twelve years old. A cross-breed. Part Border terrier, I'll bet, on account of your otter-shaped head and even temperament. And part . . . Alsatian?'

The dog looked at him blankly. Alex couldn't shake the feeling that it was eyeing him with suspicion.

'Nice doggy,' he said nervously, giving it a pat.

All at once the dog leaped up, barking, and ran onwards into the trees. Then it suddenly stopped and turned back. Alex waited for it to do something.

'What?' he said.

The dog took a step forward and turned back round. It was staring at him. Alex shifted uncomfortably.

'You want something?' he asked.

The dog's eyes widened.

'Walkies?' Alex suggested.

The dog gave him what looked like a withering glare.

'Er . . .' Alex mumbled. 'Do you want me to follow you?'

The dog's tail almost started wagging, but then it quickly made it stop. Alex smiled.

'All right then,' he shrugged. 'I guess I'm going that way too.'

The dog jumped up and down with excitement and ran back to Alex. Alex took a deep breath and looked into the forest. The trees around him hummed with the calm glow of the lantern. The barking of dogs carried long into the distance, beyond where the green light lay brightest. Alex gulped. He turned back to the dog.

'You don't know how far a dog can run in the woods, do you?' he said.

The dog stared at him. Alex rubbed his head and nodded.

'Me neither,' he sighed. 'Shall we?'

They both set out along the glowing path in the trees, running alongside the dogs.

14

Watching the esteemed members of the Order of the Sword and Torch lose every shred of their dignity in the chaos of the base was quite something. It had been hours since the Expedition had fallen apart at the seams, but the hysterical crowd showed no signs of stopping. They cried, they fainted, they tripped over their own helmets. Some quite literally ran around in circles. They weren't the only ones panicking. After only a few hours of riots most of the guards had disappeared. Reporters and cameramen who had stayed behind to film the devastation were now clambering up the sides of buildings to escape the packs of dogs gnawing their ankles. The dogs were at least having fun, but then, being dogs, they hadn't much to lose in the first place.

Perhaps the only person who remained calm was Davidus Kyte.

He stood on the edge of the bandstand, his eyes darting across the base with an expression that few could read. He wasn't really looking at the crowds. He was looking over the top of them, to the figure on the grassland slowly disappearing from view as the sun set over the rioting base. He had been looking at it all day. He stood and stared, barely blinking.

'Squiggles,' he muttered quietly.

Someone came and tapped him on the shoulder.

'Sir,' came Greg's voice. 'We've run into some problems.'

Kyte made no effort to turn round.

'Really? Problems?' he said, apparently surprised. 'What would those be, then?'

Greg paused. 'Er . . . it's the Grand High Pooh-Bah, sir. He wants to see you.'

'You don't say,' Kyte muttered.

There was an awkward silence. Kyte turned his head ever so slightly, to the great zeppelins that still lined the horizon.

'Have all the dogs escaped, then?' he asked. 'Every one?'

Greg gulped. 'Yes, sir.'

'I see,' said Kyte. He took a moment's pause. 'And . . . the others?'

Greg shifted. '. . . The others, sir?'

Kyte suddenly eyed him darkly. 'The *others*, Greg,' he repeated.

Realisation dawned on Greg's face. 'Oh! Er . . . no, sir. They're – still there.'

'All of them?'

'All of them, sir.'

Kyte turned back to the figure on the grassland. It had disappeared. Kyte's lips thinned, curling slowly into a smile.

'Excellent,' he said.

'*KYTE!*' a voice suddenly roared behind them.

Kyte stayed facing the way he was for a few moments more, before slowly turning around. On the bandstand behind him stood a small crowd of esteemed members of the Order, gazing slack-jawed in disbelief at the carnage raging across the base. They had so far managed to avoid the worst of the violence by using their deckchairs as clubs, but their ripped tailcoats and dented helmets suggested that it had been a long and difficult day.

In front of them stood another man, his helmet's plume nearly twice the size of the others and a colourful sash stained with spilt champagne slung over his shoulder. His head was very large and very red, and the expression on his face was very much like that of a man holding in his breath in case he started screaming. Kyte nodded in recognition.

'Ah, Grand High Pooh-Bah,' he said. 'I see you finally made it . . .'

We might say that the man 'exploded' at this point. But he didn't actually explode, he just shouted a lot.

'*What on earth do you call this?*' he roared, waving his arms at the rioting crowds. 'Kyte, this is . . . a disaster! You assured me last night – *assured me* – that everything was going to go off without a hitch! And now you give me . . . *this?!*'

The esteemed members of the Order beside him stepped forward in sympathy.

'An outrage!' yelled the Major, shaking his fist.

'An insult!' blustered Charles.

The others muttered in furious agreement.

'I paid you for an Expedition, Kyte!' the Grand High Pooh-Bah bellowed, his jowls slapping wildly against his neck. 'Not for you to bring it forward by six months at a moment's notice and turn us all into a laughing stock!'

Kyte sighed. 'Your Lordship, I assure you that the Expedition will still be going ahead . . .'

The Pooh-Bah's eyes nearly bugged out of his head. '*Oh no it will not, Kyte!* You are done! Finished! No more luncheons, no more research grants, no more so-called "experiments" . . . !'

Kyte sighed, and turned to Greg.

'Turn the beam on,' he said. 'And clear the runway. We'll go ahead with Plan B.'

Greg nodded and shot off the bandstand, barking orders into his walkie-talkie. Kyte turned back round to the esteemed members of the Order and gave a nod.

'Gentlemen,' he said. 'I'm very sorry, but I'm afraid I must be going now. I have an Expedition to prepare.'

With that he marched straight past them to the conductor's podium at the back of the bandstand. It was carved from solid pine into the shape of a knight. In one movement Kyte ripped open a hidden switch under the helmet. The Grand High Pooh-Bah pushed his way through the confused crowd to face him.

'Oh no you don't, Kyte!' he demanded. 'You're not going anywhere! You've got a lot of explaining to do –'

'All in good time, Your Lordship,' Kyte said curtly. 'In the meantime I suggest you hold onto something.'

Kyte flicked the switch and threw himself to the ground. The esteemed members of the Order stared at him in confusion. Then suddenly, with a great snap and shudder, the floor started shaking, and at once the entire bandstand plummeted down into the ground like a lead weight, throwing them to the floor in darkness.

Kyte picked himself up as quickly as he had fallen and stepped carefully over the tangle of deckchairs and groaning bodies. Ahead of him now lay a huge underground corridor, leading to a single lit doorway in the far distance. He marched towards it without looking back. By the time he had reached the doorway the Grand High Pooh-Bah could be heard charging after him, his breathing heavy and furious.

'*Kyte!*' he roared. '*Stop right now before I kill you!*'

'Calm down, Your Lordship,' Kyte called behind him, opening a panel of numbered buttons beside the door and keying in a code. 'Everything is going to be fine.'

'No, Kyte, you imbecile!' the Pooh-Bah bellowed, grabbing his shoulders and spinning him round. '*Nothing* is going to be fine!'

Kyte didn't blink. 'Your Lordship, if you'll just listen for a moment . . .'

'No, *you* listen!' the Pooh-Bah wailed. 'We've got a riot on the runway that's been raging all day! It's being filmed by news stations all over the world! And it's threatening to take over this base unless something's done about it! *You*, Kyte, are going to stay here and sort it out – not me! You are not going to leap onto some half-baked "Plan B" you devised while taking a break from throwing away every penny the Order has on . . . on *dogs*!'

Kyte paused, and glanced up at him.

'*Every* penny?' he muttered innocently. '*Really?*'

'Every single one!' the Grand High Pooh-Bah sobbed miserably, grabbing his hair in his hands. 'Because I was stupid enough to believe in you, Kyte! You've . . . you've ruined us!'

'Mmm,' Kyte nodded. 'Well then, I suppose, on the plus side, Your Lordship, you really have nothing left to lose, do you?'

With that he threw open the door and marched out into the glare of beaming floodlights. Ahead of them lay the runway that ran alongside the warehouses, far away from the chaos of the crowds at the boundary. Inside the first warehouse, one of the great black zeppelins was being winched down to earth. Work was going on at a manic pace inside. Packs of workmen were lugging hundreds of boxes off and throwing them under the shadow of the lowering zeppelin. Kyte stood and watched as the monstrous balloon crept slowly down towards him, filling his vision with a growing blackness.

He turned around. The esteemed members of the Order stood behind him, open-mouthed. A single Catherine wheel shot down the tarmac beside them in a stream of yellow sparks.

'An Expedition is still going ahead,' said Kyte. 'Of course, it's just the single zeppelin now instead of sixty. Such a terrible shame. From now on, we're going with Plan B. We'll have to repack the entire zeppelin and prepare it for the journey. It'll take all night – maybe even until tomorrow. I suggest you fine ladies and gentlemen leave us to it. They're going to be chaining the pack to the front any moment now.'

The Grand High Pooh-Bah snorted bitterly.

'The pack?' he said. 'Tell me, Kyte – how many dogs are left to pull that great floating bag of yours?'

Kyte looked back at him blankly.

'None, Your Lordship,' he said.

There was a roar of an engine behind them, and they all swung round. From the back of the warehouse, a great black truck was slowly creeping out into the light. It was flanked by security guards, waving the vehicle forwards with trembling hands. The back of the truck was piled up with giant cages that seemed to shudder in the flood-lights. The members of the Order glanced at each other nervously.

'I see!' shouted the Grand High Pooh-Bah. 'Then what *else* do you have up your sleeve to pull it to the centre?'

Kyte strolled up to the black truck, and the security guards parted in front of him like grass, grateful for the distance from the cages. Kyte stood behind the lorry and gazed up into the back. A smile crept across his face. He glanced up again, and waved the truck forwards.

'Plan B, Your Lordship.'

The truck slowly turned round to face them. The collected members of the Order leaped back with horror. Each cage was lined with metal bars as thick as gateposts, and padlocked shut with ten iron locks.

'No,' gasped the Major. 'It . . . it can't be.'

Before them stood row upon row of caged wolves, all black hair and heaving shoulders and spit-flecked jaws. They paced their tiny cages, glaring at the men standing trembling before them, their eyes flashing hungrily as they bared their teeth against the thick steel bars and rolled their furious eyes. The Grand High Pooh-Bah shook his head in disbelief.

'Kyte . . .' he gasped. 'Kyte, what on earth are you doing?'

At that moment, the lights in the brass statue were slammed on, and they all spun round. Its green glare was fixed on the distant forest like a searchlight. Kyte turned to the Grand High Pooh-Bah in mock surprise.

'What do you think we're doing?' he murmured. 'We're going after the boy.'

15

Alex stood in the shade of the trees, gazing out. In front of him the forest ended, and in its place a desert stretched out, on and on in great white waves to the horizon. A burning midday sun hung in the sky, drawing heat from the sand like petrol fumes.

'Oh crikey,' he said.

All around him lay hundreds of dogs, panting furiously along the farthest edge of the shadow where the trees became the desert. They sat, waiting patiently, their fur caked in dust.

'The desert,' Alex murmured. 'Just like he said.'

He rubbed his eyes. He had walked all night in the forest, and there had been no sign of his father. Alex sighed and stared over the burning sand. He was probably already halfway across the desert by now.

There was a sudden tug on his leg. Alex looked down.

The dog with the black patch was biting at the cuff of his trousers, yanking insistently.

'What?' said Alex.

The dog sat back down anxiously and turned towards the desert. Alex shook his head.

'Oh, no,' he said. 'We can't follow him now. We have to wait.'

The dog stood up and barked. Alex frowned.

'I just told you,' he said irritably. He waved his hands at the other dogs around him, lying lazily in the shade. 'We can't go now. It's too hot. See?'

Alex looked back at the dog with the black patch beside him. He couldn't shake the fact that there was something strange about it. The other dogs had completely ignored it, and it in turn had made no effort to run with them in the forest. Instead, it just spent the entire journey clamped beside Alex's leg, pulling him on whenever he tried to stop.

'Come on,' said Alex. 'Don't you want to rest, or eat, or something . . . ?'

The dog leaped onto the desert. It took a few steps forward and turned back expectantly.

'No,' said Alex. 'Bad dog. Some things you have to wait for. Bad dog.'

The dog sat down and stared at him. Alex groaned.

'Fine,' he said, turning back. 'Go on if you want. I'm

going to sleep.'

He sat down beside a tree, breathing a sigh of relief. He untied the jumper from his waist, balling it up behind his head and leaning back. Alex screwed his eyes shut against the glare of the sun. He hadn't eaten or drunk anything since he'd left the boundary the day before, and yet he somehow wasn't hungry or thirsty in the slightest. He wasn't even sure how many hours it had been since he last slept. But then, Alex thought, he *must* have stopped somewhere in the forest and slept, because he'd had the dream again, the one where he was pressed up against a wall. And memories not of walking but of lying down, with the rustle of dead leaves running up his back, as if he was being dragged along the forest floor . . .

'Sleep,' he muttered to himself. 'Just go to sleep, Alex.'

■ ■ ■

'Just go to sleep, Alex.'

Alex was allowed to stay up late, because it was the day that the Order were finally letting his father come home. Alex had even made a cake to celebrate. He'd wanted to make it in the shape of a dog, because his father liked dogs so much. Alex's mum said sternly that she didn't think that was the best idea. In the end the cake collapsed, and they had to scoop the middle out, and left a gaping hole in the centre. In a moment of inspiration Alex filled it with crisps.

They waited until long after midnight, at which point Alex's mum said he should probably go to bed. Of course, Alex was still wide awake when his father's footsteps came slowly up the stairs and his face appeared at the crack in the door, trying not to wake him.

'Dad!' Alex cried, sitting up.

'Shhh!' hissed his father, glancing quickly over his shoulder.

'You're back,' Alex said, a little more quietly.

His father smiled and pushed open the door. Even in the dim light of the room Alex could see that he had become much older over the past year. His hair was greying, and there were lines on his face that Alex couldn't remember being there before. He carefully crept over the bedroom floor and sat down on the edge of Alex's bed.

'Hello, Alex,' he whispered.

'Did you see my cake?' said Alex.

'I did,' his father smiled. 'It looks very nice.'

'We should have some now,' Alex suggested, nodding encouragingly.

'Not now, Alex,' he said. 'It's far too late. Your mother wouldn't be very happy if she knew you were talking to me. Now, go to sleep.'

He kissed Alex on the head and stood up. Alex started.

'But . . . aren't you going to finish the story?' he said.

Alex's father looked at him blankly. 'What story?'

Alex bristled. 'The one you started,' he said. 'On the night you left.'

His father shifted uncomfortably and made to leave.

'Alex, we've got lots of other nights for stories,' he muttered. 'You've got to go to sleep now. Good night.'

In a flash, Alex grabbed him by the wrist.

'That's what you said last time!' said Alex angrily. 'And then you ran away!'

His father looked shocked. 'Alex –'

'And I couldn't ask Mum to finish it because you said I shouldn't tell her about it!' he snapped. 'And now I've been waiting to hear about what happened to Malex M. Mennings for over a year, and I've waited up all night, and now you're telling me to wait even longer!'

Alex stopped and the room fell quiet. Alex's father stood looking at him for some time. His breathing was louder, more difficult now than it once was.

'You remembered all that?' he said eventually.

Alex nodded. His father paused.

'Alex, do you know who Malex M. Mennings is?'

Alex nodded. 'He's the explorer,' he said. 'The explorer in your story.'

His father paused for another moment and looked behind him at the door. He sighed and sat back down on the bed. He crossed his arms and then, after a moment's thought, and with apparent difficulty, crossed his legs too.

'OK,' said Alex's father. 'But I'm only telling you this because I owe you. Five minutes, max.'

Alex nodded eagerly. He had no idea why his father was calling him Max.

'So,' said Alex's father, 'where had we . . .'

'He'd gone through the forest,' said Alex quickly, 'and come out the other side. And he found something and it wasn't the centre of the Forbidden Land.'

Alex's father raised his eyebrows.

'Quite a memory you have there, Alex,' he said. 'Looks like you're ready to hear about how Malex M. Mennings crossed the desert.'

'A desert!' said Alex in amazement. 'So that was what was in the centre . . .'

'Well, yes and no, Alex,' said his father. 'The forest had no centre to it, really – it was like a giant ring, one so big that you couldn't see the other side of it. Just like how the Cusp is a ring around the Forbidden Land. And in fact, Malex M. Mennings realised the desert was just another giant ring inside that one. So there had to be something else inside that, too, right in the middle of it. Do you see? He just had to keep going until he found the centre. The true centre.'

'Oh,' said Alex, clearly disappointed.

'But Malex M. Mennings couldn't travel in the burning heat of the desert sun to find it,' said Alex's father. 'Not in his special suit. It would kill him, and his dogs, before they even got a mile.'

'So what did he do?' asked Alex.

'What do you think he did?' said his father. 'He looked at his dogs. And he saw how they just sat and waited in the shade. Most people would try and get over the desert as quickly as possible, but the dogs knew they could only go when it was cool. So he waited too, until the sun had set and the desert had become as cold as a grave. And only then did he travel, by the light of the moon and stars. And when the sun began to rise again the next morning, he and his dogs took cover in the shade of a dune and went to sleep, and waited for the night to fall once more.'

'But that would have taken ages!' Alex groaned.

'Some things you have to wait for, Alex,' his father said. When he spoke again, his voice somehow sounded different in the darkness. 'Some things need time.'

'So did he do it?' asked Alex. 'Did he find the centre of the desert?'

Alex's father nodded. 'In a way. Well, he found something.'

He patted Alex on the leg.

'But that's a story for another time.'

'But that was hardly any story . . . !' cried Alex.

Alex's father shook his head and stood up. 'You remember the deal. Time to sleep.'

'You promise you'll tell me the rest?' said Alex.

'Promise,' said Alex's father, walking to the door. His steps were pained. Alex sat up.

'Dad,' he said. Alex's father turned around.

'Yes, Alex?'

'I'm glad you came back.'

Alex's father smiled.

'Me too, Alex,' he said. 'I'm glad I came back too.'

With that he walked out of the bedroom and closed the door behind him.

When Alex woke up the next morning, his mother was crying downstairs. Alex's father's bags were still unopened on the kitchen floor. He had run away again.

■ ■ ■

When Alex woke up, it was night once more, and all was silent. The sky above the desert was thick with stars, more than Alex had ever been able to see his whole life.

Alex sat up and looked around him. All the dogs had long disappeared, and he was alone at the edge of the trees. The desert stretched out ahead of him, calm, rolling, empty, like a blanket settled on a bed. In the distance, a light was glowing. Alex gazed at it, wide-eyed. It was not the green beam of the base. The light was coming from inside the desert. Alex sat up, his heart racing.

'The centre,' Alex gasped. 'The centre of the Forbidden Land.'

Alex made to stand, and stopped. There was something weighing on his legs. Alex looked down. Lying alongside him, its head resting on his knees, was the dog with the black patch, its little chest rising and falling with exhausted sleep.

16

The walkway of the zeppelin reeled itself in like a curling tongue, and the doors snapped shut with a hiss.

'All aboard,' said Kyte quietly.

He stood in a dark corridor lined with wood panelling. At the end of the corridor was a set of double doors, and in front of them stood Greg. He was clutching his clip-board, his hands shaking.

'Everything ready?' Kyte barked.

Greg snapped himself back up. 'Yes, sir. We're finally ready to go.'

'Those two idiots I sent for,' Kyte said, striding towards the doors. 'Are they on board?'

Greg nodded. 'In your quarters, sir.'

'Good,' said Kyte. He stopped and looked back at him. 'And . . . Number 51?'

Greg's eyes darkened. 'In the kennels, sir.'

Kyte smiled. 'Good,' he said, turning to the doors. 'Set us off to the boundary.'

'Er . . . sir . . .'

Kyte stopped and slowly turned around. Greg shifted nervously on his feet.

'We have a bit of a problem, sir,' he said quietly. 'With the Pooh-Bah.'

Kyte barely blinked. 'What about him?'

'He's – well, he's on board, sir,' said Greg. 'With the other esteemed members of the Order. He says you're not to take off without his permission. He says he needs to talk to you.'

Kyte stood still for a moment. Then his eyes slowly began to glint.

'He's on board?' he said calmly. 'Really?'

Greg nodded. Kyte smiled. 'Set us off, Greg,' he said darkly. 'Immediately.'

Greg's eyes widened. 'Sir, I . . .'

Kyte gave him a look that told him not to argue.

'Of course, sir,' said Greg, his face turning pale. 'Right away.'

Kyte gave him another nod, and with that Greg shot off down the corridor. Kyte pushed open the doors and stepped inside.

A set of lush carpeted steps ran down from the door-way to a large polished wooden desk and a leather swivel chair. Behind them the entire wall was given up to a grand set of windows, revealing the empty runway outside scattered with wreckage. The crowds had finally been broken up, and the base was quiet once more.

In the middle of the room, two men were strangling each other.

'Mike,' said Kyte, nodding to them. 'Duncan. So glad you could rejoin us.'

The two men spun around. Kyte walked briskly down the carpeted steps and threw himself down on the leather chair. He calmly wheeled himself over to the desk and swivelled menacingly in front of them, smiling like a carnivorous fish. Behind him, the pack of wolves emerged into view, barking and snarling, slowly heaving the zeppelin down the runway, their legs powering, their chains taut almost to breaking.

'So,' said Kyte gently. 'I'm sure you've heard that the boy's now making his way across the Forbidden Land. No doubt following his father to the centre.'

The two men nodded sheepishly.

'And I hope you both realise', Kyte said carefully, 'how much of a problem it would be if either of them reached it before we did.'

The two men coughed and shifted uneasily on their feet. Kyte drummed his fingertips on the desk before him. The surface was inlaid with a large leather panel and had small recesses for buttons on either side. One of the recesses contained a hefty metal paperweight, a set of razor-sharp wolf's teeth that glinted in the lamplight. The other contained a metal egg whisk. Duncan stared at it, deeply puzzled, and had already opened his mouth to ask about it before Mike quickly elbowed him in the ribs.

'Don't you worry, boss,' Mike croaked, a light sweat forming on his brow. 'He's just a little kid. We'll catch him. And if we ever get our hands on that Headteacher . . .'

He was cut off by a sharp knock at the door. A troop of guards strode in, saluting.

'Sir!' the guard at the front announced. 'We've found a stowaway on board, sir!'

Kyte looked back at him with interest. 'A stowaway?' he repeated.

'Yes, sir,' said the guard. 'We found him clinging to the bottom of the sewage tank. Shall I bring him in?'

Kyte nodded. The doors swung open, revealing another pair of guards either side of a beaten and weary-looking prisoner. Mike and Duncan's jaws fell. The prisoner was led down the stairs and thrust forwards onto the desk. He was thin, grubby and unshaven, and smelt faintly of sewage. Kyte smiled at the familiar face.

'Ah, Mr Price,' said Kyte. 'I seem to remember that was your name, although at the time I didn't think it was worth remembering.' Matthew the Headmaster nodded grimly.

'And you're Davidus Kyte,' he said. 'Shamed ex-Head of Expeditions, last time I heard.'

Kyte laughed and swivelled back into position on his chair.

'Not quite, Mr Price,' said Kyte. 'I have some unfinished business to attend to before I give up my position. Unfortunately, it's not something you can join us for.' He waved his hands at the guards. 'Throw him out of the window.'

Matthew's eyes widened with shock. The guards grabbed hold of him and started dragging him back up the stairs.

'What?' cried Matthew. 'But – we're already in the air!'

'I have no choice, Mr Price,' said Kyte sadly. 'You see, once you cross the boundary, something still tries to push you out – even if your feet aren't touching the ground. If there are too many passengers on board then it's far too much strain for the wolves. I really can't risk losing valuable time on an Expedition because of extra weight. So long, Mr Price . . .'

'*UNHAND THAT MAN AT ONCE!*'

Everyone spun round. The Grand High Pooh-Bah was at the doorway. He did not look pleased. Behind him stood the esteemed members of the Order, nervously peeking over his shoulders. Kyte's face broke into a smile.

'Your Lordship!' he cried. 'Fellow Order members! What perfect timing. Come in! Take a seat. We'll be crossing the boundary any moment.'

Kyte swivelled the chair round to face the window. The line where the tarmac became the grassland inched ever closer. The wolves leaped and heaved down the runway, their black fur foaming with sweat. The Grand High Pooh-Bah stormed down the steps.

'What on earth is going on here?!' he cried, waving his arms at the men holding Matthew. 'Why are we moving? I never gave you permission to set off on this Expedition! Stop this at once! And what are all these guards doing on board . . . ?'

Kyte smiled. 'I thought some protection would only be fitting, Your Lordship, given that we now have so many esteemed members of the Order travelling with us . . .'

The Grand High Pooh-Bah leaned over the desk to better shout at Kyte.

'We're going nowhere, Kyte!' the Pooh-Bah roared. 'I will not let you lead a – a *manhunt* for a young child in the name of the Order. And now I find you throwing people out of the balloon, to fall a hundred feet to the ground – have you gone insane?' He drew himself up to his full height. 'I'm calling an end to all this right now!' he bellowed. 'Guards – unhand that man! We're heading back.

This Expedition is over!'

'I'm afraid I can't allow that, Your Lordship,' said Kyte calmly.

The Grand High Pooh-Bah snorted in disbelief.

'I beg your pardon, Kyte?' he laughed. 'I am your superior . . . !'

'We are in the air now, Your Lordship,' said Kyte, cutting him off. 'We are now officially on an Expedition. And I am the Official Head of Expeditions. That means that you and all the other Order members are my guests. Not my superiors. And these fine men – ' he indicated the guards surrounding the room – 'answer to me. Not to you.'

The Grand High Pooh-Bah's face fell in disbelief. Kyte smiled.

'So, for the meantime, at least,' he said, 'I'm in charge, Your Lordship.'

There was a sudden tremendous thump at the front of the zeppelin, as if the entire balloon had been hit with a solid wall of air. The esteemed members of the Order gasped in horror. They were passing over the boundary. The force of it bucked the room almost completely upright, and sent everyone to the floor. The walls and floor began to shudder, a terrible tremble that started at the front and slowly ran along the entire length of the balloon, rattling their teeth in their heads and sending the blood to the back of their eyes. Whole shelves of books came crashing down.

The zeppelin stopped shuddering as quickly as it had started. All was still. Everyone glanced at each other with fear. Through the window, the grassland stretched out ahead of them. And then slowly, like a dark cloud, it sank over them: the nervousness, the homesickness; the terrible itching in their feet. The Forbidden Land wanted them out.

Kyte was the only one who didn't seem to be concerned. He had no shortness of breath, no anxiety, no frantic pacing. And yet there was something about him that suddenly seemed different.

Through the window behind him, the shadows of the wolves could be seen ripping through the grass below like a black tide. He leaned over his desk and pressed a button.

'What speed are we going at, Greg?' said Kyte into a vase of flowers beside him.

There was a pause.

'Thirty knots, sir,' came a crackly voice from inside the vase.

Kyte gave this some thought.

'We're supposed to be doing fifty,' he said testily. 'Alex is going to get to the centre in less than five days. We need to be faster if the wolves are going to have any chance of catching him . . .'

There was a sudden commotion at the doorway. With a great heave Matthew had struggled free of the guards and was now clinging onto the doorframe beside him.

'No, Kyte!' Matthew cried. 'I won't let you get him!'

Kyte raised an eyebrow.

'*Him?*' he said. '. . . You mean, the boy?'

'That's right!' Matthew yelled as the guards tried to prise his fingers from the doorframe. 'I know what you're up to, you monster, and I'm not letting you do it! You'll have to go through *me* first!'

The threat, heartfelt as it was, was slightly diminished by the fact that Matthew had now formed a starfish shape in the doorway which the guards were trying to break by tickling him, giving him the appearance of a dog who didn't want to go in the bath.

'Yes,' Kyte said calmly. 'The boy. He trusts you, doesn't he?' He stood silently for a moment more, before turning back to the desk. 'Let him go,' he ordered the guards.

The guards stopped tickling him. Matthew looked up in surprise.

'What?' he gasped.

'*What?*' gasped Mike and Duncan.

'Mr Price has convinced me that he should remain here as our guest,' said Kyte, sitting back down in his chair. 'Which unfortunately means that we have to lose some unnecessary weight elsewhere.'

His eyes quickly set on Duncan. Kyte pointed a finger at him.

'Throw him out instead,' he snapped.

Duncan's eyes filled with horror.

'Wha—?' he wailed.

'Try to make sure he lands on something soft,' Kyte added gently. The guards started dragging Duncan out of the door.

'Mike, do something!' he cried.

'Shut up, Duncan,' muttered Mike.

Duncan was dragged kicking and screaming out the room. All eyes slowly settled back on Kyte. He was staring out the window, his eyes fixed on the green beam of light that stretched out from the base, searching the horizon. There it was again – the sense that something about him was changing. He spun back round and pressed the button again.

'What speed now?' he barked.

'Thirty-two,' came the crackly reply. 'We . . . we seem to be carrying more weight than we thought, sir.'

There was a knock at the door and everyone turned round. A guard stood in the doorway, looking slightly shaken.

'Sir,' he said. 'We, er . . . we've found another stowaway.'

Matthew looked up in shock. Kyte glanced around the room and nodded.

'Bring them in,' he said.

A number of guards led in the prisoner. They were wincing with the bruises they had clearly received in the process of capturing her. Kyte looked blankly at the furious girl standing opposite him.

'Let me guess,' he said. 'You're after the boy as well.'

'Heesh got my teesh,' lisped Martha. Kyte nodded.

'His friend,' he said. 'I see.'

Kyte pointed at Mike.

'Guards, throw him out too,' he said.

Kyte waited until Mike's wails had disappeared down the corridor, and the soft *shoomp* of a window opening and closing had passed, before pressing the button on the desk again.

'Now?' he said.

There was a pause. 'Thirty-five,' came the voice.

Kyte nodded, his face set in thought.

'Sounds like we're carrying a lot of dead weight, doesn't it?'

Kyte seemed to be in some pain. After a moment he turned back to the guards.

'Strip the zeppelin,' he ordered. 'Strip everything that isn't needed and throw it out. We've got a long way to go.'

The guards saluted and without another word started ripping the wood panelling from the walls around them. Kyte leaned over the desk, his back curled and his mouth gaping open in a ravenous yawn. Matthew looked at Kyte, at his body that even now appeared to be stretching in front of him, and suddenly realised what was so different about him. It seemed almost mad to even think it.

Kyte's teeth had somehow become sharper.

17

Alex woke with a start.

'Dad,' he gasped.

He scrambled up, looking around him. The sun was setting on his second day in the desert, and already a coolness had begun to settle across the dunes. There was no one else in sight: no other dogs, certainly not his father. All was sand. Alex groaned. He'd had the dream again.

He threw the jumper off his face, gasping for breath. He was completely bathed in sweat. Sleeping in a desert with only a jumper for a sunscreen was easier said than done.

'Hey,' said Alex drily, shaking the figure lying beside him. 'Wake up, you.'

The dog with the black patch slowly stirred and poked his head out from under the sand.

'It's time,' said Alex. 'We've got to get going.'

The dog needed no more encouragement. It shook itself and leaped to its feet.

Alex got up painfully and watched the dog disappear into the distance. It had stayed with him the whole night, walking when he walked, sleeping when he slept. The other dogs were still too far ahead. Alex could only guess they, too, were heading towards the light, drawn like all dogs to the power of the centre. He squinted his eyes against the setting sun. It was too bright to see it yet.

'Where are you?' Alex muttered, scanning the horizon.

Far ahead, the dog barked. It had stopped in the sand and was glancing back at him. Alex sighed and started walking.

'All right, all right!' he shouted. 'I'm coming.'

The dog turned back round and scampered up the dunes. Alex watched it run away. He wrapped the jumper around his head with a sigh. He still couldn't understand how he could go so long without needing food. Nothing made any sense here. He glanced up, to the horizon of sand spanning the world before him.

'He's somewhere out there,' he muttered under his breath, heaving his feet through the sand. 'He must be.'

■ ■ ■

The night after his father had run away from home the second time, Davidus Kyte appeared at the house.

He came round just before dinner, a security guard either side of him. He sat in the kitchen with Alex's mum and told her that Alex's father had been caught at the boundary again, shrieking like a wounded animal. But this time, he said, they weren't going to let him come back home. They were going to keep him at the Cusp for questioning until they found out why he was doing it.

Alex was still only five years old and he was too frightened to walk in the room, even though it was time for dinner and he was starving hungry and didn't understand why his dad had run away again. He'd sat outside the door and waited, getting hungrier and hungrier.

The argument went on until long after dinner time. Alex remembered looking through the crack in the door and seeing Kyte's face as his mother cried. Eventually, Kyte got up and started opening cupboards, and when he had finally found a plate and a big butcher's knife he sat back down at the table and helped himself to a slice of the cake that had sat there all night, untouched.

Alex had thrown the rest away. He didn't want cake after that.

■ ■ ■

Alex marched onwards, his feet sinking through the mounds of cool sand. The desert was slipping into darkness around him. In the farthest distance, a glow was appearing.

'The centre,' Alex whispered.

He had no choice. He kept walking.

■ ■ ■

The years after that were the years when everything changed.

They were the years when Alex started noticing people on the street pointing and whispering about him. About the boy with the mad father, the one who thought he was a dog. And each time Alex's dad broke out of jail and they found him at the Cusp, trying to get back in, Kyte would turn up on their doorstep, a pair of security guards beside him. And Alex would have to go upstairs to his room while his mum was asked questions that seemed to go on for hours, and there would always be more shouting.

His old room seemed far away now, farther away than it had ever been. He'd only had one photo of his dad on his wall. It was taken before Alex was born, and it was of his dad sitting in a kennel surrounded by a pack of enormous dogs. Alex's mother told him they had pulled the sledge on his Expedition, and that Alex's father had become very close to them and that was why he had started acting so strangely around people. Why the garden was still littered with patches of torn grass and soil from where he had spent days digging endless holes.

In the photo, his father had his arm around the biggest of the dogs, an Alsatian, and looked happier than Alex had ever seen him before. And Alex had thought it was no surprise his dad had run away, when there was so much shouting around the house all the time.

That was when Alex started collecting pictures of dogs.

■ ■ ■

Alex trudged onwards across the sand, his eyes set on the distant glow, watching nothing else.

'He's out there somewhere,' he muttered. 'He must be.'

■ ■ ■

Alex learned a lot over those next few years.

He learned that you couldn't always believe what people said. He learned that even when people told you that they loved you, and that they only wanted you to be happy, it didn't stop them from hurting you.

He learned that sometimes, when bad things happen at home, it makes home stop feeling like home at all. And the worst part is that once it happens you can never go back to it.

He learned that sometimes, once enough people start treating you like you're less of a person, then you start believing them.

When he was eight years old, Alex's mother told him that the bullying at school had gone on long enough, and that maybe he should try going to a boarding school for a while, one that was far away, and Alex didn't argue.

■ ■ ■

The desert was soon at its coldest. Bleak light was appearing at the edge of the world again. The glow became harder and harder to see. Alex stopped. There was no sign of his father. They had gone far enough.

'Hey,' he cried out to the distant figure of the dog. 'Stop. We have to stop.'

They both crouched in the shelter of a dune, a tiny fire of bush scrub kindling before them. Alex shivered and pulled the jumper back over him. He turned to the dog.

'I hate to say this,' he muttered, 'but I don't think we're getting any closer.'

The dog was silent. It looked idly at the fire, watching the stray sparks as they popped from the dry wood. Alex sat silently for some time. Far away, the edge of the sun appeared over the desert.

'I have this dream,' he said eventually.

The dog looked up at him. Alex paused and kicked at the embers.

'In the dream,' said Alex, 'I'm pressed up against a wall so I can't move. And my chest is hurting really badly. So I look down and I see there's this pole poking right into me, right where my heart is, so hard that it's hurting me and keeping me pinned to the wall and I can't move. And

I look along the pole, it's miles long so it takes me ages to see where the end is, and I see that it's my dad holding the pole. He's so far away that I can hardly see him.'

The fire briefly swelled in a small gust of desert wind, like a chest rising.

'And I shout out for him to let go of the pole, so I can move and it'll stop hurting me, and he says that he can't, that he has to hold it there. And so we're stuck like that until my chest hurts more and more and I can barely stand it. And then I realise that I'm not pressed against the wall at all, I'm being pressed against the ceiling. And my dad is holding me up there with the pole, not able to let go or move because the second he does I'll fall.'

Alex looked at the dog. It was lying down now, gazing into the fire.

'And in the dream he lets go,' he said, 'because he can't hold on any longer, and I come crashing down, right down on top of him, and he's holding his hands out to try and catch me and just before I hit him, I . . .'

Alex stopped himself. The fire was dying. He looked up. The thick blanket of stars was disappearing as another day began to break above them. Alex blinked, drowsily. His legs ached, and his head ached. He lay down and slumped his head in the sand. His eyes flickered.

He was in his old bedroom, the dog photos covering the wall where the old mirror stood. And beyond that his dorm room at school, and his cupboard filled with dog magazines and every present his mum had ever sent him.

He grumbled. None of those things could be here. It was the Forbidden Land again. Nothing made any sense here.

'They can't be here,' Alex murmured, 'because I'm completely alone.'

Slowly, the dog sat up and turned to him, giving Alex a smile.

'If it's any consolation,' said the dog, 'I never really knew my father either.'

Alex smiled. I must be dreaming, he thought, because dogs don't talk.

'Night, dog,' said Alex, turning away and falling asleep.

The dog sighed.

'Goodnight, Alex,' said the dog. 'Sweet dreams.'

18

'Hello?'

Far away at the perimeter of the base, a new day was dawning and the night watchman's shift was almost over. Kyte's ship had been gone for nearly two days now, and all was silent.

Almost silent.

The night watchman scanned the horizon with an unflinching gaze and slowly ate a biscuit.

'Who's there?' he mumbled.

He looked out across the turf lining the boundary, or what was left of it. It couldn't accurately be called turf now. What hadn't been trampled flat by those piling in for the ceremony had been torn apart by those charging out afterwards, and what was left of *that* had been churned to mud by trucks following incidents in the nearby town. Some troublemakers at Cloisters calling themselves the Wolf-Tiger Fighter Jet Squadron had started looting the local shops and declaring civil war on all mankind.

The night watchman sighed. It had been a difficult few days for him. The one benefit of the week's disasters was that every competent member of staff had been promoted and sent to deal with the riots, so the night watchman had been allowed to keep his job. He brushed the biscuit crumbs off his shirt and leaned forwards over the desk.

'Who's there?' he called out again. 'I can *hear* you, you know!'

Outside, all was silent. Bent floodlights flickered on and off across the mud. The night watchman listened. He was certain he had just heard *things* moving out there. Lots of things.

Suddenly the phone rang beside him. The night watchman's eyes scanned the darkness outside. He lifted the receiver.

'Security,' he said into the phone.

'Er . . .' came a quavering voice. 'Hello.'

The night watchman frowned. 'Who is this?' he said.

'Who is this?' said the voice. It had suddenly become a lot deeper. 'What do you mean, who is this? I'm your superior officer! Officer . . . er . . .'

The night watchman paused. '. . . Officer Barker?'

'Yes,' said the voice. 'Officer Barker.'

'You sound different, sir,' said the night watchman suspiciously.

'Never you mind how I sound!' the voice roared. 'If you must know, which you shouldn't in my opinion, I have contracted a terrible case of diarrhoea which has affected my vocal chords.'

The night watchman shifted awkwardly on his chair. 'I'm sorry, sir,' he muttered. 'That sounds terrible.'

'It is!' said the voice. 'But more importantly, you must now listen to me and do everything I say. I am about to entrust to you a task so secret that anyone within at least forty feet of you will have to be killed, just in case. Are you listening?'

The night watchman had broken out in a light nervous sweat. 'Yes, sir!' he boomed. He was very grateful that no one else was near him at the base. He didn't want to kill anyone. Despite the seriousness of the situation, however, the night watchman couldn't shake the feeling that Officer Barker was trying as hard as he could not to laugh whenever he spoke.

'Good!' the voice squeaked. 'First of all, I want you to punch yourself in the face.'

The night watchman paused. '. . . Sir?'

There was the sound of a heated argument on the other end of the line.

'All right, all right,' muttered the voice, apparently

disappointed. 'Forget that. Listen here – the entire Royal Family is on its way to the base for a top-secret meeting. In a minute, probably less.'

'The Royal Family!' gasped the night watchman. 'Why, sir?'

'Er . . . I'm not sure,' said the voice. 'Probably something to do with, er . . . taxes. But you're not to inform any other guards about this! All you need to do is open the gates the second you see the convoy arrive, in about half a minute, and close them again afterwards. Do you understand?'

'Yes, sir,' said the night watchman. 'The secret's safe with me.'

'That's a good lad,' said the voice. 'It'll be there in twenty-five seconds. No, wait, twenty. I should also add that in the interest of keeping a low profile the Royal convoy will be cunningly disguised as a light burgundy Citroën C5.'

'Yes, sir,' said the night watchman.

'Make that ten seconds,' corrected the voice nervously. 'It should be easy to spot because all the windows have been smashed out. In fact if I were you I'd open the gates right now.'

'Yes, sir,' said the night watchman. 'When exactly did you say . . .'

A light burgundy Citroën C5 suddenly shot past the

security booth at high speed and with the sound of failing brakes on liquid mud careered straight into the gates.

'Oh no!' gasped the night watchman. He flew out of the booth, shedding crumbs. 'Your Majesty!'

The scene that greeted him outside was horrific. The Citroën had buckled the security gates and was now almost completely upright, its back wheels still whirring at high speed and spraying the surrounding area with brown sludge. As mentioned, all its windows had been smashed in by what looked suspiciously like bullets. A crown had been painted onto the bonnet. The Queen was dragging herself out of the wreckage in a floor-length turquoise ballgown and long white gloves, whacking the driver round the head with her crown.

'You pillock, Dennis!' she screamed. 'Call that driving? That was *easily* our coolest car!'

'Sorry, Laurence,' muttered the driver.

The night watchman sprinted across the mud towards them. 'Don't worry, Your Highness, I'll . . . !'

Before he could finish the sentence the world had turned upside down, and the night watchman found himself rapidly ascending skywards. He shrieked and waited for the horrifying drop, but none came. He opened his eyes again. The world was still upside down. He was dangling from a branch by a rope snagged round his ankle. He looked down. Far below, the Royal Family were staring up at him. The night watchman could swear they were all wearing fancy-dress costumes.

'Oh wow,' said the Queen. 'Nice trap, Justin.' She turned round to the bushes. 'Come on out, guys!'

The night watchman gasped. Hundreds of boys in camouflage were suddenly emerging from the darkness on every side, their clothes and faces covered in mud. The Queen tore off her wig and stuffed it into a pearl-snap handbag before looking back up at the night watchman. Even with her expertly applied make-up it was now rather obvious that she was not the Queen of England.

'Good evening,' said Laurence Davy with a sweep of his arms. 'May I introduce the Wolf-Tiger Fighter Jet Squadron. Say hello, boys.'

'Hello,' said the army of boys.

'Hello,' said the night watchman. 'Can you let me down, please?'

'Not till you punch yourself in the face,' one of them said.

'And the bum,' someone added.

'Let's lock him in the toilet,' said Laurence.

19

The zeppelin swayed and dipped in the desert heat like a ship on a groaning ocean, and would no doubt have made anything on the shelves fall off had there been anything left on them. In the two days since they had left the boundary, Kyte's quarters had become almost unrecognisable. Gone were the chandeliers, the vases, the paintings, all thrown to the ground below. Only the enormous wooden desk had managed to keep its place, not to mention – Matthew noted with some confusion – the paperweight and the egg whisk.

He sat on the floor with the rest of the esteemed members of the Order, rubbing at his aching feet. They were all suffering from it. With each step of their journey a new symptom cropped up. A deep throbbing pain in the stomach, constant watering of the eyes, hair standing on end. Matthew hadn't been able to get the taste of lemons out of his mouth since yesterday afternoon.

A series of delicate chimes suddenly rang out and the huddled crowd of prisoners immediately fell silent. Matthew looked around at what had become of Kyte's 'guests' over the last two days. The esteemed members of the Order were frightened and shaking, stripped of their helmets and suits and wrapped in the old wolf furs that the guards had humiliatingly made them swap for their clothes. Matthew turned to Martha, sitting beside him in a heap of furs. She was the only person who didn't look in any way frightened.

'Don't worry,' he whispered to her. 'He won't make us do it. Remember, he needs us. Just don't punch him again.'

Martha shrugged, promising nothing.

In front of them stood Kyte, with his back curled in a great hunch over his desk. When he was certain everyone was listening he closed the xylophone with a set of long, gnarled fingers and turned back round to face them, his back releasing itself in a reel of cracks.

'Let's get started,' he muttered.

The prisoners looked round nervously. No one wanted to go first. Kyte rolled his eyes, huffed and pointed to a man in grey furs sat next to Matthew.

'You,' he said.

The man pointed to himself in horror. 'Me?'

'Yes, you,' Kyte snapped. 'Have you prepared your speech?'

'Er . . . I . . .' He shyly held up a crumpled sheet of paper.

'Well, go on then,' said Kyte irritably. 'Stand up, so we can all hear.'

The man got to his feet and looked around him. He was bald and visibly sweating. He straightened out his sheet of paper with trembling hands.

'H—' he began.

'Aren't you going to say your name?' Kyte interrupted.

'Er . . .' said the man. 'Reginald.'

'Well, Reginald, let's begin,' said Kyte, taking out an egg timer. 'Nice and loud please.'

Reginald looked back at his paper, which was now shaking violently, and spoke just about as loudly as you can without actually shouting.

'"Hello everyone – I'm Reginald. I think I deserve to stay on this wonderful zeppelin because of all the Order experience, know-how and problem-solving skills that I can bring to the challenges which lie ahead. Being a lawyer by day, I . . ."'

'A lawyer?' Kyte snapped. 'You're a lawyer?'

'Er . . . yes,' said Reginald.

'No,' said Kyte, shaking his head. 'Throw him out.'

Within moments the guards had dragged him out the

room. Everyone muttered in horror.

'You please,' Kyte now said, pointing at someone else and turning the little egg timer back over.

With considerable difficulty Charles got to his feet and held up a sizeable heap of papers.

'Friends,' he said loudly to the room with a dramatic sweep of his arm. 'The phrase "solid all-rounder" is used all too often nowadays . . .'

Kyte groaned and waved his hand irritably. 'God, just throw him out.'

Charles was dragged out of the crowd as quickly as the man before him. Kyte's eyes scanned the room and finally settled on someone new. He smiled.

'You,' he said.

The man got to his feet. He looked phenomenally angry.

'I'm Greg,' he snapped. 'And I deserve to stay on this zeppelin because, as I've explained *quite a few times now*, I'm the only person here capable of flying it!'

Kyte sighed. 'You're not flying it now, are you, Greg? The wolves are pulling us along quite admirably.' Kyte waved a hand to the guards. 'Throw him out.'

'*Not so fast, Kyte!*' a voice cried out.

Matthew turned round. Behind him, the Grand High Pooh-Bah was getting to his feet. He had long ago lost his special sash and his helmet. His face had managed to keep its familiar shade of braised-beef red, and his fists were clenched.

Kyte smiled sarcastically. 'Have *you* prepared a speech, Your Lordship?'

'No, I haven't!' he roared. 'I refuse to take part in this monstrous game of yours!'

Kyte turned to the guards.

'Get Number 51,' he croaked weakly, waving them away with his crooked fingers. The guards looked at each other.

'Sir?' said one. 'Are you sure you don't . . .'

'*Now!*' Kyte suddenly roared, slamming his hands down on the desk. Everyone leaped back. His eyes had clouded white with anger, and his mouth had twisted into a furious snarl. It was like something terrible was digging itself out of him. But whatever had overcome him quickly passed as he fell hunched over the desk, heaving for breath. The guards dashed up the stairs and out the door, closing it behind them. The crowd of terrified prisoners shrank back.

'Kyte,' the Pooh-Bah muttered, 'what on earth have you done to yourself?'

Kyte was now breathing calmly. He slowly raised his head to look at them.

'Pooh-Bah,' he said. 'As I've explained many times now, we have to lose as much weight as we can. The centre is trying to push us away and we're losing speed. Unless everyone can prove their importance to this Expedition then . . .'

'What about you, Kyte?' the Pooh-Bah snapped. 'Have *you* prepared a speech?'

The room fell silent.

'That's right,' the Pooh-Bah smiled. 'So far, all you've done is doom this Expedition from the word go!'

The crowd of prisoners mumbled their approval.

'He's right, you know!' said the Major, standing up. He was almost unrecognisable since he'd been forced to shave off his moustache and throw it overboard. 'What say we give *you* a quick trip out the window, Kyte?'

The guards looked at each other, growing in confidence, and stepped forwards.

'They have a point, sir,' said one of them. 'We lost a lot of men greasing up the side of the zeppelin to get over the trees. There's been no sign of the boy or his father. I really think it's time to turn back.'

'The way I see it, Kyte,' said the Pooh-Bah, stepping forward and jabbing a finger into Kyte's shoulder, 'there's far more of us here than there are of you. Democratic vote, mutiny . . . call it what you like, I don't think we need your leadership one moment longer! And what's more . . .'

'I've already prepared a speech,' said Kyte, matter-of-factly.

The Pooh-Bah smiled and crossed his arms.

'Go on, then!' he said. 'Let's hear it!'

The crowd waited expectantly. Kyte stood up painfully and leaned forwards, nodding to the egg whisk on the desk before him.

'Anyone know what that's for?' he said.

The Pooh-Bah snorted. 'Whipping cream?'

Kyte nodded. 'Exactly. Only, interesting fact: cream whips *itself* this side of the boundary. Another one of the strange and wonderful things that happen once you step into the Forbidden Land. So the egg whisk isn't really needed on board. It's a symbol, more than anything else. A symbol of everything that is wholly unnecessary once you pass over that line. To remind me, at all times, what is of no use on this Expedition.'

The crowd glanced at each other. Kyte laughed.

'Well, actually I'm lying,' he said. 'It's not just a symbol. It's a lever, disguised as an egg whisk.' He reached out and delicately placed a hand on it. 'A lever that, when pulled, drops the floor of this whole room.'

Everyone froze. Behind the doors, something was approaching, crashing against the corridor walls, getting louder.

'You see,' said Kyte, 'I don't really need any of you. I don't even need the guards. You're useless to me. All that matters is that I get to the centre before Alex or his father does. All I need are the wolves.'

The crashing in the corridor was getting louder. Shouts and cries could now be heard outside the doors.

'For now, maybe,' Greg cried, standing up. 'But how long until your precious zeppelin starts falling apart, Kyte? How do you propose to get back on a disintegrating ship?'

Kyte revealed a dazzling set of hungry teeth.

'Who said anything about going back?'

The doors burst open. The prisoners flew back with fear. At the top of the staircase stood an enormous grey wolf, twice the size of the others, straining at the collar, held by two guards with long poles. Its eyes scanned the room as it bared its teeth and flung itself against the banisters, howling, howling, howling with fury. From its collar hung a tag: *51*. Kyte smiled and pushed himself away from the desk.

'Have you ever wondered', he began, speaking over the howls of the wolf, 'why it actually *is* that we can't cross the boundary?'

'That . . . that's just the way it is,' said Greg, rooted to the spot with fear.

Kyte shrugged. 'So everyone thinks. But not me. I've spent a lot of time looking at the Forbidden Land. And I've always found myself thinking – why is it so perfectly *round*? A perfect circle. How often do you see that in nature?'

Kyte stepped carefully over the crowd of trembling prisoners, his eyes fixed on the wolf at the top of the stairs.

'The way I see it,' Kyte continued, 'there *must* be something at the centre of it. Something that doesn't want us to go near it. Keeping us a fixed distance away, on every side. Making sure us humans can't ever reach it. Pushing us *out*.'

He was at the bottom of the staircase now. The wolf had stopped roaring at the room and was now glaring at Kyte, its back curled with each heaving breath.

'Alex J. Jennings knew it, for certain,' said Kyte calmly. 'Despite all his lies about there being nothing in the centre. Tell me this – does it really seem as if Jennings is after *nothing*? He's on his way there now, no doubt strapped up to his mangy dogs . . . ! After nothing? I don't think so.'

'But then . . . what about the boy?' said the Pooh-Bah.

Kyte smiled to himself. 'Indeed. What about him?'

He raised himself up the first step. The guards holding the wolf pulled back with all their might.

'Sir!' one cried, struggling with his grip. 'Don't get any closer! It's gone mad!'

'Of course it has,' said Kyte absent-mindedly. 'I haven't fed it since we left.'

Kyte took another step forward. The wolf's eyes widened and fixed on him, its neck craning, its mouth hung with reels of saliva.

'I worked on the Jennings Expedition,' Kyte began, his gaze never leaving the wolf. 'A lot more than most people realise. Before he threw me off his team, of course. If he had only listened to me, let me help him . . . well. Things might have turned out very differently.'

Kyte fell quiet and took another step. The wolf started quietly growling.

'I wasn't there when they wound him back in,' said Kyte. 'But I learned all about it afterwards. No one had heard from him in days. Everyone expected him to come back dead. He came back alive, but absolutely raving, desperately trying to get back over the boundary. He was absolutely furious at having been brought back early.'

The wolf was straining at the collar around its neck, its back arched, its chest heaving. The prisoners watched in horror as Kyte took another step forwards.

'The question is,' said Kyte, 'why did he want so desperately to get back? What is it he's been after all this time?'

He took another step up the staircase. His eyes and the wolf's eyes were locked.

'There's no doubt about it now,' he said quietly. 'It's what I've always suspected. Alex J. Jennings saw something on that Expedition. Something that he won't tell us about. Something that he'll do anything to get back to.

He and the Forbidden Land have some kind of . . . deal. There's no other explanation for it. How else can you explain why his own son can *walk* on it, for heaven's sake! Can any of you explain it? Unless, of course . . .'

Kyte paused for a moment, and for a single second his eyes seemed to glaze over with doubt. And then he took a grip on the wood of the banister and shook it away, and it was gone. He glared back up at the wolf, his eyes pierced with hunger.

'No,' he whispered, staring into the wolf. 'There's no other explanation. They have a deal with the Forbidden Land. It's giving them something in return. And I'm going to find out what it is, once and for all. What it is that they're after. What they've always been after.'

The room was silent. Kyte breathed out, and stepped forwards.

'. . . *Squiggles*.'

With a great heave, the wolf wrenched itself free of the guards and flung itself with all its might down the staircase towards Kyte. The prisoners on the floor screamed with horror. Matthew threw himself against Martha.

'Martha, don't look!' he cried. 'Cover your eyes!'

But she sat stock still, her eyes unblinking, staring open-mouthed. Matthew turned round. The guards had stopped dead, and one by one were dropping their hands to their sides with shock.

Kyte and the wolf were embracing in the centre of the staircase. The wolf was on its hind legs, leaning on Kyte's shoulders, licking his face. Kyte turned to the room, stroking the wolf's nose calmly.

'This is Number 51,' he said. 'And he's going to stop Alex and his father from getting to the centre before we do.'

The wolf stepped gently off Kyte's shoulders and skulked down into the room. The prisoners flew back against the desk and the guards pressed themselves to the walls.

'The wolves and I are in charge now,' said Kyte calmly, following Number 51 down the stairs. 'Guards, if you would like to sit with the others and prepare your speeches.'

They didn't need asking twice. The guards dropped to the ground, quickly followed by Greg and the Grand High Pooh-Bah. Kyte sat down with difficulty in his chair. The endless desert spread out in the window behind him, the wolves below powering across the dunes like a black sandstorm.

'You can't be serious,' said Matthew emptily. 'Those wolves, they'll . . . they'll tear Alex apart.'

Kyte smiled. 'With any luck, Mr Price, they'll tear Alex *and* his father apart.' He leaned over the desk. 'All that's left is to find out who will be staying with us in the kennels when they do.'

Kyte picked up the egg timer and turned it back over.

'So,' he said, 'who's next?'

20

Far away, at the other end of the desert, Alex stood at the edge of a dune, panting. The sand ended at his feet, and before him an endless plain of water frothed and boiled before his eyes.

'The ocean,' said Alex. 'Just like he said.'

He turned back around, shaking his head in disbelief.

'And . . . and the dogs.'

All around him in every direction stood thousands upon thousands of dogs, stretching as far as the eye could see. There were dogs of every age, every shape and size, every colour, and the air was filled with their howling and whining and barking. They lined the vast circle of raging sea for miles in either direction, shifting on their feet, too frightened to take another step forwards. They were all barking at something in the distance.

There, on the far side of the ocean, stood a single dot

on the horizon. It was surrounded by a haze of smoke, almost erasing it from view. Alex's eyes flickered.

'The centre,' he whispered.

Alex stood staring at the dot for some time. Then he looked back down at the water before him. It heaved and sank in great foaming waves, crashing against the bank and sending the dogs scattering backwards.

His heart sank. There was no way he could possibly cross it. There was no way *anyone* could cross it.

So where was his father?

There was a sudden tug at his leg. The dog with the black patch was yanking furiously at his trousers again, its paws scuffling in the sand. It was the only dog in the thousands around them that wasn't standing barking at the water's edge.

'What?' Alex snapped, shaking his leg irritably.

The dog let go and bounded a few paces along the bank, looking back at him expectantly. It wanted him to follow again.

Alex sighed.

'It's no use,' he said. 'There's no way across. My dad told me all about it. He went the whole way around it looking for a bridge, or a walkway, but there was nothing.'

The dog ignored him and kept scampering on along the bank, sniffing the ground intently. Alex turned back and stared across the water.

'And when he got back to where he'd started,' he continued, 'he saw that his airpipe had caught on something out there. Something way out in the middle of the sea.'

Alex's eyes fixed on the dot, barely visible on the horizon.

'It had wrapped around it,' he said quietly. 'Whatever it was. And so he tied himself to the airpipe, and pulled himself back over the water towards it, him and his main dog. Until they finally reached it.'

Alex paused.

'Whatever *it* was,' he said. 'He never told me.'

Alex looked down at the water's edge, at the line where the desert became the sea. He stood at the exact point where his father's stories about the Forbidden Land had ended. He had no idea what lay the other side of the water. He had no idea how to get there. And yet somewhere over there now, somehow, his father was waiting.

The dog barked. Alex looked up.

'*What?*' he snapped.

The dog had come to a stop at the bank not far away and was staring at him expectantly again. Alex shuddered, barely able to hide his irritation.

'I just *told* you,' he said. 'There's no way of getting over! My dad had an airpipe. We don't. We don't even have a *rope* –'

Alex stopped himself. He looked at the dog in front of

him. It was sitting next to a large dead branch which stuck out of the ground beside him. It had been taken from the forest, carried across the desert and jammed into the bank with some force. Tied around it was a piece of rope, old and weathered, that dipped down into the water.

Alex looked at it, and back at the dog, and back at the rope. He slowly walked over and pulled it up. The rope heaved out the water ahead of him, dripping, thick with slime. Alex followed it with his eyes. It ran across the water, straight out towards the centre, and then came back again. It had caught on something out there.

'Dad?' said Alex quietly.

He lowered the rope back into the water, and stared across the waves.

'He's over there now,' he said. 'And he can't be that far ahead – not if he had to walk all the way around the ocean first.'

Alex looked down at the dog. It was back on its paws, eagerly facing the water. Alex gave the rope an experimental tug. It was slack in his hand. He shook his head.

'But we can't risk it,' he muttered. 'We need to make sure that the rope is safe before we do anything stupid like . . .'

Alex was cut off by a great splash. He looked down. The dog had flung itself into the water and immediately sunk from view. Alex leaped forward.

'*Don't!*' he cried, stopping at the bank. 'You'll . . .'

The dog suddenly appeared some distance off, paddling furiously. The current had dragged him out in a matter of seconds.

'*Are you mad?!*' Alex cried. 'Come back! Hey!'

The dog ignored him and kept paddling furiously. It was disappearing among the heaving roll of the current, almost lost from view. The dogs along the bank barked and whined, but none of them were able to take another step forward to follow it.

'Wait . . .' Alex cried feebly.

It was no use. The dog was gone. Alex stood, panting, looking at the dot on the horizon. Then he looked down again at the furious water before him.

'Oh crikey,' he mumbled.

Before he could change his mind he grabbed at the slimy rope, swallowed hard and threw himself into the water.

The second he hit it he was dragged sideways, the rope snapping tight in his hands. Alex surfaced and gasped for breath. The water was ice cold, shooting up his spine like electric shocks. He glanced around desperately. The dog was nowhere to be seen.

'Wait for me!' Alex yelled. 'Wait!'

The branch in the bank suddenly gave way and fell into the water behind him. In seconds Alex found himself floundering in the roar of the current, the rope now slack and still clutched in his desperate hands, kicking and gasping for breath. The speed of the water was unbelievable.

'*Wait!*' Alex cried.

Alex sank back under, the sound of the water pounding in his ears as he kicked his legs feebly against the surging current. The endless barking of the dogs faded into its muffled roar. He heaved himself back to the surface, taking last desperate gasps of air, until everything went dark, and all he could see was the water.

■ ■ ■

'And that,' said his father, 'is how Malex M. Mennings left behind his dogs and crossed the ocean.'

Alex's father got to his feet, slowly, shakily. He had become even older since Alex had last seen him. His hair was completely grey. The Order had decided that he was now so sick, so old and frail, that he was no longer a threat to the safety of the Cusp. They had finally allowed him to come home. When he appeared at the front door again that evening, his legs stiff and pained, it was as if he had been away for forty years instead of four. He looked down at Alex lying in bed.

'You've been very quiet tonight, Alex,' said his father.

They stayed in silence for a moment.

'Well, you're nine years old now, I suppose,' he said, and stood up. 'Maybe you're too old for stories . . .'

'Some boys at school told me about the Expedition,' said Alex suddenly. 'About what happened.'

Alex's father was silent for another moment.

'I see,' he said sadly.

He walked around the room. The walls were covered in pictures of dogs. Alex had come home one day to find his mum standing in his bedroom, just looking at them. Alex had thought she was going to cry but she didn't. That night she made the biggest dinner Alex had ever eaten in his life.

'Perhaps, Alex,' said his father slowly, 'I'll tell you everything that happened myself one day. Everything. So you don't have to hear from . . .'

'I don't want to hear any more of your stories,' said Alex.

He had raised his voice. They both fell silent, not wanting to wake Alex's mother. She had gone up to bed the moment his father had come back, and had not come down. Alex sat up and stared at the man across the room.

'You're going to do it again, aren't you?' he hissed. 'You're going to do it and you can't even lie to me.'

His eyes were beginning to fill with tears. Alex willed them away, not wanting to cry in front of him. They were both silent for a moment. Alex's father sat back down on the bed and placed a hand on his son's shoulder. The skin was already beginning to shrivel like that of a man twice his age. Everything seemed to be moving faster now.

'I'm sorry,' said his father.

'Why did you do it?' said Alex.

Alex's father said nothing.

'Why?'

Nothing.

'Was it the centre?' asked Alex. 'What you found there?'

His father smiled.

'Not really,' he said. 'It was something else. Something I had to go back for.'

Alex's father looked around the room, to the pictures that lined the walls.

'Something you lost,' said Alex.

Alex's father nodded sadly. 'Something very important to me. I didn't even realise what it was or what it meant until I didn't have it any more. Does that make sense, Alex?'

Alex nodded. He didn't want his father to know that he didn't understand.

'But I'm not going to try any more,' he said. 'I'm going to stay here, with you and your mother. You don't have to go to boarding school any more.'

'You promise,' said Alex.

'I promise,' said Alex's father. 'And I'm not going to tell you the stories any more either.'

He kissed Alex's forehead and stood back up.

'Good night, Alex.'

He made his way out of the bedroom. Alex lay awake listening to his father's slow and painful footsteps down the corridor, past the bedroom door where Alex's mother was sleeping alone, down the steps and across the kitchen, to the utility room at the back where the washing machine was kept, and where the old wicker basket filled with blankets lay. This was where Alex's father now slept.

He stayed at the house for two more days, pacing the garden and digging holes, before he ran away again.

■ ■ ■

The distant roar of the water closed in on him once more. The darkness faded.

Alex opened his eyes. The brightness of the day almost made him sick, and he shut them again, groaning. A cold wind caught his soaking jumper. His arms were dead weights.

Something was dragging him across the rocks.

Alex raised his head and opened his eyes again. The dog with the black patch had him by the collar and was heaving him inch by inch over the seaweed and stones beneath him.

'[. . .]!' said Alex. His mouth was swollen and useless. No words formed.

The dog let go and gave Alex a quick lick on the face before bounding away. Alex lay still for a moment more, his stomach churning. He had swallowed a lot of water. When the desire to vomit had passed, he slowly heaved himself up on his elbows and opened his eyes again.

He was on an island of black rock. That much he could tell. Everything else was hidden by thin grey smoke that hung in the air on every side, shielding the rest of the island from view. The distant barking of the thousands of dogs could just be made out over the lapping of the waves. Alex squinted his eyes to the distance. Through the smoke, he could just make out an enormous black shape that lined the horizon.

Alex gasped. 'The cen—'

He stopped. There was something else on the island.

There, a stone's throw ahead of him, was a small wooden hut. The door was open, and a thin stream of smoke was rising from the chimney.

Someone was inside.

Alex leaped to his feet and immediately fell over again. His legs felt like they belonged to somebody else several miles away. Gritting his teeth, he threw himself forwards and stumbled across the slimy rocks to the door of the hut. Without pausing for breath he ran inside.

'*Dad! . . .*' he cried.

He stopped. The hut was empty. A fresh bunch of drift-wood was kindling in the fireplace. On the floor in front of it lay a dog basket, piled high with ragged blankets and strewn with moth-eaten dog toys. The rest of the hut was empty, except for a tiny table and chairs made from pieces of scrap wood. The table was only big enough for a small child. Alex swayed unsteadily on his feet.

'. . . Dad?' he whispered.

'Mine, actually,' said a voice behind him.

Alex whipped round. The dog with the black patch was standing in the doorway. It had several pieces of driftwood strapped to its back in what looked suspiciously like a handmade sling. The dog shifted uncomfortably on its paws.

'Er,' said the dog awkwardly, 'you are in my way.'

Alex stepped wordlessly aside. The dog scampered past him and started chucking the wood piece by piece into the fire with its mouth.

'We leave in twenty minutes,' it said, 'so get some rest while you can. You must dry yourself, too, it will be very cold out there. Oh, and let's have some tea! Tea?'

Alex didn't reply. Slowly, he slumped onto the table beside him. Although he couldn't be a hundred per cent certain of anything any more he was fairly sure that, outside of his dreams, he had never heard a dog speak before. He was pretty convinced that he had never met one with a slight French accent either. He was also, he realised, more hungry than he'd ever been in his entire life.

'Tea?' the dog repeated.

Alex fainted.

'I will take that as a yes,' said the dog.

Part Four

The Centre

21

The boy stood at the boundary, gazing out across the grassland that rolled in great billowing sheets onwards to the horizon. He stood as close as one could to the Forbidden Land without touching it, the ends of his recently acquired trainers skirting the great curve where the concrete ended. He was unafraid. The others behind him didn't dare to step so close. But then, thought the boy, that was probably why he was Grand High Chieftain Wizard and they weren't.

'*Laurence!*' one of them suddenly cried. '*There! To the left!*'

Grand High Chieftain Wizard Laurence Davy glanced over. Sure enough, another figure was emerging from the grassland in the distance, running full pelt back to the Cusp.

He turned round, facing the crowds of expectant

children behind him. The Wolf-Tiger Fighter Jet Squadron had grown significantly in numbers since they had captured the town several days ago, and new recruits were turning up every day. The base was still in the process of being transformed into the centrepoint of their New Age revolution, and it was already looking brilliant. All the warehouses had massive swear words spraypainted on them. Dozens of boys were busy Sellotaping fireworks to the riot vans. Laurence pointed to a pair of lookouts stationed on top of a nearby barracks, their costumes decorated with cardboard and warpaint and leaves.

'What can you see?' he called. 'Is it the Dog Walker?'

They hurriedly looked down the telescopes in front of them.

'No, Your Wizardliness,' one of them cried. 'It's a man. It's an extremely hairy old man.' He paused and looked through the telescope again. 'Or maybe it's just another old guy in wolf furs.'

Laurence Davy sighed, barely able to hide his disappointment. Another member of the Order. They were all useless to him. All he needed was Alex. He turned back round. Beside him stood a line of boys, each holding a large mattress.

'Ready, men?'

'Yes, Your Wizardliness!' they chanted.

Laurence Davy nodded. 'Commence the pummelling.'

The second the man stepped over the boundary the Wolf-Tiger Fighter Jet Squadron leaped into action, walloping him repeatedly with their mattresses until he finally collapsed onto the concrete. A single wallop with a sturdy mattress, they had discovered, was sufficient to break the spell of the Forbidden Land and stop people from running home.

Laurence waved them away half-heartedly and knelt over the man on the concrete. He had the same glazed look of exhaustion and horror that marked all the people who had arrived back from the Forbidden Land over the last few days. He was gasping for breath, his arms and legs still twitching from days of running. The surface of his face was dry and caked with sand.

'Name?' said Laurence Davy.

'Wh . . . what?' said the man, his chest heaving.

'Your name,' Laurence repeated. 'What's your name?'

'Oh,' said the man. 'Er . . . Reginald.'

'Have you come from the zeppelin, Reginald?' said Laurence. 'Were you a member of the Order?'

Reginald nodded wordlessly, gasping for breath on the floor. Laurence leaned down to his face.

'Did you see him, Reginald?' said Laurence quietly.

The man's eyes flickered, confused. 'See who?'

The Grand High Chieftain Wizard gazed into his eyes.

'The boy,' he said, his face set. 'Alex Jennings. The

Dog Walker. Did you see him?'

'The boy?' Reginald gasped. He thought about it and shook his head. 'N-no. None of us did. He was too far ahead.'

Laurence Davy sighed with frustration and then stood up.

'He's no use to us,' he barked to his men, giving a wave behind him as he marched back to his position on the boundary. 'Tie him up with the others.'

A pack of boys immediately ran over to Reginald and started dragging him across the runway. Reginald groaned with confusion.

'Wait – what?' he cried. 'Where are you taking me? What's the meaning of this? What on earth are you boys doing here . . . ?!'

Grand High Chieftain Wizard Laurence Davy watched as the man was taken to the line of stakes set up along the curve of the boundary and tied up. He was now just another of the scores of prisoners captured since the Wolf-Tiger Fighter Jet Squadron had claimed the town. Laurence sighed. He wasn't entirely sure what he was going to do with them yet. They were just another step on the road towards the New Age. A time when children would rule the world, and do away with the wickedness of their elders, and the streets would overflow with super-cool skateparks and massive ramps.

He turned back to the grassland. For now, the prisoners didn't matter. For now all he needed was Alex Jennings. The boy with the power to walk over the Forbidden Land. He gazed out once more across the boundary and sighed.

'Where are you, Dog Walker?'

22

The first thing Alex realised was that he had suddenly become very cold and very wet.

I must still be in the ocean, he thought. *Maybe I never got to the island after all. Maybe I'm drowning and my life is flashing before my eyes*.

Then Alex realised that the surface against his face felt very much like wood, in particular the wood of a table that had been badly carved by a dog.

He sat bolt upright, gasping for breath. The dog stood on the table in front of him, next to an empty bucket of seawater.

'Are you OK?' said the dog.

Alex nodded, dripping water.

'Good,' said the dog. 'Because we leave in ten minutes.'

The dog jumped off the table and scampered towards the fireplace. Alex looked groggily around him. The tabletop in front was laid with a set of neatly arranged dog bowls. A battered iron pan now sat on the glowing embers of the fire, bubbling loudly. Alex's stomach moaned with hunger.

'I have made food,' said the dog, carefully stirring the pot. 'For your strength. It's not an easy walk to the centre, you know.'

Alex steadied himself on the table. 'The wha—?' he slurred.

The dog nodded out the window. Alex gazed outside. On the horizon he could still make out the great black shape that loomed through the smoke like a dead volcano. From its very top now shone a great bright light. Alex blinked. It was the light he had seen from the desert.

'Your father, he is heading there now,' said the dog, heaving the pot onto the table and ladling out some green slop from inside. 'If we hurry, we might even make it there before him.' It pushed a bowl over to Alex. 'I hope you like seaweed.'

The dog pulled up a chair and started eating. After a while it looked up again. Alex wasn't eating. He sat perfectly still across the table, staring at it.

'Yes?' said the dog.

Alex thought long and hard about the best thing to say.

'You're a dog,' said Alex.

There was an awkward silence.

'Who lives in a house,' he added. 'And makes food.'

Pause.

'And talks,' he said.

They both fell silent and stared at each other for a moment. The dog narrowed its one visible eye.

'. . . What is your point?' it said.

Alex thought about it.

'Well, in my experience most dogs don't do any of those things,' he said. 'Most dogs just bark and run around and stuff. They definitely don't build houses and cook food in them. And they don't make tea. That's just weird.'

The dog bristled and started carefully arranging its napkin over its legs.

'Well, I am not like most dogs, Alex,' it said shirtily. 'So that explains most of those things. Anything else "weird" about me that you feel is worth mentioning?'

Alex nodded. 'You have a slight French accent.'

'My father was an Alsatian,' said the dog.

Alex blinked. 'Oh.'

The dog gave him a withering look and without any further explanation launched into its food again. Alex kept staring.

'Can any other dogs talk in the Forbidden Land?' he said.

The dog glanced up. '*Non*,' it said thinly.

'So you live here by yourself, then?' he said to the dog.

The dog nodded. 'Yes,' it said. 'Just me.'

'Why?' said Alex.

The dog looked up. 'What do you mean, why?'

Alex blinked. 'Why live here all alone?'

The dog shifted uncomfortably. 'Why not?'

'Because you'll get lonely,' said Alex.

'I don't,' said the dog.

'Oh,' said Alex. 'Can't the other dogs make it over here?'

The dog sighed. 'Does it *look* like there are any other dogs here, Alex?'

Alex looked around and shook his head.

'No,' said the dog. 'There aren't. Because dogs cannot make it over the water.'

'Except you,' said Alex.

The dog grumbled. 'Except me.'

Alex paused. 'What about a name? Do you have a name?'

The dog appeared to be gritting its teeth with frustration. 'Arnauld.'

It made to start eating again, but was suddenly blocked by Alex's outstretched hand. It looked up to the boy's grinning face.

'Alex,' said Alex.

The dog looked at his hand for a moment, and then looked up again.

'No,' he said. '*Arnauld.*'

There was an embarrassing pause. Alex slowly dropped his hand. The dog made another attempt to start eating again.

'Why didn't you talk to me before?' Alex said suddenly.

The dog looked up impatiently. 'I didn't feel like it,' he snapped. 'Alex, aren't you going to eat something?'

Alex looked down at the slime in his bowl and grimaced. He might have been starving, but nobody was *that* starving. 'I'm all right,' he said weakly.

Arnauld sighed. 'Just eat. You haven't eaten for days, and we need to get to the centre as quick as we can . . .'

'Why do we have to get there so quickly?' said Alex.

Arnauld glared at him in disbelief.

'We *must* talk about this now?' he said.

'I don't see why not,' said Alex huffily.

Arnauld looked like he was trying his best not to lose his temper.

'I mean,' said Alex, 'no offence, but I don't see why I should be listening to anything you say at all. I've only known you for a few days.'

The dog raised an eyebrow.

'And also you're a talking dog,' Alex added.

Arnauld nodded thoughtfully. Then he wolfed down

the rest of his seaweed in a single gulp and pushed the empty bowl away from him.

'Correct, Alex,' he said. 'But I am *also* a talking dog who knows the only way to get to the centre.' He nodded out the window again. 'Would you prefer to go out there on your own?'

Alex glanced outside. The island had become darker since they started talking. The ground stretching ahead was littered with drops and craters and jagged edges that split into dozens of different pathways. The smoke was thick, and clung to the slippery rocks on every side.

'I thought not,' said Arnauld. 'You'll need my help if you want to get to the centre. And I leave now. So I suppose the question is, do you want to find your father or don't you?'

Alex stared at him.

'You know where he is?' he said.

Arnauld snorted. 'Of course I do. Where do you think I've been taking you this whole time? I know *exactly* where he is, Alex, and I know how to get there before we run out of time, too. So let me repeat my question: do you want to find your father, or don't you?'

Alex shifted uncomfortably.

'Of course I do,' he said quietly. 'But . . .'

'Then you have two choices,' said Arnauld, jumping from his chair. 'You can either try to find him out there on your own, or you can shut up and eat your seaweed and come with me.'

Alex looked dejectedly at the bowl of green slop in front of him. It did not look appetising. His stomach howled.

'Er . . . you don't have anything else, do you?' he asked.

Arnauld shook his head. 'You have two minutes to decide,' he said. 'I wait outside.'

Without another pause he scampered out the door and slammed it shut behind him.

Alex looked at the door for a moment. Then he looked out the window, at the distant black mass towering through the smoke. Finally he looked back down at the bowl of green slop. His stomach groaned with hunger.

With a sigh, he pulled the bowl towards him and started stuffing the seaweed into his mouth. It had already turned cold and slimy. Alex didn't care. He crammed in handful after grisly handful until there was nothing left, and then when he was done he licked the bowl clean. With determination, he stood up and strode towards the door. Then he quickly turned back and licked the pot and the ladle clean as well, before turning around and striding out again.

Arnauld stood waiting. Smoke was rolling in great gusts across the rocks behind him, dipping the distant ocean in and out of view.

'You are coming?' said Arnauld.

Alex nodded.

'Good,' said Arnauld. 'I will lock up.'

He propped a bit of wood up against the door. Alex looked at the hut. From close up he realised it looked like a very large kennel. Arnauld turned to him.

'The rest of the journey is not easy,' he said sternly. 'The rocks are slippery and it is easy to get lost, but we will have to go fast if we want to catch up with your father. Stay with me at all times. Understand?'

Alex nodded.

'Then let us go,' said Arnauld. 'Let us find your father.'

He flew off into the smoke, his claws scuttling across the slimy rocks. Alex shielded his eyes and gazed at the distant light of the centre. It glowed through the haze like a lighthouse, turning the air all around them white.

'My father,' he said.

He stepped into the smoke, his gaze fixed ahead.

23

On the farthest horizon, something appeared. It was a light, surrounded by smoke.

Kyte smiled.

'Squiggles,' he said quietly.

A desert sunset stretched before him, drenching the barren room in blood-red light. He reached out a hand, raw with sunburn, and absent-mindedly stroked the muzzle of the wolf beside him. Their gazes were both fixed on the dot on the horizon.

'Almost there,' Kyte whispered.

He lowered his hand and slowly turned his chair round to the wooden desk. It was rapidly disintegrating, as all things made from wood and metal did once they passed the boundary that separated the Cusp from the Forbidden Land. The leather surface had already been bleached white by the desert sun, and the rows of buttons were now chipped and peeling. Kyte pressed one with a long and knotted finger. A ragged wooden drawer opened beside him. A television screen emerged, its wires frayed and sparking.

Kyte smiled. The screen showed the kennels below. He could see the huddled crowd of prisoners locked inside their single tiny pen, clutching each other in fright. He could see the rows of caged wolves beside them, already harnessed up so they could be sent to the ground with the flick of a switch. He could see the two enormous wolves left free to pace the kennel walkways, stopping any attempts at escape.

He pressed another button and leaned forwards to the empty vase beside him.

'Attention,' he said.

At once, his voice boomed from all the loudspeakers on the ship, echoing down the empty corridors and blaring outside across the rolling dunes ahead. On the screen, he watched the prisoners flinch. Kyte smiled again. He picked up the vase and turned back around to face the desert. His eyes silently scanned the horizon. He licked his dry lips.

'Alex Jennings,' he said slowly. His chest heaved. 'Father and son. I know that you're out there. And I know that you can hear me. So I will say this only once.'

Kyte took another moment to collect his breath.

'Give yourselves up now,' he said, 'before it is too late. You cannot hide from me for much longer. I *will* find you. Give yourselves up.'

He paused. 'If you do not,' he said, 'then I will set the wolves on the prisoners inside the kennels. The wolves have not been fed for many days. There will be no survivors.'

Kyte turned back round to the screen on his desk. The prisoners were petrified, frozen to the ground with fear, holding each other. He reached out and touched the centre of the screen, where the teacher and the young girl sat.

'Amongst them are friends of yours, Alex,' he whispered into the vase. 'I will make sure that they are killed first.'

The zeppelin shuddered, and a great groan of bending metal echoed through the empty corridors behind him. Kyte sat and waited until it had finished. The zeppelin was falling apart. They did not have long left now. They had to move faster. Always faster.

'The ones on the ground are getting tired,' Kyte muttered, glancing behind him at Number 51. 'Time to swap over.'

He pressed another button on the desk. On the screen, the cage floors of the kennels suddenly flew open and dropped the harnessed wolves from view, their chains slowly unwinding to the sand below. At the same time, the chains in the empty cages opposite began winding in.

The zeppelin came to a stop. Then, very slowly, it began to float backwards. There was nothing pulling the zeppelin forwards any more and the Forbidden Land was trying to push them back out. Kyte turned round and faced the dot on the horizon, hidden by smoke.

'Squiggles,' he whispered.

The zeppelin suddenly jerked forwards. A new set of wolves appeared on the ground below, heaving against their chains. Kyte turned slowly to Number 51. The wolf stared back at him, without expression. Kyte smiled.

'Almost there,' he said.

The wolf smiled back.

'*Almost*,' it growled.

24

'*Almost there!*'

Alex's wet shoes slipped and stumbled across the slimy rocks. He seriously doubted that they were almost there. Arnauld had been saying that for hours.

'*For heaven's sake hurry up, Alex!*'

Alex sighed. He'd been saying that, too.

He looked up hopelessly. The dog had run ahead again, too far for Alex to see in the smoke. The rocks in front split into endless slimy pathways and wove into nothingness. He had no idea which way the dog had gone.

Alex stopped and leaned on his knees, gasping for breath. How his dad could find his way through this on his own was beyond him.

'*Hey!*'

Alex looked up. Arnauld had suddenly appeared from the smoke ahead. He looked extremely annoyed.

'What are you standing there for?' he snapped. 'No time for rest! We have to keep going!'

Without warning he shot off again over the rocks. Alex straightened up with a groan and ran after him. The dog was tireless, leaping between the slippery stones with ease, winding expertly through the knotted pathways, his nose fixed to the ground. It was all Alex could do to catch up. He ran alongside him, panting for breath.

'So how much farther is it?' said Alex.

'I told you,' said Arnauld. 'We are almost there. Look.'

He pointed to the shadow on the horizon. It was closer now, much closer. It seemed to stretch from one end of the world to the other, although Alex knew that wasn't possible. It was the smoke. Once you were inside it, there was no way of telling what was real and what wasn't.

'And when we get there,' said Alex, 'what exactly are we going to do?'

The dog cast him a glance over his shoulder. 'We are looking for your father,' he said. 'Remember?'

'So you already know where he is?' said Alex.

'Of course,' said Arnauld haughtily.

'Oh,' said Alex. 'And you're certain he'll still be there when we get there?'

The dog sighed. 'No Alex, I'm not. Do I look like a fortune teller to you?'

'Er . . . no,' said Alex. 'But you seem to know a lot about the Forbidden Land.'

'That is because I am an expert,' said Arnauld.

They came to a set of sprawling crossroads. Arnauld paused only for a moment, sniffing the ground furiously, before flying down the one that lay ahead. Alex heaved himself forward after the dog, his shoes sliding across the stones.

'How come?' said Alex.

The dog glanced over his shoulder again irritably. 'How come what?'

'How come you're an expert?'

The dog shrugged, but Alex was certain he saw his chest puff out just the slightest bit as he ran.

'It is self-taught, mainly,' Arnauld said, with a roll of his eyes. 'I have studied it my whole life. Probably the only one ever who knows as much as I do, in fact. I am one of the select few who has ever made it this close to the centre. I was even born in the Cusp, you know. At the base.'

'Really?' said Alex. 'I didn't know they had kennels.'

'They built them for your father,' said Arnauld. 'For his Expedition. Even after that failed, they kept the dogs. They used them for their research on the grassland. That was what my mother did.' He paused for a moment. 'Still does, I suppose.'

'But . . . how did you find out all of this stuff?' said Alex.

Arnauld laughed bitterly. 'You hear many things growing up in a top-secret base, Alex. *Especially* if you are a dog. No one expects you to understand anything – they might as well be talking to a stone, no? I just listened whenever anyone talked, that is all. Soon enough I heard some workers talking about a hole in the fence, and so I escaped. I have lived here ever since.'

'So how come you were at the base just now?' said Alex.

Arnauld stumbled ever so slightly on a stone. 'What, that? Oh, you know, just some . . . research. Er . . .'

'What about the other dogs at the base?' said Alex. 'Are any of them like you? Can they talk?'

Arnauld frowned. 'I told you, *non*.'

'Really?' said Alex. 'You're certain you're the only one?'

'*Yes*, Alex,' said Arnauld irritably.

'What about your mother? Could she talk?'

Arnauld was silent.

'What about your f—'

'*Good grief!*' Arnauld suddenly snapped, swinging round. 'Do you *always* ask this many questions?'

They stood still, staring at each other.

'Sorry,' Alex muttered, his face burning. Arnauld glowered at him and set off over the rocks.

'Now for heaven's sake, *hurry up!*' he barked. 'Do you have any idea what I did just to get you here? Honestly, the efforts I have made . . . it's not as if I'm not busy enough already! You must be the slowest human I have ever met – your father's probably at the centre already, and you act like we are both out for a walk . . .'

'So what if he is?' Alex snapped.

The dog stopped and turned round. 'I'm sorry?'

'*So what if he's already there!*' Alex shouted. 'You've practically dragged me here since I met you – what's the hurry? What's going on?'

If dogs could blush, Arnauld would have turned a fruity crimson.

'I did not drag you,' he said defensively.

'Yes you did!' said Alex angrily. 'You dragged me! You did it while I was sleeping in the forest too, didn't you?'

Arnauld started taking great interest in a nearby pebble.

'Well, you were coming here anyway,' he muttered. 'I was just . . . helping you along, that's all . . .'

'I don't *need* any help!' Alex shouted. 'It's *my* father! And I can find him without your help if I have to!' He waved his hand at the black shape looming through the smoke in front of them. 'I mean, it's only a mountain, for heaven's sake! Can't we just climb after him and . . .'

'It is not a mountain,' said Arnauld.

Alex sighed. 'Whatever it is! Can't we just –'

'It is a wall.'

Alex stopped. He looked back at the dog in disbelief.

'A *wall*?' he repeated.

The dog nodded. Alex gazed at the black shape, dumbfounded. It could have been half a mile high.

'But it's enormous,' said Alex.

Arnauld nodded. Alex turned back to him.

'If it's a wall,' he said, 'then – what's behind it?'

Arnauld snorted. 'Isn't that what we are all trying to find out, Alex?'

A gust suddenly parted the smoke ahead, and without warning the vast shape they had been following was revealed in front of them. Alex gasped. It was an enormous tower, jutting from the jagged rocks ahead like a split in the earth. Its walls were darker and colder and more ancient than the stones they stood on, reaching higher than ten Cloisters Schools stacked on top of one another and running in either direction as far as the eye could see. It was almost impossible to tell if it had been built by something, or if it had just always been there.

'Oh crikey,' said Alex. Arnauld trotted past him.

'See? I *told* you,' he muttered. 'We are almost there.'

25

In the bowels of the zeppelin, a crowd of prisoners lay huddled in wolfskins They sat in silence. No one felt like talking. The only sound was the slow *click*, *click* of claws on the metal walkways around them.

'Why is it so quiet in here?' said Matthew eventually.

'It's the guard wolves,' said Greg, with a weary sigh. 'They're getting hungrier.'

There was a sudden *clang* of metal, and all the prisoners clutched each other in fright. Then came the now familiar sound of unwinding chains. The prisoners fell silent. The wolves were being swapped over again. Everyone's gaze slowly returned to the floor.

Everyone except for Martha.

She sat up and watched. She had been watching for a while now. She watched as the wolves from below appeared in their cages once again, water pouring from their black fur onto the metal floor, their shoulders heaving with exhaustion. Her eyes darted from them to the empty cages opposite and back again, her brain whirring. She picked at her new set of teeth thoughtfully. She liked her new teeth. No one else did, but what did they know?

'Matthew,' she said, 'I think I have a pla—'

Matthew didn't hear her, because at that exact moment he stood up and started shouting.

'*This is ridiculous!*' he roared.

Everyone spun round to face him. Matthew's eyes flared with anger. He waved his hands at the huddled crowd of broken prisoners before him.

'Look at us!' he cried. 'Have we really come to – to *this?* We're just going to sit here and wait until he kills us?'

A guard snorted across the pen. 'What else can we do?'

'Anything!' said Matthew furiously. 'We can't just sit here and die, or . . . or wait for a young boy to get ripped to shreds! Are we really going to let that happen?'

The prisoners looked to the floor in shame.

'Well, not me,' said Matthew. 'I couldn't live with that. I'd rather die trying to stop it than live with that.'

The prisoners looked up at the man who stood above them. He was thin. He was unshaven. He was rather unfortunately wearing just socks and pants because he had given Martha his wolfskin. But Matthew Price didn't look like a man in his underpants – he looked like a headmaster. And what's more, he knew it. He put his hands on his hips and struck a noble pose.

'Well, what are we waiting for?' he said. 'We have to *do* something!'

'Exactly,' said a voice from the other side of the pen. 'We have to help Kyte.'

There was a collection of gasps and everyone spun round. From the opposite side of the pen, the Grand High Pooh-Bah stood up. He turned to the crowds with a smirk.

'You heard what Kyte said, didn't you?' he said. 'If they don't find Alex, then we *all* die. So we have to make sure that they *do* find him! In no time at all we'll be back home, safe and sound, and all this will be a distant memory.'

There was a round of appalled cries from the prisoners. Matthew shook his head in disbelief.

'You idiot,' he cried. 'You really think Kyte's going back after this is done? How could he – he'll have committed *murder*, for heaven's sake . . . !'

The other prisoners muttered in agreement. The Pooh-Bah shifted on his feet.

'Well, we don't *know* that,' he mumbled weakly. 'Maybe he doesn't want to kill him. Maybe he just wants to . . . tell him off. Or something.'

The prisoners snorted with laughter.

'Well, Pooh-Bah,' said the bespectacled lady, 'I can tell

you you're *certainly* not getting my vote at the next Order election.'

'Nor mine!' said the Major, standing to attention. His eyes were suddenly glinting with excitement. He almost looked young again. 'The Reverend's right – it's high time we stood up for ourselves! Show that idiot Kyte who's boss!'

'He's not a Reverend, Major,' said the bespectacled woman exasperatedly.

'All we need', the Major continued, ignoring her, 'is something for us all to get behind – to lift our spirits! We need . . . a plan.'

Martha stood up. Her moment had come.

'I have a plan already!' she said brightly. 'We could . . .'

'I know!' interrupted Greg, leaping to his feet. 'Why don't we . . . um . . .'

He trailed off, looking in vain for a clipboard in his empty hands. Matthew turned to the crowd.

'You're right, Major,' he said. 'A plan's just what we need.'

'I have a plan,' Martha repeated, slightly annoyed.

'I know!' one of the guards cried, getting to his feet and pointing to the Pooh-Bah. 'Why don't we use *fatty* here as bait for the wolves?'

There were a number of jeers from the other guards, and they started creeping over to the Pooh-Bah. He squealed nervously and backed away. Matthew stepped up in front of the guards.

'Gentlemen, please!' he said. 'We can't waste time arguing and turning on each other. We need to focus on coming up with a plan.'

'*I have a plan*,' said Martha through gritted teeth.

'Who made *you* boss all of a sudden?' the guard snapped, giving Matthew a little push. Matthew frowned.

'Now, now,' he muttered. 'I really don't think there's any need for that . . .'

'I don't think there's any need for your *face!*' cried the guard, lunging at Matthew.

In moments all the prisoners were on their feet, throwing punches and rugby-tackling each other. Martha sighed. She took in a deep breath and let rip.

'*QUI – EEEEET!*'

Her voice silenced the crowd like an air horn. Martha stood up, her new set of teeth gritted and glinting murderously in the flicker of electric lights for all to see.

'Good,' she said calmly. She ran a tongue carefully across her fangs. 'Now I have your attention . . .'

The prisoners glanced fearfully at the girl before them with a mouth full of razor-sharp metal wolf's teeth. Kyte had forced Martha to wear the monstrous paperweight in a bid to get her to talk for her speech. This had, of course, been a disaster. Once she had them in it had taken twelve reluctant guards, and three lost fingers, to drag her down into the kennels. She cast a quick glance over at them. They let go of Matthew and stepped back nervously.

'I have a plan,' she said calmly, teeth flashing, 'to get us all out of here *and* save Alex.'

The prisoners looked back at her warily. No one said anything.

'Well?' she said. 'Don't you want to hear it?'

One of the guards slowly put his hand up.

'It doesn't involve you fighting us again, does it?' he said.

Martha smiled and waggled her eyebrows. 'It doesn't have to,' she said.

The guards gulped. Matthew stepped forward.

'Look, let's just listen to her idea,' he said. 'Tell us, Martha – what's the plan?'

Martha cricked her fingers and placed her hands on her hips.

'First things first,' said Martha. 'We have to get out of this pen and lock Kyte in his quarters. That wolf of his, too.'

Everyone looked at each other. Matthew tried not to blink.

'Er . . .' he said. 'How?'

'Easy,' said Martha, pointing to the entrance of the pen. 'Just run as fast as you can into that door.'

Matthew looked at it. It was solid steel, and looked very hard.

'Me?' he said. 'It doesn't look like I could knock it down, Martha.'

'Sure you could,' said Martha. 'Just run at it head first.'

'Oh,' said Matthew. 'Well, er . . . if you say so.'

The crowd behind him parted. Matthew took a few steps back and squared himself up to the door. It still looked very hard. He took in a deep breath and charged.

Several seconds later he was lying flat on his back, gazing at the ceiling as it swam in front of him. Martha's face appeared in his line of view, her wolf fangs sparkling.

'It didn't work,' said Matthew bluntly.

'Luckily for you,' she said, 'that was part of the plan.'

Everyone froze. The kennels had suddenly become eerily quiet. There was no rattling of claws on the metal floor; no grinding of chains as the wolves tried to escape their harnesses. The only sound was the hungry intake of breath all around them. Matthew brought a hand up to his forehead. A red stain trickled down his fingers.

'I'm bleeding,' he muttered.

There was an almighty *bang* at the door, and everyone looked up. A snout had appeared above the doorway, gulping in great breaths and croaking with hunger.

'Oh dear,' said Matthew.

The two guard wolves were frenzying. The flavour of

fresh blood was in the air, and they would stop at nothing to get it. They dug their claws under the doorway, howling, throwing their black bodies again and again against the steel door, the scent of blood flickering madly on their tongues. The prisoners flew backwards.

'You idiot!' cried Greg. 'Now you've done it! The door won't hold them!'

Matthew stared groggily at the doorway at his feet. Sure enough, the great steel hinges and locks were beginning to buckle as the wolves outside crashed against it, howling murderously for blood. His eyes widened.

'Er, Martha,' he mumbled. 'I think we might be in trouble.'

He looked over at her. She was calmly standing beside the door, crouched down low, rubbing her hands together.

'Patience, Matthew,' she smiled. 'This is all part of the plan.'

The metal of the door buckled further. Matthew started floundering away from it. 'Martha, for heaven's sake get away from –'

With a great *bang* the lock gave way and the door slammed open. The prisoners screamed and flung themselves against the back wall. At the doorway stood two great wolves, their mouths foaming with hunger, their eyes crazed. They locked their sights straight onto Matthew. Beside them, Martha had crouched down even lower.

Matthew's stomach dropped. She was going to jump.

'*Martha, no – !*'

She jumped.

■ ■ ■

Several astonishing minutes later, the prisoners gazed open-mouthed at the young girl before them. She was standing on top of the slumped bodies of two unconscious wolves, calmly dusting off her hands. She took a moment to catch her breath, wiping a modest amount of sweat off her brow before turning back to them.

'Right!' she said jauntily. 'Anyone here know how to shave a wolf?'

Two men put their hands up.

26

The slimy stone pathway beneath them ended, and the ground became hard and dry and dead. Before them stood the vast black tower, stretching up into the clouds, its top lost to the smoke.

'Quite something, no?' said Arnauld.

Alex didn't reply. All his attention was fixed on the surface of the walls before him. He squinted.

He stepped forwards and ran his fingers over the mass of lines that were carved deep into the stone. They covered the walls from top to bottom in every direction. They were cold to the touch.

'They're squiggles,' said Alex quietly.

Arnauld snorted. 'Not quite, Alex,' he said. 'They are pictures.'

Alex looked up. '*All* of them?'

Arnauld heaved himself up onto his paws and leaned

against the wall, pointing to a single carving in the stone.

'This here,' he said, circling his claw round the shape in front of him, 'is the tower. See?'

Alex looked closer at the picture. It showed a tower, black and looming. It was set in a giant ring. Smoke appeared from the top, like a smouldering volcano. Alex looked up above him.

'That's where all the smoke comes from?' he said. 'From inside it?'

Arnauld nodded. 'Yes. Now, look at what is next to it.'

Next to the carving of the tower was another shape. Alex ran his finger over it.

'It's a man,' he said.

'Almost,' said Arnauld. 'It is, how you say, a *knight*. See?'

Alex peered closer. Sure enough, the man had a plumed helmet on his head. He carried a sword in one hand and a torch in the other. He was being fired out of a cannon.

'It's . . . the Order,' said Alex. 'Someone from the Order trying to get to the tower. Only . . .'

'Only he cannot,' said Arnauld. He waved his paw to the walls beside them. 'None of them could.'

Alex looked up, realisation dawning on his face. Next to him was another carving, of a knight on stilts stumbling towards the tower. Beside that, a knight with wooden wings.

'The Expeditions,' said Alex. 'They're pictures of all the different Expeditions.'

He walked along the wall, gazing at the carvings as they unfolded before him. Each and every attempt to cross the boundary lay before him, a thousand years of failure carved into the tower. They stretched for miles in every direction, spiralling round the entire length of the walls from the top right down to the bottom.

'And the walls . . . knew?' said Alex. 'They knew that each one would happen all along?'

Arnauld shrugged. 'Perhaps. Not quite. Each time another attempt is made, the walls keep a memory of it.'

Alex shook his head in disbelief. 'There must be thousands of them,' he said. 'I didn't know the Order had tried so many times . . .'

Arnauld snorted. 'That is because they haven't, Alex.'

Alex looked at him in confusion. 'What do you mean?'

Arnauld pointed up to the top of the tower. 'Do those people up there look like they are from the Order to you?'

Alex craned his neck and peered up to where the pictures were almost lost to the smoke. The stone up there seemed older and more weathered, but the pictures were exactly the same. Alex gasped. No, not *exactly* the same: the people were different. At first they wore suits of armour; then long flowing robes; then furs and skins of animals, and then nothing at all. Their clothing changed more and more the higher he looked, the more ancient the carvings became. Soon they were wearing strange, futuristic costumes that Alex had never seen before, until he couldn't see high enough to make them out any more.

'But . . .' said Alex. 'Those must be thousands and thousands of years old. The Order was only founded . . .'

'Alex,' said Arnauld, cutting him off. 'People have *always* been trying to find the centre. They have been trying for so long that they cannot even remember when it all started. The walls – only they remember.'

The dog started walking along them, his paw trailing on the stones.

'And none of them succeeded in getting here?' said Alex, scampering after him. 'Not one?'

Arnauld shrugged. 'There are some who made it to the island,' he said. 'A few at most. But they never made it to these walls. Lost in the pathways and smoke. Even if they *had* made it, then they would have been confronted with the final challenge.' The dog's eyes darkened. 'The Unopenable Door.'

Alex blinked. 'What's that?'

The dog turned to look at him. 'It is a door that cannot be opened, Alex,' he said shirtily.

Alex blinked. 'Why have a door if it can't be opened?'

Arnauld spoke without turning back.

'These walls are here for a reason, Alex,' he said. 'They

guard what is in the centre. And the Unopenable Door is the only way of getting through them. Apart from me, only one other person has ever found it.'

'Who?' said Alex.

Arnauld suddenly stopped, almost sending Alex sprawling to the floor. He had a single claw placed on the carving beside him. Alex knelt down and peered at it. It lay at the end of the sprawling chain of pictures that spiralled round the walls. It sat just above the ground, before the dirt hid the stones from view. The picture was like all the others. The tower stood in its great circle again, tall and black and unconquerable. Only now, Alex saw, there was a tiny hole carved into its side. He ran his finger around it.

'The Unopenable Door,' said Alex.

Arnauld nodded. 'Yes. And the two beside it?'

Alex looked closer. There were two other shapes beside the tower. One of them was clearly a dog. It was difficult to make out what the other one was. It wore a helmet, and had a long tube stuck out from its back, carved in great curls along the rock behind it.

'It looks like an alien,' said Alex.

'It is not an alien,' said Arnauld. 'It is, how you say – an explorer.'

Alex's eyes widened.

'Recognise him, Alex?' said Arnauld quietly.

He moved his claw to the next picture along. Alex gazed along the wall in disbelief. In the next picture, the Unopenable Door had once again been shut. Beside it, the image of a man in a diving suit being dragged backwards by his airpipe was now unmistakable. Alex reached out and touched the rocks.

'My . . . my dad,' he gasped. 'He found the Unopenable Door.'

'More than that, Alex,' said Arnauld. 'He *opened* it. The door which no one else could open. Do you understand what that means? In the entire history of the Forbidden Land, your father is the only one to have found a way to get past it and into the centre.'

Alex gulped. 'So . . . that's where he's going now?'

Arnauld nodded. 'Without a doubt. And we have to get there before he opens it. Once he does, we might not be able to follow him. Unless, of course . . .'

He trailed off. Alex looked at the carvings. It seemed so obvious to him now that there was almost no point in saying it. He slowly turned to the dog.

'You think I can do it too, don't you?' he said quietly.

Arnauld nodded. His eyes were glinting.

'Alex,' he said. 'I have spent my whole life trying to open that door. My *whole life*. You might be my only chance of succeeding.'

Alex blinked. 'But . . . why? Why do you need to get

in so much?'

Arnauld didn't reply at first.

'It has . . . something,' he said eventually. 'Something very important to me.'

The dog looked past Alex to the carvings on the wall behind him.

'Something I lost,' he said.

Suddenly, the air around them was cut through with a terrible roar. Alex leaped up.

'What was that?' he said.

He stopped. The ground beneath his feet was beginning to quake, slowly at first and then harder, more violently. He looked up.

'What's going on?' he cried. 'Arnauld, what's . . .'

'It is carving!' said Arnauld excitedly. 'The tower! It is making a new carving!'

Alex gaped at him. '*Making* one . . . ?'

There was another terrible roar. He flipped round. The stones of the wall behind him were bending and wrenching against each other. Tiny fragments of stone poured out from the cracks from high above and covered them. The ground shook. Alex gasped. The tower was moving.

'But . . . but why is it making one?' he asked.

'It means someone is trying to get inside,' said Arnauld.

They glanced at each other.

'My dad,' said Alex.

All at once the walls gave a final groan, and with a heave and shudder the stones at their feet corkscrewed up from the ground, wrenching up the ancient soil and showering them with dust and debris from above. Alex stumbled backwards, staring down in disbelief. Sure enough, there at the base of the wall – where the picture of Alex's father had been only moments before – lay a new carving.

They both stood staring at it for a moment. Then they furiously brushed away the unearthed soil from the freshly carved picture. It showed the tower. In its side was a hole, and in the hole was the leg of a man, disappearing inside. Arnauld leaped up in excitement.

'He has done it!' he cried. 'He has made it inside! And the door, it is only up here . . . What are we waiting for, Alex? We have got to get there now, before . . .'

All at once, the ground started shuddering again, and an almighty groan vibrated up through their bodies. Alex and Arnauld shared another glance.

'*Again?*' said Alex.

'No,' said Arnauld. 'No, it cannot be . . .'

Dust started falling down on top of them, and with another great groan the tower unscrewed from the ground once more before their eyes.

'But how?' said Arnauld. 'How can . . .'

A new picture rose from the dirt before them, packed

with soil. Alex frantically brushed it away. Beside the tower stood two new figures. A boy and a dog.

'It's us,' said Alex. Arnauld blinked in disbelief.

'Well, what are we doing?' he said. 'Are we breaking inside too?'

'No,' said Alex. 'We're . . . we're running.'

He stared at the picture in confusion. There was another shape too, carved behind the two figures. Alex rubbed his fingers over the round oval in the stone.

'It looks like a balloon,' he said.

A single bloodcurdling howl rang out behind them. Alex and Arnauld spun round. Emerging through the smoke behind them was the black zeppelin, billowing through the haze like the bow of a great ghost ship. At the front a pack of ferocious wolves tore forwards against their rusting chains, their shoulders heaving and their teeth bared and their eyes crazed with hunger as they flew across the slimy rocks towards them.

27

Alex and Arnauld stood frozen to the ground.

'Who are they?' said Alex.

'It is the humans. From the Cusp,' said Arnauld, his eyes white with horror. 'They have followed us.'

Alex sat bolt upright. 'Kyte?'

'Yes,' said Arnauld.

Alex gulped. 'Then what do we . . .'

'*Run!*'

Before he knew it Alex was on his feet, and in seconds the carvings were flashing past and blurring into one another as he sprinted round the great curve of the walls as fast as his legs could carry him.

'Where are we going?' he cried.

'Where do you think we are going?!' said Arnauld. 'The only place we *can* go!'

The zeppelin groaned in the air behind them like a

dying monster. Alex's stomach dropped, and against his better judgement he glanced backwards. The wolves had turned on the stones. They were heading straight for them.

'How much farther?' he cried, his heart racing.

'Almost there!' shouted Arnauld.

'And then what?'

'You have to try and open the door!'

'But what if I can't . . .'

'*Alex, just shut up and run!*'

■ ■ ■

'Squiggles,' said Kyte.

He threw himself against the glass. There it was. In front of him, looming like a gravestone from the smoke – the centre. He had found it.

'Squiggles,' he croaked, his back reeling.

The zeppelin suddenly turned, twisting in the air like a building on the verge of collapse. Kyte held onto the windowframe and looked down at the chains disappearing into the smoke below. The wolves were running off course. They had found something.

'The boy,' he seethed.

His teeth flashed, his mouth foaming against the glass. The centres of his eyes became pinprick knives of light. He clutched onto the windowframe.

'Faster,' he said. '*Faster, faster!*'

■ ■ ■

'Faster, Matthew!'

Matthew tore down the walkways of the kennels towards Martha, slamming shut the cage doors as he did.

'You're certain this is going to work?' he shouted, hurriedly pasting the last of the fur to his cheeks. Martha glanced back up at him. Like Matthew, and all the other prisoners, her face was now completely covered in wolf hair, held in place with thick smearings of axle grease.

'No,' she said. 'Does it matter?'

The sides of the balloon beside them groaned with strain. Its metal skeleton was disintegrating, twisting itself into threads. Matthew glanced back at the girl.

'I guess not,' he said.

Martha glared back at him through handfuls of black fur. *'Then run!'*

■ ■ ■

Another howl rolled across the stones. Alex's blood filled with dread. The wolves sounded much closer than they had only a moment ago. He could hear the scrape of their claws on the stones behind him, and the hiss of their desperate breath.

'There!' cried Arnauld. *'There it is!'*

Alex glanced back up. There, along the unbroken wall of the tower far ahead, a shadow lay across the path.

'There it is . . . !'

His voice was suddenly lost. The ground shook, and the stones began to quake and tremble beside them. Dust flew down.

The tower was making another carving.

■ ■ ■

There he was on the ground below, running through the smoke ahead of them.

'The boy,' gasped Kyte.

He threw himself from the window and onto the desk, bent double in pain, slamming his hands against the buttons on the surface. The television screen flew out of the drawer beside him, spraying sparks. The kennels appeared on the screen, the remaining wolves heaving in their harnesses and thrashing against the bars.

'Davidus Kyte!'

The shout came from outside the double doors. Kyte did not turn round.

'This is Greg!' cried the voice. 'Your office is now surrounded by a dozen guards. We've locked the doors and we're taking over the zeppelin. There's no way out. Give yourself up and let the boy go!'

Kyte turned to Number 51. He smiled.

'Kyte?' Greg called. 'Did you hear me?'

Kyte turned back to the desk, his ragged fingers slowly uncurling towards the buttons.

'Kyte!' Greg snapped. 'We mean it! Bring up the wolves and let him go!'

One by one, Kyte pressed down the buttons on the tabletop. On the screen before him the cage floors dropped, and wolf after wolf was lowered down to the ground.

'All of them,' said Kyte quietly. 'Send them all down. All of them.'

■ ■ ■

'All of them?' Martha cried.

Matthew flew towards her. 'Yes!' he shouted. 'The cages are all set!'

Martha nodded, her eyes sparkling. 'Then we just need . . .'

There was a great *clang*. Martha and Matthew froze, their eyes widening with horror. The chains in the cages beside them were unwinding.

'There's no time!' she cried. 'We have to do it now!'

Matthew started. 'But . . .'

'*Now, Matthew!*'

■ ■ ■

Alex threw himself forwards, stumbling across the path. The walls beside him wrenched and tore against themselves as they heaved out of the ground.

'We can make it, Alex!' Arnauld cried. *'Just don't take your eyes off the path!'*

A great *clang* suddenly sounded from above. The zeppelin was almost right on top of him. Alex looked up, and gasped. Through the smoke, even more wolves were being lowered to the ground from a new set of chains at the back.

'Alex!' cried Arnauld. 'Look ou – '

Without warning a rock from above crashed on the path right beside them, smashing on the stones and showering them with dust. Alex cried out, and before he knew it he was flying straight off the path and down onto the slippery stones below. He tried to right himself, but kept falling, crashing again and again down the slime of the crater that lay beneath.

He skidded to a stop and looked up in horror. Arnauld was nowhere to be seen. He was alone.

'*Arnauld!*' he cried. 'Wait . . .'

A howl rang out. Alex spun around.

There, emerging from the smoke across the stones, were the wolves. They were heading straight for him.

Alex turned and flew up the walls of the slimy crater as fast as he could, his breath heaving. Up ahead, the walls of the tower reappeared in the smoke.

'Arnauld!' he cried. '*Arnauld!*'

He looked behind him and gasped in horror. The wolves were tearing up the slope towards him at a furious pace, their teeth foaming, their eyes rabid with delight. Alex made to stand up but his feet slipped beneath him and he came crashing down once more.

'*Arnauld!*' he cried.

The wolves sensed their moment. One by one they leaped through the air, splaying their claws and opening their mouths for the kill.

'*Arnauld . . .*'

The wolves came roaring down upon him, and Alex closed his eyes.

28

Alex waited.

And waited.

He kept his breath held and his eyes clamped shut, waiting for the end to come.

Only it didn't seem to be coming.

Eventually he opened his eyes.

He was lying on the stones. The wolves stood in front of him, their mad jaws snapping furiously only inches away, their claws thrashing hopelessly through the air. Only they couldn't move. They heaved and heaved against their harnesses, but it was no good. They couldn't take another step forward.

Above them, the zeppelin had come to a complete stop. A new set of chains had appeared, dangling down from the kennels at the back. And they weren't being pulled forwards by the wolves. They were being pulled backwards. The zeppelin was stuck in mid-air.

Alex's gaze ran down the new chains. Another pack of wolves stood on the stones in the far distance. They were heaving the zeppelin away from the centre with all their might, fighting against the wolves in front.

'*Alex!*'

Alex looked up. Two more wolves were slowly being lowered by chains through the smoke above him. At least, they looked like wolves. They looked quite like people, too. In fact, the more Alex looked at them, the more he thought they just looked like people with handfuls of wolf fur cackhandedly glued to them. His jaw dropped.

'Martha . . . ?!' he cried. '*Mr Price?*'

Martha grinned and waved a hairy arm.

'Right first time, Alex!' she shouted. 'Sorry about the disguises – it was the only way we could trick Kyte into sending us down! Looks like they hit the ground just in time.'

She pointed to the pack of prisoners in the distance, heaving the zeppelin away from the centre, their faces and bodies also pasted with poorly glued fur. 'Is that the boy?' cried one, whose fur had been artfully arranged into a whiskery moustache. 'Is he safe?'

'He is, Major!' shouted Matthew. 'We were just in time! Keep pulling!'

'It's not as if we have a choice!' snapped the Grand High Pooh-Bah, pointing at his feet as they paced furiously on the stones against his will, already bewitched by the power of the Forbidden Land.

'Oh pipe down, you whining old codger!' snapped the Major. He shook his fist in triumph. 'Good on you, Alex! Well done for getting so far!'

'Yes Alex, well done!' said a wolf wearing spectacles.

'Hear, hear,' another added, with a hiccup.

Alex gaped at them. 'But . . . what are you all doing here?'

'What does it look like we're doing, Alex?' Martha snorted. 'We're going to pull this heap all the way back home. We're rescuing you!'

She landed gently on top of the wolves in front and started hopping between their furious and snapping heads like they were stepping stones.

'All of it my idea, if I do say so myself,' she said proudly. 'We shaved all the wolves and locked them up in the pens. The guards have already surrounded Kyte in his quarters and barricaded him inside. He won't even be able to control the ship once we rip out the main switchboard.'

Alex frowned. 'What's the main switchboard?'

A large metal box suddenly landed beside them, shattering on the stones. Martha grinned, her metal teeth sparkling. 'That.'

'But how are you going to get back?' said Alex.

'The power of the Forbidden Land, Alex!' said Martha,

pointing at the ground. 'Once us *normal* people step on the surface we run all the way home – remember? With that lot pulling us backwards we'll be back at the Cusp in a couple of days.'

The wolves at her feet suddenly roared with anger and heaved themselves forward against their chains. Martha rolled her eyes.

'Speaking of which, I think they need a bit of a hand,' she said. 'You still have my teeth, don't you?'

Alex grinned. He reached into his pocket and held up the two tiny pink curves on his palms.

'They're a bit dusty,' he said apologetically.

'Brilliant!' said Martha.'Well, look after them for me.' She flashed her new metal fangs. 'I want to keep a hold on these bad boys for a while longer.'

With that, she leaped onto the ground. In a snap the force of the Forbidden Land took over and she was pacing across the rocks at lightning speed towards the other prisoners, her chain snapping taut in mid-air. The wolves were suddenly hauled backwards again, their paws slipping on the stones.

'That's it!' shouted Matthew from above. 'Keep pulling, everyone! They can't keep it up much longer!'

Alex looked up. Matthew was still descending towards the ground above him, shedding fur and pinwheeling his arms gracefully.

'Hi, Mr Price,' said Alex.

Matthew looked down and smiled.

'Hello, Alex,' he said sheepishly. 'Sorry you have to see me in my underpants.'

'That's fine,' said Alex.

'It's a long story.'

'I'm sure it is.'

There was an awkward pause. Matthew sighed.

'Er . . . before I get going, Alex, there's something I need to say to you,' he said. 'I . . . I'm sorry. I should have listened to you. I should never have let Kyte take you away like that.'

Alex blushed. 'Don't worry, Mr Price, you don't need to –'

'No, I do, Alex,' Matthew interrupted. 'I do. Had I known the truth, of course, I never would have done it, but that doesn't really mean much now. I'm sorry I let you down. I've been so worried about you.'

Alex started. 'You . . . you *have*?' he said.

Matthew laughed. 'Of course I have, Alex! Martha too . . . I mean, why else would we have come all this way?'

Alex was speechless. He started fumbling with his jumper.

'Wow,' he said. 'Thank you.'

'It's nothing, Alex,' said Matthew. 'Although you could make it up to me by having a word with Mrs Beaumont when we get back. I think I might be in a bit of trouble with her.'

Alex shifted awkwardly.

'Er . . . I'm not going back, Mr Price,' he said.

Matthew's face drained.

'What!?' he spluttered.

'I'm sorry, sir,' said Alex. 'I can't. I have to find my father.'

The wolves started skidding backwards inch by inch. Matthew looked down nervously. His feet were almost skimming the stones. 'Alex, listen to me –'

'You see, he's all I have left now,' he said. 'There's nothing for me back there.'

'Alex, you idiot,' Matthew snapped. 'I haven't just chased you across a forest and a desert and an ocean for you to say you have nothing. I'm your friend. So is Martha. And none of *those* people would be pulling a zeppelin backwards for you if they didn't think you were worth something, too. OK?'

Alex was lost for words. 'But . . . but my mother, she . . .'

'It was all lies, Alex!' said Matthew 'Everything Kyte told you was lies. Your mother never gave you up. She loves you! She's probably worried sick about you, for heaven's sake . . . !'

Alex stared back in disbelief. Matthew sighed and reached out a hand. He placed it on Alex's shoulder.

'Look, Alex,' he sighed. 'Just . . . do whatever you need to do. But don't forget to come home.'

With that, he finally gave up the doomed attempt to keep his feet from touching the ground and let go of the chain. He came crashing to the ground and bounced off it like it was a trampoline, speeding off and scattering the wolves behind him like bowling pins.

'That's it, Reverend!' cried the Major from up ahead. 'Come on, everyone – give it everything you've got!'

With a sickening *crack* Matthew reached the end of his chain and the entire zeppelin lurched backwards in the air. The prisoners pulled and tugged and heaved and hauled until they were fit to burst. The wolves tried to fight them, but it was hopeless. One by one they collapsed on their backs, gasping for breath. With a cheer the prisoners charged, dragging the exhausted wolves backwards across the slimy rocks and heaving the zeppelin away from the centre once and for all.

'So long, Alex!' cried Matthew.

'*Bring back my teeth!*' Martha cried.

And with that, the smoke swallowed them up, and they vanished from sight.

Alex's eyes flickered across the smoke, gazing at the point where his friends had disappeared. He lifted his hand and waved.

'Bye,' he said quietly.

He turned around, and stepped slowly to the side of the crater. He heaved himself back up to the dusty path and looked around him. Arnauld was nowhere to be seen.

'Arnauld?' he called out.

There was no answer. Alex spun round.

'Arn—'

He stopped.

There, in the wall in front of him, stood a door. It was made of the same stone as the wall, and was darker still. Alex stood staring at it. There was no doubt what it was.

He reached out, and opened the Unopenable Door.

It slowly swung open.

Inside was a long, dark tunnel. At the end stood a pool of dull grey light.

'Arnauld?' Alex called out.

There was no answer. He stood staring into the grey light at the end.

'. . . Dad?'

Silence. He gazed down the tunnel. The grey light seemed almost to glow.

If you go in now, said the voice, *you might never be able to get out again*.

Alex slowly stepped inside. It was cold and damp.

'I'm not going back without him,' he said.

He carefully unpicked a single thread from the bottom of his jumper and tied it to the handle of the door. Then he turned back to face the pool of grey light.

And what if you don't find him? said the voice.

Alex shrugged. 'Then I'll find what he kept going back for,' he said.

Step by step, he walked towards the light, his footsteps drumming off the tunnel walls.

29

The tunnel ended.

Alex looked ahead of him and saw nothing. The centre was greyness. Nothing was visible. He could barely even see the ground. He looked up. Even the black walls were swallowed up by it.

'It's not smoke,' said Alex. 'It's fog.'

He looked down at his jumper. The bottom few rows had already unravelled. The thread stretched out behind him, back to the door.

He gazed out into the fog. It was all-encompassing. He reached out a foot carefully and patted it onto the ground. The earth was hard and dead beneath him.

There was only one way to go now. Alex put his hands to his sides, breathed out and stepped towards the centre. The walls disappeared behind him.

■ ■ ■

His father's ward was almost empty.

There was a time when it would have been filled with cards and flowers, but nobody sent them any more. It was as simple as a child's room. A bed; a table; a window. Alex's father lay on the bed in the centre of the room, breathing, breathing, all his attention focused on breathing. His eyes were closed. His hands trembled slightly. On the wall above his head was a dog calendar.

'Mr Jennings,' said the nurse. 'Your son is here to see you.'

Alex's father opened his eyes weakly and lolled his head on the pillow. He tried to fix the doorway in his sights.

'Alex,' he said quietly.

His father was very sick. He had a mask over his mouth. His left hand held tightly onto the metal side of the bed. It had a plastic tag around it. A machine against the wall hummed.

'You've come to visit me,' he said.

Alex said nothing. He stepped into the room, towards the bed.

■ ■ ■

Alex was enveloped by the fog.

The jumper had unravelled to his chest. Each step forward picked off another line of hooks, unwinding through the grey behind him, linking him to the past by a single string. The air was silent, as grey as the fog. Only his breathing, his heartbeat, his footsteps, made any sound here.

He kept walking.

■ ■ ■

Alex sat beside the bed. The door behind him closed softly.

His father was little more than a skeleton beneath the soft hospital sheets now. He turned to look at Alex.

'Well,' he said weakly. 'You look very smart, in your new uniform.'

The room was silent. His father's breathing was hollow inside the plastic mask.

'It must be the holidays,' he said.

'No,' said Alex. 'It's a school day. I'm not supposed to be here.'

Alex's father frowned. 'What do you . . .'

'I've come to talk to you,' said Alex.

The room was filled with the hum of the machine beside them. Alex's father stared at him.

'Alex, you can't just . . .'

'No,' said Alex firmly. 'I want to talk to you.'

Away from the darkness of his bedroom, in the bleak and unforgiving light of the ward, the true extent of how much his father had aged since Alex had last seen him was shocking.

Alex now realised why his mother had said she didn't want him to go to the hospital.

'I want to talk to you,' said Alex, 'because I'm not going to wait for you to come home again. I'm not going to wait to listen to your stories. You're going to tell me everything now.'

Alex's father said nothing. His chest rose and fell, as delicate as a paper bag.

'And then when you're done talking, you won't ever see me again,' said Alex. 'So make it good.'

Alex sat calmly on the chair, staring at his father. He had known for a long time what he was going to say. He wasn't going to get angry. He wasn't going to cry. His father gazed back. Then, very slowly, he pulled off his mask.

'What do you want to know?' he said.

■ ■ ■

Alex kept walking.

Stitch by stitch, the jumper unravelled.

■ ■ ■

'Why did you do it?' said Alex. 'Why did you keep running away?'

Alex's father heaved out a breath. He tried to bring a hand to his face, and gave up.

'The centre,' he said eventually. 'I had to find the centre.'

Alex nodded.

'And did you ever find it?' he said.

Alex's father paused.

'Yes,' he said quietly. 'Yes I did.'

Alex stared at his father.

'Was it worth it?' he asked.

Alex's father looked at him. His eyes saddened, like a flicker in the light of a candle. He shook his head.

■ ■ ■

Step by step, stitch by stitch, Alex grew closer to the centre.

There were no walls around him now. There might not even be ground.

Alex kept walking.

■ ■ ■

Alex threw his hands against the bed, grabbing the metal frame, shaking it with fury.

'Then why go back?' he cried.

It was too late to stop trying now. Useless tears rolled down his cheeks.

'Alex,' said his father. He tried to put out a hand, but Alex tore it away.

'Why go back,' Alex repeated, his eyes furious and hurt, 'if there was nothing there?'

'Because of what I'd lost,' cried his father.

■ ■ ■

And then, all at once, it was happening.

Far away, in the fog ahead, a shape was emerging from the darkness.

■ ■ ■

'You must have lost something very important,' Alex screamed, 'to do what you've done to me.'

'I did,' Alex's father said. 'Oh I did, I did.'

■ ■ ■

And with each step forward that Alex took, with each new line of stitches unstitched, the shape grew closer, clearer, less grey. It rose out of the fog in front of him, as if from the bottom of an ancient well.

Alex looked down.

■ ■ ■

'Then what was it?'

'I can't.'

'What was it?'

'I . . .'

'Tell me.'

'Squiggles,' his father cried.

He rolled on the bed, his knees up to his chest, rubbing his hands over his face in misery, sobbing. Alex stared at him, horror-struck.

'Squiggles, Squiggles, Squiggles, Squiggles.'

Alex turned and ran. He hadn't known it then, but it was the last time he would ever see his father, and it was the last image of him that he would carry, the sight of him crying on the bed.

■ ■ ■

And the last of the stitches gave way.

A single thread stretched back from his neck now, swallowed up by the grey behind him. Only the collar of the jumper remained, holding him on the spot.

A pair of bodies lay at his feet. One of them was his father. The other one was a dog. Both were dead.

Alex looked silently down at the dog. He had known it his whole life, from the photograph on his bedroom wall. He knelt down and placed a hand on its chest. The fur was thick and matted, and very old. It had not been dead for long.

Alex searched around its neck until he found the worn metal tag. He held the collar up to the light.

SQUIGGLES

'It was his dog,' said a voice in the fog.

Alex didn't look up immediately. He stayed kneeling on the ground, looking down at the tag in his hand.

'His dog,' the voice repeated. It was harsher than a whisper, but not much louder. It somehow sounded like two different voices. Slowly, Alex looked up.

On the other side of the bodies, outlined in the fog, was a figure. It was a figure in the sense that Alex had no idea where the great grey wolf before him ended and the man hunched on its back began.

'Who would have thought?' said the voice of Davidus Kyte.

Alex didn't move from the ground. He stayed crouched. He felt that something terrible would happen if he looked directly at the figure opposite him. Alex stared at the ground instead.

'I mean,' Kyte continued, 'to come all the way back *here*? To spend years and years of his life escaping and being caught . . . for a dog? I never would have guessed. No, it never once crossed my mind, Alex. Not once.'

'You can walk on the Forbidden Land,' said Alex calmly.

The figure stopped.

'Yes, Alex,' said Kyte. 'I'm afraid your friends had no idea. I doubt they would have locked me in a room with a trap door if they had known.'

The figure stepped forwards. The remains of a rotting parachute dragged in the dust behind it. Alex fixed his gaze on the ground, his whole body trembling.

'If you're going to kill me,' said Alex calmly, 'then just get on with it.'

The figure stopped. It craned its neck for a moment. Alex knew that it was looking at him through the fog. He kept his gaze fixed on the ground.

'Kill you?' said Kyte, his voice empty of any emotion. 'No, Alex. I'm not interested in that any more. Up until a few moments ago, of course, that was my exact intention. But now . . . well, there doesn't seem to be much point, does there? Not now we both find ourselves in the same position. Not now I finally understand everything.'

The figure almost made to laugh, and then stopped. It held for a moment beside the bodies, silently looking down at them. If Alex could have made out its face, he would have sworn it was smiling.

'You know,' said Kyte, 'I remember the very first day I met your father.'

Slowly, the figure began to creep around the bodies in the fog. Alex followed the shape out the corner of his eye. The legs of Number 51 walked, but with each step Kyte's spine seemed to curve up, as if part of him was walking with it.

'I was working in the laboratories back then,' he said. 'I

ran the experiments at the second base when your father became Head of Expeditions. He came to find me – said that he had heard about what I was doing to the dogs in my tests. He wanted to shut me down. And that was when I explained what I could do for him, if he would only let me try.'

The figure came closer towards Alex, the terrible wolf and the man on its back walking as one.

'There was a way, I explained,' said Kyte slowly, 'that a man could fool the Forbidden Land. Fool it into believing he wasn't quite human. Fool it into letting him step over the boundary without being thrown straight back out again.'

Alex was trembling. He still could not see the face that was talking. In the fog, it was easy to believe that Kyte didn't have one any more.

'All it required', Kyte croaked, 'was to take away a human part of himself. And replace it with something else.'

In the corner of his eye, the figure was getting closer.

'All it took was the heart of a dog,' he said.

Alex froze. Slowly, he looked down to the two bodies clasped in the fog before him. He looked from his father to the dog, and from the dog to his father, and how they lay perfectly together on the cold dead ground. Alex struggled for breath and fell back. It was almost as if they were trying to put themselves back together again.

'No,' he gasped.

Kyte laughed.

'That's exactly what *he* said, Alex,' he smiled. 'He said I had gone too far . . . told me I was out of my mind. He shut down my laboratory and threw me out of the Expedition right there and then.' The figure gazed back down at the bodies. 'Only it seems . . .' He laughed. 'It seems as if he had a change of heart.'

Alex shook his head in horror, his stomach churning. The bodies lay before him, man and dog, dog and man.

'No – no, he wouldn't . . .'

'Yes, Alex,' said Kyte, creeping closer. 'He did. He was desperate to succeed. At any price. And who can blame him really? It was a perfect plan, so long as nobody knew. Both he and the dog could walk on the Forbidden Land without being pushed out – once safely out of sight of the crowds, of course. And both could be switched back round again before they came home. No one would ever need know the terrible secret . . . of the man with the heart of a dog . . . and the dog with the heart of a man.'

The figure staggered slowly through the fog towards him, Kyte's wrinkled hands clutching at the fur on its neck.

'Only it didn't quite work out like that, did it?' he said, his dry breath heaving. 'The dog never came back. He was locked inside the tower when they reeled your father back in. Couldn't even open the door to get out. And that was when it all began to go wrong for your father. Doesn't it all make sense now? The faster ageing, the madness, the desperation to get back at any price . . .'

The figure suddenly stopped dead, throwing its head up in the fog.

'*And yet it never occurred to me, Alex!*'

The voice came out almost as two voices, so close to a laugh of genuine happiness that it was sickening to hear.

'All those times I questioned him, *all those times* – I never once thought that maybe, just maybe, he could have gone through with it. He never breathed a word of it. But then, how *could* he have told us? That really would have been the end of it, for him and for you, for the whole Order even. I understand it now. He was just trying to buy time, a little more time, just enough to get back into the Forbidden Land without being stopped. How was I supposed to know it was for . . . for his *dog*? His dog!'

The figure had turned towards him.

'But I see now,' it heaved, catching its breath through the laughter. 'It was the part of himself that he gave up. The key to the whole mystery, the whole terrible mess. The part that he would go through anything to get back. Only *now* can I . . . truly understand.'

Alex looked up. The figure took another step forward,

the shape of its two bodies rippling in the grey before him. His body flooded with horror.

'You . . . you did it too,' said Alex. 'You swapped hearts with . . . with *a wolf*.'

'Yes, Alex,' said the figure. 'I gave up everything for it too – just like your father.' He laughed. 'It turns out he and I have a lot more in common than any of us realised.'

The figure grew clearer, step by step across the bodies. Alex tried to look away.

'And me . . .' Alex cried, his voice breaking. He almost couldn't bring himself to say it. 'I can walk here because . . .'

The terrible figure was before him now, their eyes locked. When Kyte finally spoke, Alex realised that both the mouth of the man and the mouth of the wolf were moving at the same time.

'Because, Alex,' said Kyte's voice, 'you are your father's son.'

Alex shook his head.

'No,' he said weakly.

'*Yes*, Alex,' the voices hissed. 'You alone were born with it. You will never have to go to the lengths that your father had to go through . . . what *I* had to go through, just to find the truth. Just to get where we are now. And we have nothing to lose, Alex. Nothing! We're closer to the centre than anyone has ever been. Closer than *he* ever was. The two of us can finally finish it, to go on where he never could . . .'

Alex suddenly flung himself up from the ground, pushing back the monster in the fog.

'*No!*' he cried. '*You're nothing like him!*'

Alex's eyes burned with anger. He stood up to the hunched beast before him.

'He was a good man, and you're . . . you're a *monster*!'

The figure was silent for a moment, and then suddenly burst out laughing.

'You defend him!' it cried in disbelief. 'The great explorer! The man who abandoned you for . . . for a dead dog! Who spent your whole life running away from you . . . !'

'He did not run away,' said a voice behind them.

Kyte swung round, its body now moving in ways that Alex could not understand. A figure was walking towards them in the fog.

'Who's there?' Kyte hissed.

The figure emerged from the grey. It was the dog Arnauld. He was standing on his hind legs.

'He never ran away from you, Alex,' said Arnauld.

'*Leave us!*' Kyte growled, his back coiling with fury, his two voices seething.

Arnauld walked towards the bodies lying on the ground before them.

'He was trying to undo what he had done,' he said. 'He spent his entire life trying to come back here and fix what had happened. To put them both back together, and to become human again. To live long enough to see you grow up . . .'

'*Leave!*' Kyte suddenly shrieked, throwing himself at the dog. Arnauld flung himself backwards just in time.

'Alex, your father – he never wanted to get back to the centre,' he cried. 'The thing that he lost was you. All he wanted was to get back to you, before it was too late. Please – do not make the same mistake he spent his whole life trying to fix.'

Alex looked at the bodies on the floor, at the broken man and dog, and put his head in his hands. In the fog, the monstrous body of Kyte wrapped itself around him. Alex felt the wet heat of its breath on his neck.

'Don't listen to the dog, Alex,' Kyte hissed. 'You don't need him, or your father. We don't need anyone. Not where we're going.'

'You do not need to go, Alex,' said Arnauld. 'You can turn away. Look at what happened to them.'

Alex gazed down at the floor, his eyes flooding with tears. A hand of dead skin and broken claws came to stroke his face, slowly twisting his head from the bodies.

'You can't turn away from it now, Alex,' Kyte hissed. 'The centre . . . it's right in front of you.'

'Alex, please,' Arnauld begged.

'If you turn away now,' said Kyte, 'then everything your father died for was pointless.'

'*No!*'

Alex tore the last shreds of the jumper from his neck and flung himself headlong into the sea of greyness around them, his eyes streaming.

'Alex, don't!' cried Arnauld. 'Come back!'

'No,' Alex sobbed. 'I won't let him die for nothing.'

The greyness once again enveloped him, and before he knew it Alex was running again, running towards the centre of the endless fog.

30

The grey became darker, with every step darker, harder to see, harder to feel. Even the ground felt like it wasn't there any more. He was alone.

'Where is it?' Alex cried. 'Where is it?'

He ran, thrashing in the darkness.

■ ■ ■

'Alex?'

Someone was walking towards the door. Alex said nothing. The footsteps got louder.

'Alex . . . ?'

The door slowly opened. A tired hand fumbled for a light switch, and it came on with a snap.

Alex looked up. He was hunched on the floor of his bedroom, still in his school uniform. His eyes were red from crying.

'Hi, Mum,' he said.

A woman stood in the doorway. She was wearing the bathrobe Alex had bought her for Christmas. It was white when Alex bought it. It was stained lots of different colours now, because Alex's mother always wore a bathrobe when she cooked. She rubbed her eyes and smiled.

'Hi, pudding,' she said.

'I ran away from school,' said Alex.

'You don't say,' said his mum.

Alex looked down at the carpet. In front of him lay a pile of torn-up photographs and posters. On the top lay the photo of his father in the kennels, ripped into tiny pieces. Alex looked up.

'I'm sorry,' he said.

Alex's mum walked over and put an arm around his shoulder.

'I think you need a sandwich,' she said.

They went downstairs. Alex's mum put on the radio while she made him a sandwich. Alex sat at the table. The kitchen hadn't changed since he'd left for Cloisters. The only difference was the new fridge, which was much smaller than the old one. It had a photo of Alex on it.

His mum walked over to the table with the sandwich and sat opposite him. She picked up a knife and started cutting it. Alex glanced up.

'I went to the hospital,' he said. 'To see Dad.'

Alex's mother dropped the knife. She glanced up.

'I asked you not to go there,' she said.

'Well I went anyway,' said Alex.

He looked away. His mother didn't speak for a while.

'He's sick, Alex,' she eventually said. She was almost angry. 'He's very, very sick. I didn't want you to . . .'

'I never want to see him again,' said Alex. 'I hate him.'

He stared down at the table. Alex's mother paused for a moment, and picked up the knife.

'That's no way to talk about your father,' she said quietly.

Alex glared up at her. 'Why not? Why shouldn't I hate him after everything he's done?'

'Because', she said, 'I know what it feels like to love you as much as he does.'

They looked at each other over the table.

'When you love someone like that, Alex, you have to make hard decisions. Very, very hard ones. Ones that you don't want to make, sometimes ones that you would rather die than make, but you have to anyway. Because they're for someone you love. Because they might be the only right thing to do, even if it means they hate you for it.'

She carefully cut the sandwich into two halves and gave him one of them. Alex held it.

'That's why you sent me away, then,' he said angrily.

Alex's mother nodded. 'Yes,' she said. 'It was. Because I didn't want you to see this any more. Because I did everything

I could to try and make this a happy place for you, and I failed.'

His eyes reddened. 'It's not your fault,' he said quietly.

'Maybe not,' said his mother. 'But I had to give you somewhere else. Somewhere you could run away to.'

Alex sat in silence. She reached out and rubbed his hand.

'And whenever you want to come back here,' she said, 'whenever you're ready, you come back. Any way you have to. And I'll be here.'

She stood up and switched off the radio. Alex sat holding the sandwich, his eyes fixed on the table. His mother walked up beside him and gently turned his head to face her. She looked straight into his eyes.

'I love you, Alex,' she said. 'Don't ever forget that I love you.'

With that she gave him a hug and walked out the kitchen.

When she came downstairs the next morning Alex was gone, along with all his school things. On the table was the uneaten half of the sandwich. Next to it lay the photograph of his father in the kennels, covered in thumbprints from where he had spent the night piecing it back together with pieces of Sellotape.

■ ■ ■

'Mum,' he said.

He came to a stop in the darkness.

On every side of him was grey. There was no break in it, no way of seeing through it, no way of removing it. Alex stood, panting for breath. Then he stopped.

Something was breathing behind him.

He turned around. In the fog behind him stood the figure. It was hunched over, heaving for breath, staring at Alex.

'I'm not going any further,' said Alex.

The figure arched in the haze. Some part of it was dying, or all of it.

'Alex,' it gasped. 'Not now. We're almost there. We're so close.'

Alex gazed at the figure. It was almost as if it was falling apart in the fog, away from itself, lost in the gulf.

'No,' said Alex. 'No. I'm going home.'

Alex stepped towards the figure, and its shape emerged from the grey. It was different now, decrepit and broken. It was the sorriest thing that Alex had ever seen in his life.

'You would go back instead,' it mocked from its sunken eyes, 'and live in ignorance.'

'Yes,' said Alex. 'I would.'

He turned once again and looked into the thickness of unending grey that surrounded them.

'I just don't think there's anything out there,' he said quietly.

He turned back. In the fog before him, the figure rippled and swayed, its two chests heaving with painful breath.

'You understand', said the voice, 'what it is that you're giving up.'

Alex nodded. 'I do.'

'I see,' it said.

The figure turned from him and slowly began to sink away in the fog.

'Then enjoy your life of never knowing, Alex Jennings. Live in the shadows out of choice. But I won't.'

Its steps were more pained now, its shape less and less like two distinct shapes and more like an unrecognisable whole.

'Because there must be an answer out there,' said the voice hollowly. 'There must be.'

Alex stood and watched as the shape disappeared into the fog of the centre. In a moment it was gone utterly, enveloped by the greyness.

31

Alex walked back through the grey. Slowly, step by step, the mist began to lift.

Soon new shapes began to emerge before him. From out of the haze Arnauld appeared, standing beside the two bodies that lay together on the ground. Alex smiled.

'Arnauld,' he said.

The dog glanced up. 'Alex!' he cried. 'You came back!'

He ran over and threw his front legs around Alex.

'I was knocked out by a rock when the tower shook! And when I woke up I could not find you, and the door was open, and . . .'

'You can stand on your hind legs, too?' said Alex.

Arnauld nodded sheepishly. 'Er, yes. I can.'

They both fell silent. Alex's gaze fell down to the dog that lay on the ground beside them.

'He was your father, wasn't he?' he said quietly.

Arnauld nodded.

'Yes,' he said. 'He met my mother at the kennels on the base. Just before the Expedition. She said he had gone to find the centre, and that he just . . . never came back.'

Alex smiled. 'So that's why you can talk,' he said. 'You're part dog, and part . . .'

The two looked at each other and froze. They each knew what the other was thinking, but in a second it was gone. It was something that couldn't be said, or wouldn't. They both gazed back at the bodies.

'So what do we do?' said Alex.

'We bury them,' said Arnauld. 'Together.'

It was many hours before they had made a hole big enough for the two bodies. When it was done they were covered in grey dust, darkened by the sweat of their faces. They stood for a while beside the hole, gasping for breath, and wordlessly began to lower the two bodies inside.

Alex held his father in his arms. The body was lighter than he could have ever imagined. He gazed down at his calm, sad face, and had no idea what to feel looking at it. In a way, it was as if his father had died a long, long time ago, and only now was Alex able to see him again. It was the closest that he could remember being to him. His heart was heavy with many things.

Alex kissed his father, and closed his eyes, and with a final squeeze of his hand he crawled out of the hole.

Arnauld stood waiting for him.

Alex got to his feet. 'Do you want to say anything?' he said.

Arnauld thought for a while. In the fog, it was difficult to tell what his face was doing. He looked down at the body of the dog.

'I am sorry that I never met you,' said Arnauld. 'I wish that I had been able to talk to someone about what it feels like. To not understand dogs, and yet to not understand people either. To not be either one.'

He picked up a small handful of dust in his paw, and scattered it inside. He turned to Alex.

'Do you want to say anything?'

Alex shook his head. 'No,' he smiled. 'That was perfect.'

Together they filled the hole, until it was just ground again.

■ ■ ■

They wound themselves back along the thread of Alex's jumper, their steps heavy in the grey of the fog. Soon they were back at the entrance to the tunnel, creeping towards the light of a new day.

They came outside. Alex closed the door behind them.

'So how did you do it?' asked Arnauld. 'How did you open the door?'

Alex shrugged. 'I just opened it,' he said. 'I thought you said it was called the Unopenable Door.'

'I did!' Arnauld snapped. 'I mean . . . it is. Well, I guess I am the one who called it that.' He blushed. 'So . . . how does it open?'

Alex pointed to the door handle.

'Circular door knob,' he said. 'Dogs can't open them. They don't have the thumbs.'

He waggled his thumbs. Arnauld looked down at his own paws despondently.

'Oh,' he said. 'Well, that is quite something.'

They walked back through the slimy rock pathways until they came to Arnauld's hut. It had been trampled into firewood by the wolves. They both stood and stared at it. The plank of wood Arnauld had used to lock the door still jutted up out of the rocks uselessly. He sighed and picked it up.

'I suppose I will not be needing this any more,' he said gruffly. 'Is it possible you could help me to, how you say, do a little rebuilding? It took me many years to learn how to use a screwdriver . . .'

He looked back to the boy. Alex was gazing over the surface of the tumbling water, the remains of his unravelled jumper rolled into a ball in his hands.

'You are going home,' said Arnauld.

Alex nodded. There was another thread running from

him now, from his heart across the water, through the forest, an invisible line back to the people who loved him. Alex turned to the dog.

'Come with me,' he said. 'If you want to.'

Arnauld shook his head. 'No,' he said. 'I cannot.'

Alex's face fell. 'Why not?'

Arnauld drew a breath.

'When I met you at the base,' he said, 'I was not there for research. I had just . . . given up. I could not take it here any more. I thought that maybe I could go back – to try being a dog again. But it did not work. It could not. There is no place for me there – not for something like me.'

They fell silent, staring across the water.

'You could stay with me, you know,' said Alex, stepping forward.

Arnauld looked up. 'I'm sorry?'

'Stay with me,' Alex repeated. He shrugged. 'I mean, you'd probably have to cut out the walking-on-your-hind-legs thing, but otherwise it'd be fine. Oh, and probably the talking, too.'

They looked at each other.

'So where are you going to go?' said Arnauld.

'Back to my mum's,' said Alex.

'Oh,' said Arnauld. 'And . . . she would not mind?'

Alex shook his head. 'You'd like her. She's nice.'

Arnauld thought about it for a moment. He shrugged. 'OK.'

Alex grinned. The two of them walked towards the line where black rock became water. Alex took in a deep breath and stood at the edge, his eyes fixing across the water.

'Oh, and by the way!' said Arnauld. 'The answer to your question – it is "halfway".'

Alex looked gormless. Arnauld rolled his eyes.

'*Halfway*,' he repeated. 'How far can a dog run into the woods, remember? "Halfway."'

Alex frowned. 'Really?'

'Yes,' said Arnauld, steadying himself on the edge. 'After that it is just running back out again, no?'

He threw himself into the water and was carried away by the tide.

■ ■ ■

'Dad.'

'No, Alex, bedtime.'

'One last question!'

'There's never just one last question with you, Alex.'

'No, I'm serious. Just one more, then I'll sleep.'

'If I promise to answer it, will you promise to sleep?'

'Most certainly.'

'Fine, one more. Go on.'

'What's the most frightened you've ever been?'

'That's a tough one.'

'. . . Was it when you went into the Forbidden Land?'

'Oh no, Alex, we're not talking about this . . .'

'Why not?'

'Well, we're just not. Your mother and I have talked about this and we decided that you're four years old, and you're not old enough to hear about those kinds of things.'

'But you promised you'd answer my question!'

'That's cheating, Alex. I'm not allowed to tell you about when I went into the Forbidden Land.'

'What about when you were coming out of it? Are you allowed to tell me about that?'

'Very clever, Alex.'

'Oh, come on. What was scary?'

'Well, all of it was scary, Alex. But if I'm honest, coming back out was a lot scarier than going in.'

'Why?'

'Well, because I knew what I had to go back to, that's why. When I was going in, I was more excited than anything. I had no idea what was at the centre. The whole world lay before me. But coming back out again, I knew I had to face everything that I had left behind. And that was really scary.'

'Really?'

'Oh yeah. Remember, back then, Alex, I hadn't met your mother yet. You hadn't been born yet. I didn't really have

anything – I was very alone. Maybe that's why I had gone out looking in the first place.'

'But then you met Mum, and everything was fine.'

'Yes, you're right. Exactly. It was.'

'Hooray!'

'And then you were born, Alex, and it was even more fine!'

'And then they lived happily ever after!'

'Yes, Alex, you're right. They did. And I'm not sure about you, but that sounds like the end of a story to me. Good night, Alex.'

'Good night, Dad.'

32

Another morning sun rose over the Cusp. Sunlight sparkled on the fragments of broken glass littering the runways, and great shadows were cast across the gutted sides of broken warehouses. Matthew and Martha stood at the edge of the boundary, gazing over the grassland that rippled in the morning wind.

'There he is!' cried Martha. 'I see him!'

Matthew smiled. She was right. Far on the horizon, a figure had emerged from the grassland, running towards them. Matthew squinted.

'There's something else with him,' he said.

'Looks like a dog to me,' said Laurence Davy.

Matthew glanced at the boy beside him. 'Any chance you can let us go now please, Grand High Chieftain Wizard?'

He nodded to the ropes that tied him and Martha to

the giant wooden stake. Laurence Davy shook his head apologetically.

'Sorry, Mr Price,' he said. 'Not quite yet. We need to have a chat with the Dog Walker first.'

'"We"?' said Matthew.

Laurence pointed to the crowd of armed children behind him. There were thousands of them now, filling the entire base. They were all covered in pieces of make-shift armour, their faces decorated with warpaint, wielding sticks and toy guns. Their eyes were fixed on the two figures running across the grassland towards them.

The boy and the dog reached the boundary. Slowly, nervously, they stepped onto the concrete of the base and looked up at the crowd. You could have heard a pin drop.

'Er, hello,' said Alex, and gave a wave.

There was silence. Alex looked at Arnauld and gently kicked him in the ribs.

'Oh,' said Arnauld. 'Er, woof.'

The crowd suddenly erupted with cheers. Handfuls of rose petals rained down. Laurence Davy stepped forward, his face set with humility. Slowly, he bowed down to Alex. The crowd quickly followed suit, and soon the base was filled with thousands of bodies bowed down to Alex.

'Alex Jennings,' said Laurence Davy nobly. 'Dog Walker, Triumphant King of the Forbidden Land, we welcome you back to the world of men with open arms.'

'All hail the Dog Walker!' chanted the crowd.

Laurence Davy stood up and clasped Alex by the shoulders.

'I ask you to join our crusade,' he said, 'and help us lead the New Age onwards into victory.'

'That's OK, Laurence,' said Alex. 'I just want to go home, if you don't mind.'

'As you wish,' said Laurence Davy, bowing gracefully. 'Any other requests, Dog Walker?'

'Um . . .'

'Hi, Alex,' said Matthew.

Alex looked over to where Matthew was tied to the stake. He was just one of several hundred prisoners tied up along the great curve of the Cusp. They included Martha, and Greg, and the night watchman, and Steph, and Mike and Duncan, and all the members of the Order, and everyone else unfortunate enough to be captured by the Wolf-Tiger Fighter Jet Squadron on their unstoppable rise to power.

'Yes I do, as a matter of fact,' said Alex. 'I'd like you to let all the prisoners go, please.'

Laurence Davy swung round.

'Release the prisoners!' he cried. 'By order of Alex Jennings the Dog Walker!'

The ropes tying Matthew and Martha to the stakes were quickly cut. They ran over to him.

'I don't believe it!' Martha cried. 'He's back, and he's lost the jumper too. A perfect ending.'

'Hi, Martha,' Alex smiled. 'Did I miss anything?'

'Oh, not much, Alex,' she snapped sarcastically. 'Got my teeth?'

Alex handed her the pair from his pocket.

'About time!' Martha groaned, spitting out the metal wolf's teeth. 'I mean, they're great for biting stuff, but you can't eat a toffee to save your life.' She nodded at Arnauld. 'Nice dog, by the way.'

Arnauld blushed. 'Woof,' he said, his tail wagging. 'Woof woof woof.'

There was a tap on Alex's shoulder. Alex turned and faced Matthew.

'Hi, Mr Price,' he smiled.

'Hello, Alex,' he smiled back. 'I'm so happy you decided to come home.'

'So am I,' said Alex.

'We were really worried when we found out Kyte had escaped,' said Matthew. 'Do you know where . . . ?'

'No,' said Alex firmly. 'I don't. But I don't think he'll be coming back.'

Matthew nodded. He paused for a moment, unsure if he should continue. He cleared his throat.

'And . . . your father?'

Alex gave him a look that managed to tell him not to

ask any more questions.

Around them, the other prisoners were being cut free. Steph and Greg gave each other an embarrassed wave.

'So what are you going to do now, Alex?' said Martha. 'Go back to school?'

'I doubt it,' said Matthew. 'It's been burned down.'

'Oh,' said Alex. He looked at Martha and Matthew. 'Do you . . . do you both want to come back to my mum's with us?' He pointed to the dog beside him. 'I mean, she's probably wondering where I am.'

Martha and Matthew looked at each other and shrugged.

'Sounds good to me,' said Matthew.

They made to leave, but before they took even a step they were mobbed by a crowd of excited children.

'Alex!' one shouted. 'I can't believe it's actually you!'

'You're a hero!'

'So did you see it?' one of them cried, jumping forwards. 'Did you see what was at the centre?'

A hush fell over the group. Alex looked around.

'Yeah,' he said. 'I did.'

Everyone gasped. The crowd around them had suddenly grown, and they were all jostling to hear what Alex had to say.

'What did you see?' someone cried out.

'What was there?'

'What was in the middle?'

The shouts grew over each other. Everyone was pushing and shoving, desperate to hear Alex talk. He shrugged.

'There wasn't anything,' he said. 'There wasn't anything in the middle.'

There were shouts of disbelief.

'You're joking!' said a boy next to him, poking him in the ribs a little harder than Alex would have liked. 'Seriously, what was in the middle?'

'Nothing,' Alex insisted. 'I'm being serious – there was nothing there, just fog . . .'

His voice was slowly lost in the shouting crowd.

'Was there a monster?' someone shouted.

'Another world?'

'Piles of money?'

'No,' said Alex. 'Listen, please . . .'

But in the excitement they had all started shouting at once, imagining what could be in the centre.

'*Please* . . .' he cried.

Suddenly, someone grabbed a stick and held it up in the air like a torch, and pointed out his sword. Everyone laughed, and started doing the same.

'No!' Alex cried. 'Stop, there isn't anything there . . .'

But no one was listening any more. One by one they charged down to the boundary and stood in a line where the concrete met the grass, crying out across the grassland, swords in hand, whooping and laughing.

'Stop!' Alex cried. 'Don't you believe me? Stop . . . !'

Alex started to run after them, but was stopped by a tug on his leg. He looked down. Arnauld was shaking his head gravely.

'Alex,' he said. 'There is nothing you can do. Leave them.'

'But . . .'

'*Alex*,' said Arnauld, pulling at his leg. 'Please – let us go home.'

Alex paused for a moment and turned back to the fences. They were destroyed now, and the gates were hanging wide open. Matthew and Martha stood waiting for them.

Alex gulped and walked away from the boundary. He met the others silently, and the four of them walked out the gates together.

'You're quite a celebrity now, aren't you, Alex?' Matthew smiled.

Alex shrugged, embarrassed. 'Yeah, I guess,' he said.

'I guess your mum will be wanting to hear all about it,' said Matthew.

Alex smiled. 'Yeah,' he said happily. 'She will.'

'Alex . . .' said Martha suspiciously. '. . . Did that dog just *talk* to you?'

Just before they hit the Outskirts, Alex turned back

to the crowd of children he had left behind. They were still at the boundary in their makeshift armour, crying out over the grassland. Even more had joined them now. Hundreds and hundreds of them ran around the great empty curve of the Cusp, thousands of them bellowing across the divide, spinning in circles, waving their swords to the land beyond the woods, to the land they could not see.

Q&A

Get to Know . . .

Ross Montgomery

How long did it take you to write *Alex, the Dog and the Unopenable Door*?

It took about two years in total, from when I wrote the first word to when it was finally sent off to publishers. I was working as a teacher at the same time so I could really only write it in school holidays. My friends were very nice and let me stay in their houses so I could focus on writing, and not get distracted by other less important things like marking schoolwork or paying electricity bills.

How did you come up with Alex as a character?

My experience of teaching over the last few years has helped me meet lots of different children. There's an Alex in every class: imaginative, vulnerable, struggles to stop talking.

Do you love dogs as much as Alex?

Almost. My main birthday present last year was getting to go to the dog show in Earl's Court so I could walk around, asking people if I could stroke their dog. The trick is to try and do it without looking completely mad. This is harder than it sounds.

Do you have a dog?

Not yet. I'm going to wait until I have my own house so it can savage my furniture rather than my landlord's.

What's your favourite breed of dog?

After several months of negotiation and a few threatening emails, my publisher and I have agreed that we will reduce my original extensive answer to just one breed. There's no way I could have a favourite, so I'll just choose one from the pile in front of me . . .

The Brussels Griffon. Sensitive, self-important, gets on well with ferrets. Looks like a wise old elf who smokes a pipe and grants you wishes.

Have you ever been in trouble with the police?

When I was seven I put gravel down the church toilet. The organist told me that the vicar would probably call the police when he found out. As of publication, they still haven't caught up with me.

You're a teacher – are you nice like Matthew?

I'd like to think so. I imagine the children I teach would say I'm more like Davidus Kyte!

How did you come up with all the different lands in the story?

I wanted each land to be as different as possible from the one before it. I honestly can't remember if they were based on anything, or if I just made them all up. Having said that, I should mention now that I don't know if it is best to travel across a desert at night-time. Always check with your local scientist before embarking on any expeditions.

Where did you get the idea for the unopenable door?

I liked the idea that something as simple for us to use as a round door handle is an unsurpassable obstacle to a dog

– much like how, in the book, a dog can travel across the boundary without any problems, but humans can't take a step over it, and can't understand why they can't.

What would you ask a dog if you discovered it could speak?

"What's the deal with eating poo?"

When did you know you wanted to be an author?

I wrote a story in infants' class one day, where one of the characters repeated something extremely rude about taxes that I'd overheard my dad saying the night before. I proudly informed my mum about this on the drive back home. She did a U-turn and drove back to school at about a hundred miles an hour so she could rub it out before the teacher saw it. I had discovered the power of writing.

What's a typical working day like for an author?

8.00am wake up bright and early for productive day of writing

8.01am go back to sleep
10.00am sit in front of computer and look at blank page
10.01am look at pictures of dogs on Google instead
11.50am finally start writing
12.00am well earned lunch
1.00pm delete all writing from the morning in disgust
1.01pm look at blank page
1.06pm wring hair
1.07pm kick wall
1.08pm rub cream on swollen foot
1.10pm promise to write more tomorrow when foot stops hurting
1.15pm to evening visit funfairs

How do you come up with ideas for your stories?

If you're anything like me, you'll get an idea one day – just a little one – and think nothing of it. Then it grows over time. Sometimes it's on its own, sometimes it's with a little help. Most of the big decisions I've made about my stories have been when I'm sitting alone on a bus.

Are you influenced by any other authors?

Hundreds and hundreds of them! Nothing helps you come up with ideas like reading a fantastic book, or poem, or article. It doesn't matter what you read, so long as you love it – it all helps.

Which were your favourite books when you were a child?

The first book I ever truly, passionately loved was called *Ging Gang Goolie It's An Alien.* It's about an alien that loves sausages who comes to destroy Earth and then bumps into a group of rubbish boy scouts who are on a camping trip. It taught me everything I need to know about how to spend hours carefully writing a story in your neatest handwriting, and then throw all the paper into the air instead because it's really funny.

What ingredients, in your opinion, does a good book need?

If you can surprise the person who's reading, that's always good. There are a thousand different ways to do that. My sister is a teacher too, and she showed me a

Sherlock Holmes story written by one of her pupils. It turned out in the end the killer was J. Sainsbury, the man who started Sainsbury's supermarkets. It doesn't matter how long I write for: I could write a thousand books, and I will never come up with an ending as good as that.

Do you have any tips for new writers?

It's a really boring tip and gets said all the time, but it's because it's the best one: write loads. Don't worry about making mistakes or getting it perfect – just keep writing stories that you love, and think others will love, and you'll work out everything you need to know along the way.

What do you like to do besides write?

I like to walk around aimlessly, muttering under my breath and looking like I have something extremely important to do.

Are you able to tell us anything about your next book?

Absolutely not! It's top secret – kept under lock and key in my house. My publisher has assured me they won't publish an extract of it on the next page, under any circumstances. To be on the safe side it's probably best if you don't turn over the page – just in case they have. I know I can trust you.

Don't miss the next exciting book from Ross! Here's a sneak preview from the very first pages of *Tornado Chasers*…

This notepaper is kindly provided for the inmates of
THE COUNTY DETENTION CENTRE
Use one sheet per week
No scribbling

Dear Warden,

If you're reading this letter then it means I've finally escaped.

It also means you've found the secret place behind the loose tile above the sink, which means you'll have also found the mouse traps I put there before I left. ~~Sorry about~~ Actually I'm not sorry about that.

When I first came to the County Detention Centre, you said I had to tell the truth about what happened - when it all began, who did what, why we did it, why it ended the way it did. 'Write it down,' you said. 'Make a poem about it all. Turn it into a story if you have to. But one way or another, you have to tell us.'

And so I did. I sat down, and I wrote a story - about everything that happened, from the beginning to the end, as best as I could tell it. The only way I could tell it. And here it is - every last word.

Which brings me to the question I know you're desperate to ask: if I've run away, then where have I run away to?

Well, you're just going to have to read my story, aren't you?

~~LOVE~~ YOURS SINCERELY,

INMATE 409

The Tornado Chasers

Owen, Callum, Orlaith, Ceri and Murderous Pete are **The Tornado Chasers** – five children who are sick of their bullying schoolteachers and their overprotective parents. But most of all they are fed up of living in a place where the threat of tornadoes means that they're forced to spend every evening and weekend at home.

But . . .

The Tornado Chasers have come up with an insane plan to escape. And soon they'll be propelled into a world of adventure, superheroes, ravenous bears and raining biscuits. Finally, each one of them will be forced to face their greatest fear . . .